Sisters of the Vine

A Novel by

Linda Rosen

Black Rose Writing | Texas

The author grants the final approval for this literary material.

First printing

This is a work of fiction. Names, characters, businesses, places, events, and incidents are either the products of the author's imagination or used in a fictitious manner. Any resemblance to actual persons, living or dead, or actual events is purely coincidental.

ISBN: 978-1-68433-670-8
PUBLISHED BY BLACK ROSE WRITING
www.blackrosewriting.com

Printed in the United States of America
Suggested Retail Price (SRP) $18.95

Sisters of the Vine is printed in Adobe Jensen Pro

*As a planet-friendly publisher, Black Rose Writing does its best to eliminate unnecessary waste to reduce paper usage and energy costs, while never compromising the reading experience. As a result, the final word count vs. page count may not meet common expectations.

Praise for

Sisters of the Vine

"*Sisters of the Vine* is not only a beautiful tale of self-discovery and reinvention, but one of female triumph, too. Filled with characters you'll love, and some you'll love to hate, this feel-good story will have you raising your glass to the heroine and her delightful crew."

–Hannah Mary McKinnon, bestselling author of *Sister Dear*

"A novel about vineyard life and family, Linda Rosen's delightful and poignant *Sisters of the Vine* is for wine-lovers."

–Laura Dave, author of *Eight Hundred Grapes*

"If you enjoy sistership stories, great domestic fiction, or wine, you'll relish *Sisters of the Vine* - an uplifting story that kept me engaged throughout! Just like the best wine, this novel will linger with you long after you finish."

–Lainey Cameron, award-winning author of *The Exit Strategy*

Sisters of the Vine

"A woman is like a tea bag.
You never know how strong it is until it's in hot water."
—Eleanor Roosevelt

CHAPTER 1

The locomotive rumbled past, rattling the nursery window. Its piercing sound echoed as it travelled down the tracks. Where was everyone going? Where was *she* going?

Liz froze, waiting for the baby's wail, then looked over her shoulder and sighed. Bethany was fast asleep in her crib, her little knees tucked under her belly, her tushy up in the air. Resting on the Winnie the Pooh sheet, dropped right on top of Eeyore, was her pacifier with the flesh- colored rubber nipple. The binky always slipped from her tiny lips when she settled.

Sweet, three-month-old Bethany, born the same day Alan Shepard, the Mercury Seven astronaut, was launched into space. As America celebrated the historical flight, Liz and Rick reveled in their own joy, dreaming of where their life would now take them.

Liz pressed a palm to her heart and let out a soft sigh, relieved the clanging hadn't woken her baby. She pulled back the dotted swiss curtain on the nursery's window and gazed out at the long line of train cars on the track just beyond the apartment's small parking lot. How long will it take this one to silence? she wondered and winced, noticing the grit on her finger tips. Rubbing her thumb against her other four fingers, she tried to wipe them clean. She looked at the window sill covered in soot. A bitter tang filled her mouth.

At night, the hushed sound of the train moving from Ulster County to Putnam and down to Westchester was romantic, just as Liz had imagined when they first moved into the apartment. Now, its clicking metal wheels and blaring noon whistle threatened to wreck the baby's midday nap, and Liz desperately needed her to sleep. When she napped, so did Mommy – or she tried to. Piles of laundry and bottles to sterilize – not to mention vacuuming, cleaning the bathroom, and dusting – usually kept her from putting her head on the pillow. Although Liz loved taking care of their home and their baby, she hated having to clean the filthy windowsills with their grimy coating, and today Rick wasn't even around to help. Usually, on weekends, he took Bethany out for their daddy-daughter walk so Liz could make the apartment shine. Today, though, he was off on a fishing trip with one of his fellow teachers.

Liz bent over the crib and tucked the handmade blanket around the baby. Her sister, Kristin, had chosen the perfect colors to crochet – mint-green and yellow, matching the walls and carpeting. Liz patted her daughter's tiny rump and whispered, "Sleep tight, Bethany. I love you."

Bethany, a name that evoked elegance and grace. The three syllables rolled off her tongue like a whisper. Liz was always partial to the name; it reminded her of the tall, slender gal from high school who never had weight problems, unlike herself. And Rick was right. It was chic – "too chic," as he put it – yet that's just what she wanted, even if he didn't.

Liz quietly walked out of the nursery, leaving the door half open. She walked across the hall, but before she had a chance to enter her own bedroom, the train whistle resounded, practically shaking the walls. She stopped dead. As expected, Bethany cried out. Liz hurried back. She rubbed her daughter's little head and placed the pacifier between her lips. Her mouth, like two tiny bows, pursed in and out. She quieted and Liz sighed. That was easy, she thought. Not like yesterday when the baby screamed every hour on the hour, whenever the train rolled by, its whistle like a trumpet cutting through the humid summer air.

On days like that, Liz was desperate to move and she didn't care where as long as there were no trains in the vicinity. She wished for cool breezes to waft through open windows and gently swish the curtains rather than the blaring noise and the dirt. She had planned to talk to Rick about it last night when the baby was finally asleep, but by the time she got Bethany down for the night, Liz was fried. A quiet smoke sitting on the steps outside the garden apartment with her tall, handsome husband, whose well-defined arms felt so good against her skin, was all she wanted.

Liz managed to doze off for a bit while Bethany slept. The short snooze revived her, giving her enough energy to tackle the bathroom and kitchen. With the floors sparkling clean – up to Rick's demands – and the lemon scent of Pledge throughout the apartment, Liz collapsed on the couch with a Winston and mused about how she would spend the rest of the afternoon once her baby woke. She needed to get out, which surprised her. All along, she had believed being a housewife would be enough. It had been her dream, why she dropped out of college after only one year to marry Rick. Yet, after twelve weeks with a newborn, Liz realized she missed working more than she ever could have imagined. Even though it would be at nursery school where she would be with more children, Liz longed to get back to work. She could bring Bethany with her; she'd even checked with the director. But would Rick agree? She was afraid to bring the subject up.

CHAPTER 2

The pungent aroma of fish wafted through the front door. "Hey, Liz, I'm home and I've got dinner," Rick shouted as he wiped his feet on the entryway rug.

With the baby on her hip, Liz hurried from the kitchen. Rick stood proud, holding out a large package wrapped in oil-stained brown paper. "Bluefish, all cleaned and filleted," he said. "Ready for the broiler and lots more for the freezer."

That species was not Liz's favorite, but her husband loved it. Actually, he loved anything fresh. Rick was not a fan of store-bought fish or store-bought vegetables. "If you could have your own cow," she'd once said to him, "you'd be the happiest guy around."

"No," he'd answered. "Because then I'd have to kill it to have a hamburger." He'd told her she could buy beef at the Grand Union, although someday soon, once they bought the land he so desperately wanted, she wouldn't be buying any vegetables. "We'll grow our own and live off the land," he'd said, giving her nose a tender tap.

Liz kissed his sweaty cheek, and Rick handed her the fish. He rubbed his smelly hands on his thighs and reached for his daughter. "You go separate the fillets and start dinner," he said. "I'll keep this little lady busy."

Rick walked off with Bethany tucked in his arms. Liz figured it was better not to say anything about washing his hands. Pick your battles, she told herself as she listened to him jabber on about his day.

"Daddy caught lots of fish today," he said, smiling at Bethany's peachy-pink little face. "Real big ones. One day I'll take you fishin' . . ." The baby cooed and looked at her daddy with big blue eyes, the same sapphire color that Liz's mother had. Entranced by her daughter's wide eyes focused on Daddy, Liz felt that familiar ache in her chest, the one that grabbed her every time she thought about her mother never knowing her beautiful granddaughter. Cancer had taken her mom from Liz shortly before the end of senior year in high school, before Liz had even met Rick Bergen. She always wondered if her mother would have liked her choice of husband. Liz knew her mom wouldn't have been pleased with her getting a wedding band before a college degree, just as her dad hadn't been. They'd always said Liz should marry a man she could count on. And then there was that teaching license they always mentioned, so she'd have something to fall back on. Liz bristled merely thinking of those words. She believed the first part had come true. She could count on Rick. He was steady, even with his big dream. He'd promised he would continue working until the day came they could actually live off their land, and if it proved they financially could not, then at least they'd nourish their bodies from it. But the part about her getting a teaching license – well, not so much. A nursery school job would not bring her a pension, a word her parents used that Liz never was able to wrap her head around. Shaking those disturbing thoughts from her head, Liz let the heartwarming twosome of daddy and daughter strolling off together seep into her skin. Then she turned and walked into the kitchen, the place where Rick seemed to like her best, other than their bedroom.

When dinner was over and the dishes were done, it was bedtime for the baby. Liz placed the finished bottle on the little table next to the rocking chair and lifted her sleeping daughter. She stood rocking her, making sure she was deep in sleep, then laid her in the crib, gently, like a treasured piece of fine china. She leaned over and turned the knob on the mobile. Winnie the Pooh, Eeyore, and baby Roo twirled above the yellow crib. She watched Bethany's little torso lift and lower with each breath. When she tucked her knees under her belly and lifted her bottom in her favorite sleeping position, Liz knew it was safe to leave.

She flopped onto the living room couch, put her feet up on the pine coffee table, and peered at her husband reclining on the Barcalounger, eyes closed. In his hand was a glass half-filled with a toast-colored liquid, not his usual after-dinner cup of coffee.

"What's that?" she asked.

"What's what?" Rick opened his eyes and looked around the room.

Liz pointed. "In your glass."

"Oh. The guys were sayin' today how they loved a shot of scotch after a long day on the water. It keeps the mellow mood goin'."

"Mellow. How nice."

5

"You shoulda seen it, Liz. The sun was shining, not a cloud in the sky, and the fish were biting. It was perfect."

Strains of a Mozart sonata from the Winnie the Pooh mobile softly filled the air. "Yes, perfect," Liz said shaking her head, though her husband didn't see that. His eyes were closed again as he lay back swallowing a sip of his mellow libation. "After I cleaned the bathroom and washed the kitchen floor, Beth and I went to the park."

"Good," he murmured from the depths of mellow. "I'm glad my girls got out today."

Liz let the violins and flutes play. Between the relaxing music and Johnny Walker, she judged her timing was right.

"Rick, honey," she said, her voice as soft as the sonata. "I want to go back to work."

He opened his eyes. "Seriously? We've talked about it. You're done with that."

The evening train rumbled past, shaking the bay window. The curtains fluttered. "I know we did," Liz said once the clatter subsided. "But I really want to. I asked the director and she said I could take Bethany with me."

The lounge chair banged as Rick shot up straight. "You asked the director?"

"Yes. I called her this afternoon." Liz picked at her cuticles. "She was excited – said they'd love to have me back – I would even have my same class. They'd move the new teacher to another room."

"It's Saturday, Liz." His eyes narrowed. "You don't make business calls on a weekend."

"I've got her home number." Liz pasted a smile on her face. "You know we're all friends. Nursery school is different."

"I don't like the idea. I told you I didn't want my wife workin'."

"I know. Just think of it this way. We'd save the money I make and buy that farm you want – sooner rather than later."

"Buy the farm." His words were more of a snort than a statement. "So now you're changin' your mind about that too. Seems like you did a lot of thinkin' while you were cleaning that toilet."

CHAPTER 3

"This is the one that guy told me about," Rick said as he turned off the Post Road onto a dirt lane. "It's got twelve acres of good, rich land, and the pumpkins are already planted."

"Punkins. I want punkin," two-year-old Bethany called from the back seat.

Liz turned around and smiled at her daughter bouncing up and down like a Spalding, that pink rubber ball Liz played with as a child. "The pumpkins aren't ready yet, honey." She pointed to the freshly tilled earth. "See those little green shoots coming out of the dirt? That means they're baby plants. When they grow real big, we'll buy some." She turned back and looked out the windshield. Great. What am I supposed to do, make jack-o'-lanterns and sell them for Halloween? Trees lined the road, some budding with spring growth, others totally bare, with broken limbs and dead branches strewn in between.

"I don't know, Rick." Liz shook her head. "This place doesn't look very well cared for." Just like the other two farms they'd looked at – dead trees, scruffy land. Other than Bethany loving the kitty cats, as she called them, on the previous farms and wanting to roll down the hill, nothing was promising. Liz had told Rick each time, "I'm not some pumpkin bumpkin. That's not what I want to sell." He'd laughed at her phrase. "Don't worry, honey," he'd said. "First we'll grow our own food. We'll eat off the land before we start livin' off it. That okay with you?"

Eating off the land, as long as it was vegetables, was fine. She'd even can them, like she'd promised, but no way was she collecting eggs from a chicken coop or milking a cow. There was a reason God made supermarkets.

She kept quiet as the car crawled up the craggy road. One more pothole and the tires would burst. This isn't what I want, she thought. Not wanting another argument, she swallowed the words. "Give it a chance," Rick had yelled when they parked at the last farm, when Liz didn't even want to get out of the car. That house had been in shambles, with broken windows and cracked shingles and steps in dire need of repair. This time she vowed to walk around and be nice, listening to the realtor pour praises on living in the Hudson Valley and feeling the earth under your feet. Liz was willing to live on a farm, to smell that earth, even to dig her fingers in it rather than dusting it from window sills, as she'd told the realtor when they made the plan to meet at the farms rather than driving together. It was easier for them with Bethany in tow. She'd even turned her father down when he offered to babysit so she and Rick could visit the farms without worrying about her. Liz wanted her daughter to get some fresh country air in her lungs. "It's an adventure," she'd said. Yes, it was an adventure, but she wanted something she would love. This ramshackle house, desperately in need of a paint job, right smack on the dirt road lined with dead trees, was not it.

While walking the grounds with the realtor and going through the two-bedroom decrepit abode, Liz kept a polite smile on her face. She tried to find something nice to say so Rick couldn't accuse her of hating everything. "The views are beautiful," she said, reaching up and lovingly rubbing his shoulder as they stood outside the old barn, high on the hillside overlooking the valley below. There was absolutely nothing else to compliment. She thanked the realtor for her time and for putting up with a two-year-old. "I'm sorry I had to keep chasing her. She obviously likes running through the high grass here."

The realtor waved away her apology. "She's adorable," she said. "I'm sure she'll love living out here in the country."

Liz nodded and glanced at Rick, who seemed entranced with the view of the river in the distance. "Well, thank you. Rick and I will talk about what we've seen and get back to you."

They all walked down the rutted road to their respective cars and said good-bye. Liz helped Bethany climb into the back seat. When both Mommy and Daddy were settled in the front, Rick turned the ignition on. He left the gear shift in park and turned to Liz.

"It's obvious you didn't like it. What's the sense of looking at anything else? Nothing seems to appeal to you."

"Oh, come on, honey. That's not fair. I love the view. I wish there was something on a hilltop overlooking the river, like this one, but with decent land and a house that doesn't need tons of work."

Rick let out a huge sigh. "I'm tired, Liz. Let's call it a day. I'm just . . . I don't know. Maybe it's not worth it. I don't think you're gonna like anything."

With her toes curling in her Keds, she wondered when he would ever believe she really wanted to move. "What about the one without a realtor?" she said.

"You mean the one in that tiny hamlet you heard about at nursery school?"

"Yeah."

"No. I don't trust that."

Liz knew Rick didn't want anything to do with the place she worked, or the fact that she was working, but a suggestion for land that he wanted? "Oh, come on," she said. "What do we have to lose? We're just looking."

"Maybe another time. Not today."

Refusing to look at him, Liz leaned back against the passenger seat. She wanted to spit. Why does it always have to be his idea?

CHAPTER 4

"Slow down," Liz said. "It's supposed to be the first right turn after you see the silo." Set back way off the road stood a tall steel cylinder next to a dark red barn. Rows of corn, with its silk draped like fine long threads, filled the land all around it. The noonday sun brought brilliance to the green leaves. "Just like in the song," Liz said. "This corn really looks as high as an elephant's eye."

"Elphants," Bethany said. "Tigers too, Mama?"

"No, sweety. No tigers or elephants," Liz laughed.

Rick shook his head and glanced at his wife. A loving smile filled his face. "Or maybe cows for Mommy to milk."

She gave his arm a little shove. "Stop it." Happy laughter filled the car as Rick turned onto the gravel road.

It had taken several late-night discussions over the past two months for Rick to agree to visit this farm. Finally, after a few guys at his school – longtime residents of the Valley – also recommended it, he had Liz make the phone call. "After all, the owner is selling it herself," he'd said, as if Liz hadn't already told him.

For the next quarter mile, all they saw were rows of tall corn stalks with a barn and farm house in the distance, like a Norman Rockwell painting. Liz looked through her open window imagining a big kitchen table covered in a red-and-white-checkered cloth and curtains billowing in the soft breeze. Rick slowed down as the road curved left. Huge maples and oaks, much larger than the trees that grew in her dad's suburban back yard, lined the road on both sides, creating a green, leafy canopy. After about a half-mile drive up an incline, the vistas opened to a vast expanse of emerald green. "Gorgeous," Liz said. Rick stopped the car and they stared out at the rolling hillside. The sparrows' song twittered in the air.

"Out," Bethany said. Her loud voice shook them back to reality.

"No, no, honey. Not yet." Rick took his foot off the brake and started forward, crawling along the winding road. It curved right in a gentle descent. Open, empty land filled the right side. "It must be that farmer's land," Liz said. "The one with the corn."

"No, look out there." Rick pointed to a house in the distance. "It's another farm, just nothin' growin'. Or at least not here."

The road leveled off. Rick continued driving a short distance, his foot barely on the gas when, on the left, set back off the road, they spotted a charming cottage. Blue shutters against a fresh coat of white paint. An open porch, the perfect spot for a rocking chair.

"Oh, so sweet," Liz said. "That must be it."

Rick steered the car to a cleared space across the grass on the right side of the house, where an old Ford station wagon was parked next to a pickup truck. "Someone's home," he said as he shut the engine. "Maybe she's got company, 'cause I don't think an old lady would be drivin' the pickup."

Liz helped Bethany out of the car. "Stay with Mommy," she said. "You can't go running off here exploring." With her hand tight on her daughter's, they headed across the gravel toward the front door. Before they got there, the loud clang of a screen door slamming drew Liz's attention to a woman coming from the side of the house.

"Can I help you?" she asked. Petite, with gray hair and a handkerchief stuffed in the rolled-up sleeve of her print blouse, the woman coming toward them reminded Liz of her grandmother.

Rick's voice boomed through the country air. "We heard you're sellin' the place and wanted to take a look."

"Are you the nursery school teacher?" the lady asked, looking directly at Liz.
"Yes."

"Well, how do you do? I heard you were going to come by some day. Just didn't realize it was today."

Liz winced. "Oh! I'm so sorry," she said, and glanced at her husband who had insisted there was no reason to make an appointment.

"She wants to sell," he'd said the night before when Liz suggested they call first, "then she should be home. And if not, we'll look at the land anyway." Rick shoved his hands in his pants pockets and stood tall, shoulders pulled back.

"No worries, honey. My friend at church told me to expect you, said her daughter told her you'd be coming one day." She bent a little closer to Bethany, who was digging her sandals in the dirt. "And what's your name, sweetheart?"

Liz introduced her family to the woman, ending with "And I'm Liz."

"And I'm Mrs. Lambert. Come on in, I expect you want to see the house."

The Bergens followed Mrs. Lambert through the side door. The hinges squeaked and the door closed with a bang, but no one said a word. They stepped directly into a cheery yellow kitchen with a small round Formica table in the center. The seats on the wooden chairs were covered in a matching yellow-and-red vinyl print. There was no room for that big farmhouse kitchen table with the checkered cloth that Liz had envisioned. The plywood cabinets were painted cherry red and the floor's wood planks gave off a lemony scent. The worn oak looked like it had been walked on for many years.

Mrs. Lambert led them into the living room. "Oh, what a beautiful fireplace!" Liz said, admiring the stone walls and the mantle centered on the long wall opposite the entrance.

"That's about two hundred years old," the older woman said. "The story goes that the original owner took the stones from the river and built it himself."

"Wow!" Rick said. "That means the house was here during the Revolutionary War."

"I suppose it does. My family has been living on the land since the 1800s and the people before that were here a long time. This house seems to get passed down generation after generation." She glanced at Bethany and smiled.

Liz lifted the toddler. There were lots of breakable pretty knickknacks at her reach, probably antiques.

"How long have you had the farm?" Liz asked, shifting Bethany to her other hip.

"Oh, let's see. My husband and I took it over from my parents sometime in the early Thirties after my father died." Mrs. Lambert gazed off in the distance, as if the answer would come from the large sycamore tree shading the front window. "But I grew up here."

Liz assumed it was hard for the sweet old lady to sell her childhood home, one her grandparents had even lived in. And, she wondered, if the house was so old, what kind of repairs would it need – and would they be on-going? Bethany squirmed. Liz put her down, but kept a tight hold on her hand.

"It used to be a dairy farm," Mrs. Lambert said. "My husband, though, never wanted to be a farmer. And he definitely did not want to deal with cows, so shortly after we moved in, we sold them off. We ran the hardware store in town. We raised our kids here, and we grew lots of vegetables." She gave Bethany, who was swaying side to side and shuffling her feet, a little tap on her head. "The children loved running all over the place, up and down the hills, playing in the barn . . ."

Liz wanted to hug the old lady. She looked lost in happy memories; a gentle smile spread across her soft, wrinkled cheeks.

"But now it's time for me to move on. My husband died a few years ago and this place – not the house, that's not too big – but all this land – it's just too much for one old lady."

"You've been taking care of all this yourself?" Liz couldn't imagine an eighty-year-old woman – and she had to be at least that – mowing all that grass.

"Up 'til about a year ago, I did. I have a riding mower, and I'll sell you that too, if you want. I used to climb on and mow all the time, singing to the trees. No one could hear me – well, other than the birds. Then it just got to be too much. I'm afraid everything's a mess out there now."

"How many acres do you have here?" Rick asked, staring out the wide picture window.

"Thirty-five. But a lot of them are woods. And on top of the hillside where it flattens out, there's about thirteen acres of good, rich soil. The cows used to roam there, and my husband always said it was well fertilized." She let out a little giggle. "Come, let me show you where we had our vegetable garden. That's also beautiful soil."

Rick practically skipped out the door following Mrs. Lambert. He turned his head toward Liz walking behind with their daughter. "She's already got a vegetable garden," he whispered.

"Had," Liz said, with a slight smile.

Rick walked the perimeter of the large rectangular patch, his hands forming imaginary rows in the air. "The tomatoes were over there," Mrs. Lambert said, pointing to the spot where Rick was standing. "Tomatoes, peppers, zucchini, beans . . ." She clicked off each with her fingers. "I can't remember everything we grew, but it was a lot." She scanned the yellowed vines tangled with dried out brown stalks and clover running amok, massed together like green scatter rugs strewn about. "It needs a good weeding, doesn't it? I'm sorry. After my husband died, I just let it go."

Rick stooped and sifted the dry, dark-brown earth through his fingers. "I can make this come alive," he said to no one in particular.

The sweet elderly lady placed a tired hand on Liz's shoulder. "How about I wait for you inside?" she said. "Take the baby up the hillside. Let her run around a little. You should see the view from there."

Mrs. Lambert walked off, and Liz and Rick took Bethany by the hand, one on each side. They ran behind the house and up the hill. Halfway there, Rick lifted his daughter onto his shoulders, and they climbed the rest of the way marveling at the verdant land spread before them. At the top, off to the right, was a stone bench under a tall, impressive oak tree. Liz brushed acorns off the seat and sat. She lifted Bethany to her lap and, together, they enjoyed the cooling shade from the ancient, leaf-filled limbs. Birds hidden in the branches sang softly, a lovely concert in a tranquil setting.

After several quiet minutes, Liz got up and lifted her daughter to her hip. She walked over to Rick who was gazing all around him at the vast open space. They stood together in the silence looking out toward the Hudson River in the distance, flowing downstream.

Liz put Bethany down and glanced up at her husband, who had a wide grin spread across his clean-shaven face. "Let's go tell her we'll take it," she whispered. Rick nodded. The Bergen family made their way down the emerald green hillside to present their offer. "I love the house," Liz said as they scrambled along, holding tight to Bethany's tiny hands. "And you can have your vegetable garden. A huge one. And one of these days we'll figure out what to do with the rest of the land."

CHAPTER 5

Her foot was on the gas, her hands on the steering wheel, but her mind was in Dallas. Liz turned at the corner. Gravel crunched under the tires as she drove along their mile-long road with its bank of trees creating a forest effect on both sides. She slowly pulled into her parking spot, turned the ignition off, and sat back, amazed they'd made it in one piece.

"Mama," two-year-old Bethany whined from the back seat. "We home."

"Yes, sweetheart. We are. Let's go see Daddy." She pulled the keys from the ignition, then slowly walked around the car and helped her daughter out.

It was four o'clock, one hour since Liz had learned President Kennedy was dead. Assassinated. A crazy gunman shot him through the head, his blood seeping into his wife's pink suit. Liz had been on the floor with her preschoolers, building a tower out of wooden blocks, when the director came in, bent down, and gave her the news. "The President's been shot." Liz couldn't focus on the children; she only wanted to call Rick. They both adored Jack and Jackie and believed he was the best president in their lifetime. The Cuban Missile Crisis was a close call, but he got them through it without a bomb dropped. And Liz was thrilled when John John was born though she cried when Jackie lost the other baby. She was unable to fathom why anyone would kill their handsome president.

Bethany toddled up the walk to the side door. Liz watched her little bottom wiggle. She was just six months younger than John John. So sad, that little boy wouldn't grow up knowing his daddy. She placed her hands on her stomach and thought about the baby she was carrying. She prayed nothing would happen to Rick – that this little boy or girl inside her would grow up with a loving father, just as she had.

"Go find Daddy," she told her daughter as she pushed the door open and helped the little girl over the top step. "Give him a big hug."

Later that night, with Bethany asleep in her crib, Winnie the Pooh snuggled in her little arms, Liz climbed into the bed she shared with her husband, something Jackie would no longer be able to do. She slid under the blankets and nestled against him. Rick had been in bed over an hour while Liz, two months pregnant, cleaned the kitchen, took the garbage out, and made sure all the lights were shut off.

With her freshly lotioned hand, Liz stroked her husband's well-toned flank. He let out a soft sigh and turned toward her. His breath bathed her face. His fingers played with the elastic on her panties, then made their way down to her rounded belly. His titillating strokes teased and brought her hips closer. Pleasuring her with his finger, he kissed her soft lips. His tongue played with hers. It drifted down her cheek and tickled her ear. Like a feather, it brushed along her neck. His body slid lower and he tasted her nipple. Warmth spread through her loins. With a satisfied moan, she turned over and mounted him, letting her tongue taste his salty skin.

"Mama!" A cry pierced the air. Liz shot up, arms straight and tight, pushing against the sheet. The wail got louder. Her name stretched out. "Maaa Maaa."

Rick wrapped his arms around her, pulling her back. She wiggled from his grasp. "Don't go." He said, his voice husky.

Already climbing off the bed, Liz shook her head. "She needs me."

"So do I." His throaty whisper from before turned harsh. "Let her cry."

She bent down and kissed his forehead. "I'll be right back."

Rick grabbed the pillow from behind his head and turned over. He punched it down and dropped his right cheek in its crevice. As Liz neared the door, she heard him mumble. "Don't bother. She needs you." The sarcastic tone made her bristle. It was the same one he used every time she gave Bethany more attention than him.

CHAPTER 6

Autumn turned into winter and Liz went through her days unable to get the picture of JFK Jr. saluting his father's flag-draped coffin out of her mind. Whenever Rick and Bethany were together, her heart swelled with love. And when the baby in her womb kicked or pressed against her breast bone so hard, she pictured a little foot bursting through. She tenderly stroked her belly. In a few months they'd be a family of four. Sure, she knew Rick was annoyed with all the time she devoted to their daughter, and he'd be even more jealous once this baby was born, but the women at work told her it was normal. "Just make sure you give him special attention too," they said. "Get your father to babysit. Put on some lipstick and go on a date together." Liz wished she had her mother to talk to, to find out how she had managed to keep her father happy with three kids running around sucking up all the energy in the house. It was hard enough with one and lipstick didn't seem to do the trick.

As the ground thawed and spring arrived, Liz, with her big belly, spent weekend mornings weeding their garden while Rick dug out another space for even more vegetables. "I'm gonna move the peppers over here," he said as he turned the rich brown earth over with a pitch fork. "That'll make room for more tomatoes in that patch." He pointed to the large plot of land where Liz was pulling out chickweed and all those other pesty, unwanted plants.

"What do we need more tomatoes for?" Rick knew she didn't want to sell their crop at farmers markets. It wasn't that she wouldn't like the extra money; she just refused to stand in heat or rain hawking their wares. "And how much sauce can we possibly make?"

"Plenty," he said. "It'll take us through the whole winter. You can make tomato soup, too, and that dish with the zucchini and eggplant, whatever it's called."

A coworker had given her a recipe for ratatouille last summer, their first on the farm, when they were inundated with tomatoes. Though cooking was not Liz's forte, Rick devoured the colorful sautéed dish and said he could have it every night. As long as it was homemade, he would have anything every night. Liz wouldn't have minded canning their vegetables, putting them up for winter as farm ladies of the past had done, if Rick only helped instead of peering over her shoulder criticizing her slicing and dicing methods and inspecting the jars. As if her sterilizing methods weren't good enough. This coming fall, with a new baby, Liz certainly wouldn't have time to stand in the kitchen boiling mason jars. She'd be sterilizing bottles. Stewing tomatoes, much less making pots of soup, was out of the question. She hoped Rick wouldn't make a big fuss when she bought Campbell's.

On Father's Day, Liz woke early and got Bethany out of bed. In their soft furry slippers, the most comfortable for Liz despite the warm summer day, they padded into the kitchen and prepared a special breakfast for Daddy. Pancakes, his favorite, with homemade syrup they'd bought last fall from a neighbor who tapped his own trees. The eggs came from another farmer down the road, something Liz bought for special treats. She had to beg Rick to understand it was easier to pick up a dozen when she shopped at the A&P rather than running back and forth to a neighbor to buy freshly laid. Thankfully, he acquiesced and didn't insist on milk directly from a cow.

"That smells good," Rick said, stepping into the kitchen. "Bacon?"

"Yeah, Daddy. Just for you and me."

Rick looked at his wife standing at the stove rubbing her lower back. "You're not having any?" Concerned eyes met hers.

Liz shook her head and kept rubbing. Bacon fat splattered from the pan, and she lowered the flame. "My stomach's bothering me."

Rick raised his brow and Liz shrugged. She didn't want to say anything in front of her daughter. Bethany was constantly asking when her brother or sister would arrive, and Liz didn't want to get her hopes up. "Should I call your father?" Rick asked.

"He's coming later," Liz reminded him. "But maybe it's a good idea."

An hour and a half later, Lou showed up. He took Bethany to the playground in town. Liz had cleaned the kitchen, gagging from the odor, but wouldn't let on that she needed Rick's help. Dishes were a woman's work and the kitchen a woman's domain, as her husband believed.

Later that afternoon Rick and Lou were watching a baseball game, the second of the Mets vs. Phillies doubleheader. Liz knew her husband would be engrossed in the game, coaching from the living room couch, so she took Bethany into the bedroom with her to rest. The three-year-old had too much energy for a woman in her ninth month keeping track of her contractions. So far, they were a half hour apart. No need to mention it to Rick yet. He was whooping and hollering, having the best day, as he'd said earlier – "Breakfast with my two beautiful girls, then a doubleheader. What could be better?"

"Strike three. Incredible!" Liz heard Rick's shout through the closed bedroom door. "Lizzy," he yelled. "Come out here. Bunning's pitching a no-hitter!"

Liz didn't budge. She stayed on top of the covers, her legs splayed apart, her hand low on her belly, a low moan emanating from her throat.

"This is history in the making, Liz," Rick yelled. "You gotta see it."

Liz heard her father's voice. "Maybe you should check on her."

"Nah. She's okay. She just doesn't wanna watch."

A moment later, the bedroom door opened. "Are you okay, honey?" Lou asked coming to the side of the bed. He bent down and whispered, "Should I take Bethany?"

Liz drew a deep breath and nodded. Her father rubbed her shoulder then walked to the foot of the bed and held out his arms to his granddaughter. "Come on, sweetheart, let's you and me go get McDonald's." The little girl squiggled her way down the bed with a happy squeal. "If you're not here when we get back," he said, giving Liz a wink, "I'll know where you are." Grandpa and Bethany walked out, leaving the door open.

Liz lay back against the pillows. A strong pull, like a tight fist, grabbed her belly, twisted, and squeezed. Eyes scrunched shut, mouth wide open, Liz panted, hard and fast. A few moments later, the contraction over, Liz let out a long, slow breath and glanced at the clock on the night-table. 2:15 p.m. She focused on the open window across the room. The view of the grassy green hillside relaxed her. Liz closed her eyes and just as she was dozing off, another contraction grabbed her insides, turning them upside down. Forcing herself to breathe, she groaned through it, then checked the clock again. 2:30. "Rick," she called, as loud as possible. No answer. "Rick," a little louder this time.

"What?"

"Come here."

"Wait. Just one more out."

Swallowing hard, Liz pushed herself up, dragged her legs over the edge of the bed, and, with a deep grunt, stood and slowly made her way to the door. "No," she said holding on to the brass knob as if it could keep her up straight. "It's . . ." A wave of pain hit. Intense. She doubled over.

CHAPTER 7

Noah ran around the kitchen, his paper crown with the number two emblazoned on the front. "Two. I two," he shouted as he circled Liz, who was licking the chocolate icing she'd just made off her finger.

"Yes, you are, sweetie. Now go find Grandpa and let Aunt Kristin and Mommy get your birthday cake ready."

The excited boy toddled off to the living room where Grandpa Lou was talking with Kristin's boyfriend. Liz wiped her finger on her apron, then turned to her sister.

"So, Krissy, you've graduated, and, my God, you and Jimmy have been together since your first week at college, so . . . when's the wedding?

Kristin's mouth fell open. "Seriously? You know I'm going to graduate school."

"Yeah. That doesn't mean you can't get married. You love him, right?"

"Sure I do. But I want a career." Kristin drew back and rolled her tongue over her lips. "I'm . . . I'm sorry, Lizzy," she stuttered, "but I'm not like you. School's important to me. I worked hard for my degree and I want more. I refuse to be totally dependent on a man."

Liz bristled.

"Oh, Lizzy, I'm sorry. That was harsh." Kristin reached over and placed a comforting hand on her sister's arm.

Liz shook her head, turned, and opened the utility drawer pulling out a light-blue icing spatula, a gift from her bridal shower.

"I know marriage was more important to you than college," Kristin continued, her voice to Liz's back. "Though I've always wondered, if Mrs. Bergen hadn't said that at your engagement party – that you should quit school – would you have?"

Not able to look at her sister, Liz kept her eyes on the blue scraper with the ivory colored plastic handle adorned with gold tulips and hex signs. It matched all the other utensils that hung from their own metal strip under the counter. "Yeah," she shrugged. "Probably."

Kristin pulled out a kitchen chair and sat. "I swear, I'll never forget Dad's face that day. Remember it? He didn't like that glitzy golf club, or how the Bergens paid for the whole affair. And then, to top it off, Rick's mother got bombed on Bloody Marys. And when she yelled across the table that you didn't need a college degree . . . whoa! I can still see Dad sitting there. He shot up ramrod straight. He was furious. Though, always the gentleman, he didn't say a word."

Liz blew out a short breath. Oh, yes, he did, she said silently.

"And when she said you were going to be a housewife and take care of *her* Richard, I cringed. And Dad and Ken . . . I don't know who was more stunned – our father or our brother."

"I know Daddy was disappointed in me," Liz said, turning to her sister. "But he's so proud of you, Kris. You should have seen him when you walked across that stage last week in your cap and gown, getting your diploma. He was beaming!"

"Oh, Lizzy. He's proud of you too."

Liz lowered her head. Her index finger picked at the hard skin around her thumb. She remembered all her father had said that night. It may have been six years ago, but she would never forget his words or the disappointment on his face.

* * * * *

Seated on the living room couch, Lou filled his pipe. He and Liz were the only ones home after the long day celebrating Liz and Rick's engagement at the Bergens' golf club. "Turn off the television, Lizzy," he said, putting the pouch of Amphora aside. "I want to talk to you." His tone was more serious than Liz had ever heard before.

She uncurled herself from the club chair and glanced at her father as she walked across the room. "I know," she said. "You don't like Rick's parents."

"No. That's not it." Lou patted the tobacco down and struck a match. The delicate aroma filled the air.

Liz pressed the off button on the TV and watched the screen go black. "Then what is it?" she asked and walked over to her father. She stood right in front of him, watching him take a long, slow drag on his pipe.

Lou settled back against the tufted sofa and patted the seat next to him. "Come sit." Liz angled herself on the edge of the cushion, facing him. She watched the smoke curl around his face as he exhaled.

"I hope you're not planning on quitting school," he'd said. "It was your mother's biggest dream. She wanted you to have a college education and make something of yourself."

Liz stiffened. Her mom had been a housewife, so why wasn't it okay for her?

"It's true, Mom loved being a homemaker," Lou said, "but she was sorry she hadn't gone to college like some of the girls in her class. It was the Depression, so there was no issue about it. Her parents didn't have much money, and she needed a job." He shrugged. "And then we got married and Ken was born, and then we had you. Make no mistake," he pumped the air with his pipe. "Mom loved taking care of her family – there was nothing more important to her – but she wanted to get a job one day, maybe go to school and get her degree. Then the war came and everything changed."

Lou sat back against the couch and carried on in a wistful voice. "I was away for two years, and when I came back, like all the women of the time, she stayed home and made a career of being a wife and mother. Life was good for us," he said, his eyes misting over. "But like many of the women, your mother wasn't satisfied." Liz looked at him like he was batty. The magazines back then sure didn't show unhappy women. "Yeah, I know you wouldn't have thought so, but you've got to understand that while the war was on, even though Mom stayed home to raise you and Ken, many women worked. They did the jobs the men had been doing, even in factories. And then when we came home – and with the GI Bill – the women had to go back to the kitchen."

"Yeah, so why's it different for me? Mom liked being home." Liz couldn't help her sarcasm, even though she was well aware she was baiting her father and honestly did understand what he meant.

"Elizabeth," Lou said, dropping his pipe in the ashtray. He got up from the couch and walked to one side of the room, then the other, all the time shaking his head. His eyes met his daughter's. "Just because your mother was happy being a homemaker doesn't mean she wasn't frustrated." He stepped closer and stood at the edge of the cocktail table. "And she was planning on getting a job." He flipped his hands in the air. "There just weren't any. The men were back. And it wasn't only jobs they took, it was college."

He sighed and sat back on the couch. "And then we had Kristin. A surprise, yes," he giggled, "but a delightful one." A smile of love tinged with sadness softened his face. "Mom put off college again, thinking that once Kristin got a little older, she'd . . . well . . ." An exhausted sigh escaped his lips. "The cancer had other ideas." Lou turned to face his daughter straight on. "Oh, Lizzy, I promised your mother I'd take care of you. She was so glad you were growing up in easier times, that you could go to college, have a career. Don't blow it. Get your degree."

CHAPTER 8

Forcing that disturbing memory from her head, Liz removed the wax paper covering the birthday cake she had baked with flour, sugar, even fresh eggs and butter from their neighbor. "So I am a housewife," she said to her sister, still seated at the kitchen table. "Like Mrs. Bergen wanted. Just between you and me though, I'd like it better if I didn't have to take *so* much care of her son. It'd be nice if Rick would help out once in a while. Where is he anyway?" She slid the plate holding the birthday cake closer to her.

"He's up on the hillside with Ken. Our big brother wanted to see your land," Kristin laughed. "He can't believe you're actually going to grow something – you, who hated digging in the dirt. You never even made mud pies with us."

"Damn. Rick's probably giving him an earful." Liz imitated her husband's voice: "My wife won't plant anything here – says she has no time. Like she's so busy."

"Well hell, you are. Just look at the bags under your eyes."

"Gee, thanks."

"Seriously, Liz. You look exhausted. I know you've got two kids, so why are you doing this?" she asked, pointing to the cake.

"Because your wonderful brother-in-law is too cheap to pay for a store-bought cake." Liz waved her hand in the air. "I'm sorry. I shouldn't say those things."

"And also, what do you mean you don't want to plant anything Rick wants? You've got a huge vegetable garden."

"We sure do," Rick bellowed as he strode into the kitchen. "The tomato seeds are already sprouting and with the peppers, zucchinis, beets . . . all the plants . . .

it's going to be great. He opened the refrigerator, grabbed two beers, and popped them open with the church key from the drawer.

Liz sighed and cocked her head. "Two?"

"Yeah." Rick growled. "One's for Ken. He's on his way down from the hill. I beat him." He turned to walk out the door and threw his parting remarks over his shoulder. "We'll be out back. Figure you don't need us for a while."

With the icing spatula clenched between her fingers, Liz tried to keep her voice sweet, speaking to her husband's retreating back. "So what does Ken think of your idea about planting the entire top of the hillside with tomatoes?"

"The entire hillside?" Kristin said. "Isn't it kind of big?"

"Thirteen acres," Rick answered with a shrug. He turned to face his sister-in-law and wife, clutching the bottles of Schlitz tight in his fists. "We can handle it easy. We'll can some and sell some fresh, right off the vine."

"Are you out of your *mind*? I may not know anything about farming, but that sounds like a *hell* of a lot of tomatoes. I know you always said you wanted to live off the land, but…"

"You're right," Rick cut her off. "You don't know anything about farming."

Liz's mouth fell open. Rick had always been so sweet to Kristin. Why the sharp tone? And was he totally insane? There's no way they would plant thirteen acres of tomatoes. Maybe one acre, but she didn't even want to do that.

Not backing down, Kristin asked, "You think the tomatoes will bring you enough money to live off the land?"

"Jeez, you sound just like Ken." Rick took a swig of beer. "And yes, I think they will."

Liz stood back listening to her sister and husband go at it. "Are you going to quit your job and stay home canning tomatoes, making sauce, and soup?" Kristin asked. Rick's answers floated in the air as Liz imagined cans of Bergen tomato sauce, their own label, on grocery store counters. She held in her laughter. He is absolutely insane! We'll be drowning in the stuff, engulfed by tomatoes, red fruit filling up every space in the damn kitchen. She spread chocolate frosting smoothly on top of the yellow cake. Focused directly on the work, she tried again to make her point, and not gouge the cake. "Rick, honey, you know I don't want to spend my weekends at farmers markets."

Rick threw her a pill of a look. "Yeah, yeah," he said. "I've heard all that before." He turned and walked out of the kitchen. The screen door slammed behind him.

Kristin peered at Liz; concern hooded her eyes.

"Forget it, Kris. It's an ongoing argument. And he's supposed to be the math teacher. I don't think he's calculated the amount of tomatoes in one row, much less thirteen acres. I let him go on, but it'll never happen."

Toddler giggles filtered in from the living room, lifting the heavy atmosphere in the kitchen. With the tip of her finger, Liz fixed the divot she'd dug in the cake. She knew her little guy would be thrilled when he saw it, no matter how awful the frosting looked. If only she was able to make her big guy as happy. "For the past three years," she said, standing back checking her work, "ever since we moved here, I've been trying to come up with something to plant. Rick wants it so badly. But everyone grows tomatoes and apples, and, come October, pumpkins are everywhere! They sure don't need ours." She leaned back against the kitchen counter, letting the spatula dangle from her fingers. "Maybe when the kids are older . . ." her voice trailed off as she thought about how exhausted she was – too exhausted to even think about what they could put in the ground on the hillside. But she would never tell Rick that. He'd say she should quit her job, and that was not about to happen. Even if it was with more children, it was her outlet, another hat that she wore. She wasn't just Rick's wife and Bethany and Noah's mommy. Betty Friedan had it right. Kristin had given her the book, *The Feminine Mystique*, and she devoured it. Practically every page was dog-eared. Liz recognized herself in the women Friedan wrote about, even though she wasn't a college graduate. Nursery school may not be considered a career – it certainly didn't bring in much money – but it did give her an identity. She was doing more than laundry and washing dishes. When the realization had hit her that she didn't want to only be a housewife, adrenaline tingled through her veins. Who was this woman named Liz? It certainly wasn't who she thought she was.

CHAPTER 9

Liz took three blue candles, one for good measure, from the little box, placed them on the cake and, with it all lit up, brought it to the dining room. Her whole family and Kristin's boyfriend, Jimmy, were squeezed around the pine table the previous owner had left. That, and some other furniture, all free, had made Rick very happy.

Everyone sang happy birthday while Jimmy strummed the guitar. Liz placed the cake on the table in front of the birthday boy, who bounced up and down in his booster seat.

"Not bad," Liz's brother said, licking chocolate icing from around his mouth. "I didn't know you had it in you, Lizzy."

Lots of yums and mmms from around the table told Liz they all agreed. Even Rick gave her a thumbs-up, which made her feel pretty proud of her attempt at baking from scratch. And Noah was the most pleased. His little fingers dug in and stuffed mounds of yellow cake into his little mouth, smearing the icing over his cheeks, all the way up to his eyes. Liz laughed and gave him a kiss on top of his head. When it appeared there wasn't another spot to cover, she gently took the plate from the birthday boy, got a wet dishtowel from the kitchen, and wiped his face clean.

It was time to open presents, so everyone made their way into the living room. Noah sat on his father's lap while his mother unwrapped the first gift. Liz cut the tape on the enormous cardboard box, then tried to extricate another large box from it. Her brother came over and together they pulled out a package wrapped in Mickey Mouse paper and tied with a big blue ribbon. Ken stepped back and watched, along with everyone else, as Liz untied an enormous satin bow. She handed it to Noah who was more interested in the ribbon than whatever was in the box.

"Who's that from?" Rick asked, surveying the room. No one answered. They'd all brought their presents with them.

Liz ripped a card off the wrapping paper. "To my adorable grandson," she read, then looked at Rick. "You've *got* to be kidding. How does your mother know he's adorable? She's never even seen him."

Rick shrugged. "Pictures, I guess." His dejected sigh said it all.

Liz pried open the large gift box. "Wow!" she said. "Noah, look what Grandma sent you." She pulled out a red tricycle and everyone oohed and ahhed. Everyone except Bethany. The five-year-old stared at her mother, eyes squinted. "Who's Grandma?" she asked.

Good question. Liz turned to face Rick. She lifted a brow and waited.

"Grandma is my mommy," Rick told his daughter. "She lives in Florida, very far away. That's why she's not here today."

"But she's never been here," Bethany said.

Right you are, Liz thought, feeling her jaw tighten. Rick's mother had moved to Florida shortly after her husband died, just a few months after Rick and Liz's wedding.

"Can we go to Florida?" Bethany asked, her eyes bright with excitement.

Rick stared at the pile of presents, then grabbed one wrapped in paper covered in balloons of red, yellow, and blue. "Here, Noah," he said, "let's see what's inside." Liz glared at her husband, her brow practically touching her scalp, as he continued to watch Noah tear through the wrapping. The air was heavy with silence. Then Rick looked at his daughter. With a tiny shoulder shrug, he simply replied, "Maybe. Someday."

CHAPTER 10

Rick bounded into the house banging fluffy white clumps of snow from his boots.

"Take them off," Liz called from the kitchen. She heard her husband grumble from the tiny hallway at the side door where they hung their coats. In stocking feet, Rick stood at the entrance to the kitchen flashing a piece of paper.

"What's that?" Liz placed the TV dinners in the oven and closed the door.

"It's a phone number that might just be our answer for the hillside." He took three long strides to the refrigerator.

"What are you talking about?"

"I heard something today. And I want you to hear me out." Holding the refrigerator door open, he continued, "I know you say there's no time to take care of more crops, but this is exciting."

Liz's chest tightened. "Here we go again," she silently said. "Another bizarre idea." She turned to take the silverware out of the drawer. "Can it wait 'til later?" She didn't want to argue just before dinner.

"Christ!" Rick yelled. His face closed like a fist, his upper lip curled. He grabbed a beer from the fridge, slammed it shut, and snarled as he walked off. Liz heard the kids run to him as he stepped into the living room. She pictured him patting Bethany's head when he said, "Hi, kiddo."

Later, after dinner was over and the kids were in bed, Liz sat on the couch and lit a Winston. Rick watched her every move from the club chair across the room.

"What are you staring at?" she said.

"You. I want to tell you what I heard today, but I want to make sure you're in a good mood."

"What's that supposed to mean?"

"I don't want to argue, Liz. I want to tell you about this experiment and have you listen."

"I always do."

"No. You don't."

"So now who's arguing?"

Rick held up his hand. "Forget it. Let's start over. A guy at school today told me about an experiment Cornell University is doing." He stopped and looked at his wife, his eyes open wide.

"Go on."

"Well, it seems our land is perfect for growing grapes – hybrid grapes."

"What's that?"

"It's the cross breeding of two different species of grapes, French and American. Cornell's been doing it, and they're looking for more farms to join the experiment. Our climate is perfect for them. Plus, there are no other vineyards around here growing them."

Grapes. Now that's classy. A smile spread across her face.

"Is that a yes?" Rick asked, sitting up straight on the edge of his chair.

Liz nodded. Rick jumped from his seat and bounded across the room, slid onto the couch, and grabbed her in a giant hug. "Thank you! It's gonna be great, Lizzy. I know it is."

Liz sunk into his arms, her body warm and tingly. Everything would be perfect now.

CHAPTER 11

"Your soil and climate are ideal for our varietals," the Cornell botanist said. In the humid greenhouse, Liz stood next to Rick, a very sleepy Noah on her hip, and listened to the man speak about why they should seriously consider joining Cornell's experiment. "And our Seyval Blanc grape produces good sugar. It has the perfect acid balance to make a fine wine." Liz shifted the drowsy boy to her other hip and drew in a deep breath, as if she already smelled the heady scent. She gazed out the large glass walls across from her. Fluffy white snow covered the hills of upstate New York, and Liz imagined their own hillside, just before harvest, with rows of grapevines filled with plump, luscious fruit. If only she could call her dad right now and shout out the news. "I'm going to grow grapes! French-American hybrid grapes!" A smile spread across her cheeks. Maybe now he'll be proud of me.

Rick, with his hand firm on Bethany, who was shuffling her feet and swaying side to side, turned toward his wife. "Hold on," he said, his tall, lean frame intimidating. "I know we want to do this, but we've got to be able to sell the fruit, and you said you didn't want to sell anything."

She bit the inside of her cheek, then looked him directly in the eye. "This is different," she said, enunciating each word. "We're not taking these grapes to farmers markets or setting up a stand on the corner selling them like lemonade." Clutching her toddler to her chest, she stepped toward the window, closer to her fantasy vineyard, then turned to Rick. "I'm sure there are winemakers that'll buy them. We will be the only ones in the valley participating in the experiment. And, who knows, maybe we'll make a little wine ourselves."

"Oh," he chuckled. It sounded like dry dirt where flowers would never grow. "So you don't have time to can vegetables 'cause you work so hard at that nursery school, and now you're willing to make wine?" He looked down at his daughter, who was twirling her foot, watching her red Keds go round and round. "Mommy doesn't have the faintest idea how to even begin making wine," he said. "Isn't that funny?"

Liz narrowed her eyes. The high spirits she'd had a moment ago dissolved. The air in the greenhouse was much warmer than Rick's tone, no matter how he tried to lighten it with that little glint in his eye. And making fun of her with their daughter? Her stomach knotted. She and Rick had discussed the idea of growing grapes after they'd called Cornell's extension service, before making the long ride to Geneva. They were in agreement, or so she believed, no longer arguing about apples or pumpkins or what to plant on their acreage. So what's with the sarcasm?

Liz forced the skepticism off her face and the distaste off her tongue. She came back to Rick and, with one hand, clasped his. "We can do it, honey. Just like you wanted, we'll live off the land. We'll find buyers for the grapes. You're good at that kind of thing." The creases in his forehead relaxed, as she knew they would. "Rick, we've got the perfect setting and the soil is right." For confirmation, she glanced at the botanist holding a small peat pot with a tiny bit of green sprouting from the dirt. He nodded. Liz held her chin high and looked up at her husband. "See?"

Rick flicked his eyes from the botanist back to his wife and his little boy asleep in her arms. He was silent but nodding his head ever so slightly. Liz kept quiet. She knew when to let him make the decision. "Okay," he finally said. "We'll do it." But as quick as a bee sting, he pointed an accusing finger in her face. "Remember, though, this is an experiment, and experiments can fail. You have to keep your job."

Liz almost laughed. Now he insists I keep my job? Well . . . let him think it was his idea all along.

CHAPTER 12

Monday, after returning from their trip, Rick went back to his teaching job at Hudson Vocational Tech and Liz to nursery school. The plan was they'd both ask everyone they came in contact with if they knew anyone who could teach them how to grow grapes. Cornell had given them a pamphlet, but they needed guidance. There was so much to learn.

At three o'clock Liz gathered up Noah, drove the few miles to meet Bethany at the school bus, then took both kids with her to the grocery store. There was no reason to hurry home. Rick wouldn't be there. He never got home until about five, and there was nothing to do but throw in a load of wash and put the meatloaf in the oven. But as she drove up their gravel road and pulled into her parking spot, Rick's truck was there.

"Hey," he called, coming out the side door.

"You're home early," Liz yelled back as she walked around the car to open Noah's door. Everything okay?"

"Sure is. I've been waiting for you." He stood on the top step watching her gather the kids and open the trunk. "What took you so long?"

Jeez, she thought. He has no idea. Noah and Bethany ran ahead, across the driveway, kicking up gravel with their little sneakers. She loaded three brown bags filled with groceries into her arms, her pocketbook hanging from her shoulder and Bethany's book bag dangling from her fingers. At least Rick held the door open for her. She dropped the packages on the kitchen counter and hung her coat on the back of a chair.

"So, after asking all the teachers and secretaries, it was one of the custodians who told me about a grape grower," Rick said, watching Liz put boxes of cereal in the pantry. "Matt Woods. He lives in Pine Bush."

"Where's that?"

"About twenty-five miles from here, on State Road 52. I'm going to call him – see if he'll teach us how to plant the vines."

"Isn't that kind of far? There's no one closer?"

"Come on, Liz. You know how friendly these people have been."

Liz remembered how no one had welcomed them. No one had brought a cake when they moved in or rang their bell just to say hi. Possibly it was because they were a mile off the road or maybe because they were new – that their family hadn't lived in this tiny hamlet for generations. These people baffled her. How's it possible to live somewhere – anywhere – and not have friends other than the women from the nursery school who she never saw outside of work? There were a few high school friends she kept in touch with, but sadly, no one lived near here.

Liz folded the paper bags and stashed them under the sink. "Well," she said, straightening up. "I really am glad we've got someone to call. I batted zero on that." She shook her head. "You did good." A smile filled her face and she raised her shoulders like Bethany does when she's all excited over a new toy. "We're going to have a vineyard, Rick."

He leaned over and gave her a little kiss on the tip of her nose. "As long as he shows us how to do it."

CHAPTER 13

The late afternoon spring sun swept shadows across the land. Liz stood on top of the hillside inhaling the loamy scent of the earth like an expensive perfume, its dark, rich soil her hand lotion. "I feel like I'm living in a bubble," she called over to Rick sitting on an army blanket playing cars with Noah. "And I never want it to burst."

Rick looked over at his wife, who was dancing with excitement, ready with string and chalk. He handed Noah a red metal Matchbox car. "Here, buddy," he said. "I have to help Mommy. We'll have another race real soon." Rick got up, finger-combed his hair, and walked toward Liz.

"Stand right there," she said, pointing to a spot across from her.

"Remember, Liz, Matt said the lines have to be perfectly straight."

"I know. So move a little to the right."

With a pinched expression, Rick moved slightly over.

"There," Liz said. "That's good." She bent down and anchored her string in the ground and slowly, very carefully, totally focused, pulled the string all the way across to her husband, then lifted her head. "Does it look straight?"

Rick checked her work. "Yup."

With the chalk between her fingers, Liz crawled backward along the ground making a straight white line next to the string, a quarter mile long, just as Matt had taught. A perfect row where they would plant their first vines.

Liz and Rick worked together on this Monday afternoon, alternating who crawled along the ground, while their kids played. The sun, on its downward slope, was sinking below the horizon as they completed the second row. Liz stood and dusted the dirt from her dungarees. "I guess we should go in and feed the hungry," she said, although she would much rather stay and work.

"I'm famished." Rick said. "We'll finish tomorrow."

"You sure have high hopes. Don't forget, we have to dig the stakes in."

"Yeah, I mean the rows. By the end of the week, working together, we should have it all done."

Liz loved the sound of that. It's what they'd dreamed of from the minute they decided to plant grapes. Every afternoon, after school, they met on the hillside and plotted out their vineyard. By Thursday, the five rows were drawn and the stakes, which would support the growing vines, were dug eighteen inches into the earth.

"Whew!" Liz got up and brushed the dirt from her hands. "Done!" She bent backward and reached her arms toward the evening sky, stretching out the kinks.

"I'm beat," Rick said. "Tomorrow we'll start attaching the wires."

"And then," Liz added, "when the vines grow, we'll tie them to those wires, like Matt showed us. Do you remember how?" Rick nodded, and she looked over at her children stuffing Graham crackers in their mouths. Once again, it was dinner time, her least favorite hour of the day. "Come on," she called. "Clean up your toys. It's time for tomato soup and hot dogs."

Rick threw her a look, his upper lip curled. Then he scooped up Noah and sat him on his shoulders. Liz and Bethany grabbed the blanket and toys, and the four made their way to the house. Halfway down the hill, Liz stopped and turned around. The redwood stakes stood straight and tall, six feet high, in perfect lines. Her heart filled with pride as she imagined her baby vines growing to maturity, their shoots attached to their wire supports, tied in a "Y" formation, like arms reaching out enfolding the fruit. Just like parents, she thought, then turned back and followed her family home, ignoring the annoyed expression on her husband's face.

CHAPTER 14

The next afternoon, with the sun warming her bare arms, Liz trudged up and down the chalk lines winding the hundred-pound roll of support wire around the redwood stakes. Rick's unexpected faculty meeting, and then drinks with the guys after, left her working solo. She didn't want to be angry. It was his job, after all, but she couldn't help it. This was hard work and they were supposed to do it together.

She looked up for the umpteenth time to check on her kids on the old blanket in the shade of the maples. Bethany remained sprawled on her belly, engrossed in her new coloring book, while Noah, coated in cracker crumbs, played with his cars. Back to work, Liz stretched the wire across and wound it around the next stake. Out of the corner of her eye, she saw her little guy toddling over to where the hill started its gradual downward slope.

"Stop right there," she called. "Don't go any farther."

"I not." The little guy pointed his finger out toward the base of the hillside.

"What do you see out there?" Liz asked. "Are there pirates?"

"No pirates. A truck. A really big one, Mommy."

Liz straightened and looked over to where her son was pointing. From her vantage point at the top of the vineyard, she only saw their house and the old gray barn in the distance. She walked over to Noah for a closer view of the road. He was right. An orange tractor was parked there. On her private road. Why? She watched a man climb out and wave a straw hat in her direction.

"Can I help you?" she shouted.

"It's me, Mrs. Bergen. George Franklin from down the road." He put the hat back on his head. "What're you doin'?"

Liz didn't recognize the tall, lean man in coveralls. They shared a small portion of the dirt road, at the end of her lane, where it came off the paved town street, but they'd spoken only once or twice since she and Rick moved in. Just a quick "hello," and his warning: "Be careful of the divots. You need to get yourself a truck."

"I'm planting a vineyard. Want to come up and see?" The invitation wasn't necessary as Mr. Franklin was already halfway up the hill, and Liz was still a little wary. She wondered if he'd come to spy on them. As far as she knew, no neighbor ever drove up their road. No one ever knocked on the door or rang the bell, but she was glad of the opportunity to finally chat with one.

"I'm actually laying out the wires to, eventually, tie up the vines," she added as he reached the top where the land plateaued.

"Yeah, heard you were doin' somethin' here. And who's this little man?" he asked, opening his palm toward Noah.

Liz introduced them and Noah whispered a hello. "And that's my daughter over there. When she's coloring, nothing else matters."

He nodded and pointed to the wire cutter clutched in her right hand. "What's that for?" Liz looked down at her fingers, as if she'd forgotten the cutter was there. She released her grip, letting the tool dangle. "I need this to cut the wire, the end piece, on each row."

The neighbor stood next to her, his eyes taking in the newly laid out vineyard and the wooded area behind. "You do all this on foot?"

Liz shrugged. "Yep."

"Where's your tractor?"

"We don't have one." She quickly added," yet," positive he was wondering what kind of farmer doesn't own a John Deere.

"You can borrow mine," he said with a slight lift of a shoulder, though his tone wasn't bubbling over with warmth.

"No, no, that's not necessary." Liz's words came tumbling out. "That's so kind of you, but really I'm okay."

"Yeah? It sure looks like you could use the help."

Liz wasn't sure if he was being condescending or just matter-of-fact. It didn't matter. Sweat was dripping down her face, soaking her bra and the waistband on her Wranglers, and it was tiring running back and forth pulling the heavy wire, plus she'd only completed two rows so far and the sun would soon set. But she didn't want to sound weak. And, she refused to stop. She picked at the cuticles on her left hand and swallowed her embarrassment. "Well, if you insist, but I've never driven one."

"I'll drive and you can stretch your wires." The neighbor trotted back down the hill before she was able to ask how many people fit in his tractor. What would she do with the kids? She watched him climb in and turn the wheels. Noah jumped up and down shouting "big truck, big truck," as it came up the hill.

"Hop on," the farmer said.

Liz pointed to her kids. "What about them? Can they fit? I can't leave them alone."

"Yeah, right. I'll hold the little guy on my lap. I used to do that with my own boy."

"But . . ." Liz had lots of questions. She mumbled them to herself, not wanting to sound unappreciative or that she didn't trust him or think it wasn't safe. She looked over at Bethany, then up at her neighbor.

"No room," he said, shaking his head.

Liz scrunched her face. She didn't like the idea of leaving her daughter in the vineyard while the tractor moved up and down the rows. With its constant click clack whirring sound so loud, she'd never hear Bethany if she called out. Plus, she wasn't sure Bethany would stay put if she wasn't around. The five-year-old loved exploring the woods.

"Honey, take your crayons and stuff and go sit on the bench. I'm going to work from up there on Mr. Franklin's tractor." Liz pointed to the paint-peeled vehicle.

Bethany looked over and saw her brother about to get into the tractor. "No! I want to go too. Why does Noah get to go?"

"Sweetheart, there isn't enough room for all of us. You'll get a ride later, when I'm done." Oh, this is so frustrating, Liz thought. Rick should be here. She blew out her aggravation. "Come on, sweety, please listen to me. Go on up to the bench and stay there until the tractor stops and I get off." In a chipper tone, she added, "And make Superman's tights a real bright red."

Liz watched her daughter collect her books and Crayolas and slump off to the coziest place on the farm with the old stone bench nestled under the trees, set back off the vineyard. It was at the very top, but close enough where she could keep an eye on her, even if she wasn't able to hear her. Then Liz lifted Noah and climbed into the narrow passenger's seat.

"Easier if he sits here," George said and reached for the excited little boy. "I'll drive real slow."

The farmer drove up and down the rows letting Noah keep his pudgy hands on the steering wheel while Liz pulled the wire taut. As they reached the end of the fifth row the tractor stopped again, for a moment, to allow Liz to wind the wire around the post. "What kind of grapes you gonna grow?" he asked, the first words he'd spoken since they began the ride. Liz explained about Cornell's experiment as they turned right, heading to the next post. "These are Seyval Blanc. Next year, we're going to plant two more acres with another varietal, Cabernet Franc. That's for red wine. We want to start small and see how it goes. I know they're not the usual grapes grown in this valley," she said. Mr. Franklin only shrugged.

Liz wondered if he didn't like that they were growing something different. People are resistant to change, but he didn't have a vineyard, so why would that matter? Or maybe he didn't like the university connection. Whatever it was, he didn't ask any more questions. He just drove, occasionally talked to Noah, and let her do her work.

As Liz continued pulling wire off the large roll and winding it around the stakes, she kept an eye on Bethany, absorbed in The Man of Steel, and smiled as Noah squealed whenever they turned a corner. Maybe now that Mr. Franklin's here and sees we're planting grapes, the neighbors won't see us anymore as city slickers who think rural life is nirvana. Liz had overheard those words in the A&P last week and was sure they were talking about her. She'd never considered herself that way, and she definitely didn't look like one, with her red bandana soaking sweat from her forehead, her dungarees worn thin at the knees, and her hands work-worn and filthy.

Less than a half hour later, the job was done. The birds twittered and, although it was a lovely sound, Matt had warned they could be disastrous to her fruit. She'd have to check with him for ways to keep the sparrows and starlings from eating her grapes. He'd said they were a nightmare to vineyard owners, but at the time she was more interested in what had to be done first. It would take four years for the fruit to be ready for harvesting. She'd worry about the pests then. Now, the wires were attached to all the stakes and it was time to get the baby vines in the ground. At least Rick would be around for that.

Liz reached across the front seat for Noah. "I'm so glad you stopped by," she said. Mr. Franklin smiled, patted Noah on the back, and handed him over to his mother, who was thinking about their other neighbor – the man whose land abutted theirs. She wasn't sure she should broach the subject, but she was anxious to know about the curmudgeon. Every time she saw him, even when he was walking along the edge where their properties came together, she'd call out hello and wave and he'd just stare at her. Not a nod, not even a grunt. Was he deaf? Or did he just not like new people in the neighborhood? She'd barely managed, "If you don't mind—" when Mr. Franklin cut her off.

"Glad I could help. Gotta be gettin' home now."

Liz stepped down from the tractor and tapped the side of it. "Thanks again," she said, swallowing her curiosity. Not wanting to impose, she didn't ask if he'd give Bethany a ride. Unfortunately, this probably won't be the only time I'll disappoint her, Liz thought. She looked up at her helpful neighbor. "I truly appreciate your help and hope we'll see you again soon." She led Noah aside and watched Mr. Franklin drive away while making a promise to herself. One day, I'm going to have my own John Deere and assist someone else, some woman just like me who's starting out in a new venture.

CHAPTER 15

Liz stood at the bathroom sink, the dark circles under her eyes reflected back from the mirror above. She reached across the vanity and tuned the transistor radio to WINS. Damn it! The meteorologist never said the words she wanted to hear. She rinsed out her mouth, covering the sink in foamy toothpaste, then stormed out and flipped on the TV in the kitchen. Maybe the *Today Show* would have better news.

Despite the fact that newly planted grapevines were watered when they were initially put in the ground and only for a few weeks after, Liz wanted to give her babies a drink. Only two months ago she'd planted them and they seemed to be growing nicely, but now she was losing sleep, petrified they wouldn't survive. July had already brought two weeks of high heat and no rain, and there was no sign of even a drizzle in the forecast.

"Shut the TV," Rick said as he walked into the kitchen dressed for work. The summer semester was well underway, and school was where he spent his days, often well into the evening. "You're only making yourself nuts, Liz. Give it a few more days. The rain'll come."

As he walked out, Liz seethed. Why does he always have to be so damn confident everything will be fine? Needing a more compassionate voice, she called her father.

Before she even finished "hello, how are you?" Lou jumped in enthusiastically. "Lizzy! I was just about to call you. Figured I'd take a ride and visit. I'm on vacation this week."

"Oh, that would be wonderful, Daddy. Come today, please. And stay over. Stay the whole week."

"You sure? All week?"

"Absolutely. It'll be great to spend time with you and have an adult around."

"What do you mean? Where's Rick?"

"At school. He's always there. He's a very dedicated teacher." She hoped her sarcasm didn't come through.

"Oh. Well, at least while I'm there you can go do whatever you have to in the vineyard. I'll stay with the kids."

"That's if I still have a vineyard. It hasn't rained in weeks." Liz told him her fears. Less than two hours later, she heard the crunch of his car's tires on her gravel road and ran outside to greet him.

"Oh my God," Lou said. He stood next to his car, staring up at the vineyard. "The grass does look like hay. But isn't it true that too much rain is bad for grapevines? That it can be disastrous?"

Tears bubbled in the corners of Liz's eyes. "Yeah, but these are baby vines."

Lou shut the car door with one hand and pulled his daughter to him with the other, wrapping her in a big bear hug. "You're doing great, Lizzy," he murmured. With tears pouring down her face, she sank deep into his comforting arms. "The rain will come, honey. It's going to be fine. You and Rick are doing a terrific job." Liz stiffened. Why did he have to bring Rick's name into it? Couldn't she, as a woman, be doing fine herself?

A moment later, the screen door slammed. Bethany ran toward them with Noah toddling behind. "Grandpa!" she shouted. "Wanna take a ride in our golf cart?"

Liz pulled back from her father's arms. Unaware of how his words disappointed his daughter, Grandpa Lou stepped forward to block the children's view of their mother as she quickly dried her eyes with the back of her hand.

"Sure. That's a great idea," he said, ruffling Bethany's brown curls. We'll go look at Mommy and Daddy's grapevines." Wanting some attention, Noah tugged at his grandfather's pants leg. Lou scooped him up and tickled his belly, Noah squealing with delight. "First, help me bring my suitcase in. Then we'll take a ride."

Despite his belief that Rick was an integral part of the vineyard, and his assumption that she wasn't able to do this without him, her father's patient demeanor and her children's happy giggles calmed Liz. Each morning she walked up to the vineyard, leaving her father to give the kids breakfast. She inspected the vines for insects, made sure birds weren't pecking at the tiny stalks, and walked back to the house dejected. There was nothing she could do. Rick insisted she not water them. Besides, how was she going to get a hose all the way up the hill?

Since there wasn't any work to accomplish in the vineyard, Liz tended Rick's vegetable garden in the morning, taking her time pulling weeds, staking the tomatoes, and watering while her dad played ball with the kids. Her fingers hungered to be in the dirt, and Rick didn't seem to mind that she'd done the much-needed work. In the afternoons, she and her dad took the children to the nearby lake. Lou splashed in the water with his grandchildren and, later, prepared dinner using fresh vegetables and herbs from the garden while Liz bathed the kids. Life was much easier with her dad around. Still, she wished it was her husband helping out. When he had agreed to teach summer school, she never expected he'd be gone so many hours.

At the dinner table, Rick forked a mouthful of ratatouille. "This is delicious," he said, wiping a stray piece of eggplant from the corner of his lips. "You should teach your daughter to cook."

Liz noticed her father's pinched expression as he nodded a thank you. She wondered if Rick caught it. And what did he mean her dad should teach her to cook? She had made that dish so many times and Rick said he was sick of it. Earlier, when she came into the kitchen and saw the frying pan filled with zucchini, eggplant, tomatoes, and onions, she kept quiet. She didn't want to hurt her dad's feelings, plus she was glad she wasn't the one sweating over the stove. If Rick was tired of it, so be it. He should be home to give his opinion. But none of this was worth arguing over. Liz was just glad Rick had come home for dinner these past two nights – that he'd given up his poker games to be there while her father was with them. And she was happy that he was home to say good night to his kids. Last night, when she went in to kiss Bethany good night, her heart warmed seeing Rick cuddled up reading *Madeleine* to their daughter. Beth looked so happy with her little doll in her arms and her daddy next to her.

On the third day of Lou's visit, Liz woke to the patter of raindrops on the bedroom window. Life was good again. Her vines would live and she'd be back in the vineyard taking care of them, even if it was by herself.

CHAPTER 16

Summer came to an end – too fast for Liz, who was loving the long days and the sun's warmth seeping into her hard-worked shoulders. Back to teaching nursery school, her time in the vineyard was curtailed. She sorely missed the hours spent among her vines after the rains woke up the earth and hurried home each afternoon to check them, just as mothers check on their babies. Were they growing as they should be? Were they getting enough nourishment? Did they look healthy? Even with the kids playing nearby, it was peaceful on the hillside. She loved walking along the rows, imagining even more rows of plants eventually filling all thirteen acres. She played out scenarios in her mind of harvesting the fruit with Rick at her side just as they had planned. She wondered how much money they'd make selling their grapes and hoped it would be enough for Rick to stop working such late hours. He claimed that was why he was so crabby. But until the grapes brought in money, he'd have to keep working late. On Halloween night, while they were getting ready for bed, he yelled at her about all the candy the kids got. She screamed, "You're always so angry. What's with you?"

"I'm stressed out."

"So, come home earlier. You didn't even see the kids in their costumes. You don't have to stay every day for extra help."

"I get paid for that, Liz. And we need the money."

Liz thought teachers were paid a yearly salary, but Rick said private schools worked differently. Instead of arguing further, she lowered her voice and merely said, "Well, hopefully, we'll be able to do what you've always wanted – live off the land – when this crop comes in. Then maybe you won't be so testy."

Rick threw a shoe across the room, just missing her head. He stormed out. Intense heat smacked Liz to the core and radiated through her body. She grabbed her cigarettes, her hand shaking as she lit the match, and tried hard to stop the tears.

A week later, on a crisp November Sunday with a musty scent in the air, Liz and Rick raked leaves together. Liz was happy, yet she was unable to shake her fear. He seemed to be in a good mood, but there were so many dead leaves encroaching on the vines and filling the rows, the job was overwhelming. Liz was afraid he'd snap.

"How about we just do a little today," she suggested, "and get Kristin and Jimmy to come next weekend to help?"

Rick straightened and bent backward, stretching his spine. "Good idea, 'cause the game goes on soon. You can stay, if you want. You seem to be very capable handling everything here anyway."

Liz swallowed hard. She almost choked on the words she wanted to spew. What the hell does that mean? If you'd come home earlier, I wouldn't have to do everything myself. But no, you only want to work up here on weekends. Well, my dear, grapevines are like children, they don't only need your love on Saturdays and Sundays. She blew out a heavy sigh and, with hands gripped tightly to the rake, dragged a bunch of leaves into a pile. Rick leaned against his rake, watching her. He was done. No way was she staying up here alone again. Liz rounded up the kids and the four of them trotted down the hill together, as if nothing was amiss.

CHAPTER 17

The mattress bounced. Liz opened her eyes. Rick, in his jockey shorts and T-shirt, was seated on his side of the bed, his back to her. The clock radio showed 1:15 a.m. She hadn't heard him come in this time, already used to his coming home at these god-awful hours. It had been going on all week, and, once again, Liz couldn't decide if she should say something or pretend sleep as she'd been doing. How long could a poker game take, she wondered? And why were they having a tournament on week nights when they had to get up early for school?

Rick slid under the covers, pulling them to his neck. Liz turned toward him, drawing her knees to her chest like a sleeping baby, hoping he'd bend over and at least kiss her on the forehead. When they were first married, they never went to sleep without a good-night kiss, even if one of them climbed into bed before the other. When had that stopped?

It's incredible how fast he falls asleep, Liz thought, hearing her husband's soft snore. Like nothing matters to him. Or it's the beer. The stink from his open mouth was there again. Smoke mixed with Schlitz. But there was something else. Liz lifted herself onto her elbow, bent closer, and sniffed. What's that sweet scent? It was sort of familiar, but where had she smelled it before? She turned away and scooted farther to her side of the bed, trying to name it. Finally, she threw the question out of her head. She needed her sleep. At 3 a.m. it still gnawed at her. She took some deep breaths, trying to relax. She counted backward from one hundred. It must have worked, since the next time she looked at the clock it was 4:30 a.m. And then again, 6 a.m. How was she going to function? She lay in bed staring out at the darkness when finally, sun glared through the slatted blinds and the alarm pierced the air. Rick reached over and slammed it off.

"Good morning," Liz said pulling the covers tight around her, wishing she could fall back to sleep. She was not ready to put her bare feet on the cold floor and face the day. "You came home really late last night. I don't know how you can get up and teach today." Silently, she wondered how she was able to. "Don't you have a hangover? You smelled like a brewery and . . ."

"Jeez, Liz. Can't a guy have a few beers?"

"Of course. It's just . . . I don't know how you can get up in the morning. Who played? Just the guys?"

Rick sneered. "Why're you asking?"

"Nothing. Forget it." Did she seriously want the answer?

"Christ, Liz. What do think? Other women were there?" Rick shook his head, stripped off his T-shirt, tossed it on the floor, flung his legs over the side of the bed, and stormed off to the shower. Liz got out of bed and picked up the shirt. Again, that sweet smell from last night hit her in the face.

CHAPTER 18

"If only I could paint," Kristin said as she took in the vibrant colors carpeting the vineyard. She pulled over a pile of crisp leaves and dumped it at the end of the grassy row on top of the one Liz had started. Each row of grapevines was separated by a lane of grass making the hillside into stripes of emerald green and rich chocolate brown. No sooner were the leaves off the rake and Kristin cleaning another spot than the kids ran over and jumped into the pile. Liz glanced at Rick, his head focused on the leaves. She hoped he hadn't noticed. It was a mess. Leaves were spread all around. They'd have to start all over again, but she didn't mind. The music of children's laughter made her smile – until Rick shouted. "Enough! Damn it, Liz. Can't you control them?"

Kristin shot up straight. Her head jerked back. She stood stock still, gripping the rake as her eyes flicked back and forth between her sister and brother-in-law.

Liz felt her cheeks flush. "Come on, kids," she said, trying to sound like nothing had happened. "Aunt Kristin and I are going back to the house to get some lemonade. Jump in the golf cart. You can pick out the cookies."

Liz knew her sister was stunned by Rick's tone. Kristin had heard his sarcasm before, but never witnessed him yelling at her or the kids. She hoped Kristin wouldn't ask any questions – or notice his bloodshot eyes, either. Liz wished she could forget about them too – or understand why her husband was drinking so much.

"What's going on?" Kristin asked as she pulled out glasses from the cabinet above the sink.

"Nothing. What do you mean?"

"Hey, guys," Kristin said, giving a big smile to her niece and nephew planted in front of the cabinet waiting for cookies. "Why don't you go watch TV while Mommy and I get everything ready? Then you can carry the cookies to Daddy and Jimmy."

Bethany and Noah ran off into the living room. Kristin turned her eyes on her sister. "Don't give me that bull. I can tell it's not nothing."

Liz shook her head as she pulled boxes of Mallomars and Chocolate Snaps from the pantry. "I don't know. Rick is working so hard, staying late at school and going out for beers with the guys after, and I'm stuck here doing all the work. Remember, he was the one who wanted this farm, not me. And now, it's like the earth is part of me. It's gotten under my skin. I love it and I want to see it flourish, but he's never around to help. I do everything."

"Everything?"

"Yeah. I expected to be the one taking care of the kids and the house, but the vineyard? I thought we'd be doing it together. That *was* the plan."

Kristin narrowed her eyes.

"What?" Liz asked.

"The kids? Aren't you supposed to do that together too? Isn't he the father? Why doesn't he help out?"

"Men don't do that."

Kris gave her another incredulous look.

"Yeah, I know Miss Feminist. And don't compare Daddy. He's different. He treated Mom like a princess. Most men don't do that. They don't cook dinner or read the kids bedtime stories like he did . . . well, Rick did do that one time . . . but they sure don't clean the house. They expect their wives to do all that. But I'm taking care of the vineyard too."

"Where did you ever come up with those ideas? Life isn't *Father Knows Best*, Liz. It isn't a TV show, and we're certainly not in Victorian times anymore. You're not the nanny and you're not the hired hand. Get Rick to help. And what about his drinking? You think I don't see his eyes? Is he like his mother?"

Liz slumped down on a chair. She buried her head in her hands and the tears flowed. Kristin slipped into the chair next to her and put an arm around her older sister. "I don't know what to do," Liz said as the crying slowed to sniffles. "Sometimes he scares me, but I don't want to lose him."

"You're not going to." Kristin's voice was as warm as molten chocolate. "Rick loves you."

"I'm not so sure anymore," Liz said, her face still down. She wiped her eyes, then looked at her sister. "I don't know where he was this week. Every night, he came home so late and when I asked why, he blew up. So it's better if I keep quiet and just keep doing what I'm doing."

Kristin drew her sister into her arms. She held Liz and rocked her as the tears flowed again. "No," she said. "It's not better. If he's drinking, it's only going to get worse. You know that."

Liz drew back from the embrace and nodded. "Yeah, I do. That's why I need to give him space, not get him aggravated." She wiped the wetness from her cheekbones. "Everything will change when the vines mature and we sell our beautiful grapes. I have to believe that."

"But that's not for another three years."

"I know." Liz stood and went back to the pantry. "That's why I have to pick my battles."

"I get it." Kris joined her sister at the kitchen counter. "Keep it peaceful," she said as they placed the cookies on a plate. "Just don't let him walk all over you. Rick needs to do his share. And not only on the farm. Times are different for women now."

"Okay, Gloria Steinem. I hear you. It's just so hard for me. I want my marriage to work." Liz popped a Chocolate Snap into her mouth, then another. She chewed and swallowed then, wiping crumbs from her lips as if erasing guilt, looked directly at Kristin and said. "Do not tell Daddy about this. Please. Never."

CHAPTER 19

Autumn turned to winter and work in the vineyard slowed. Liz knew their varietal was hardy for their climate. The botanist at Cornell had told her that the Seyval could stand temperatures down to minus ten degrees Fahrenheit which, thankfully, was not a usual occurrence in the Hudson Valley. Still, she insisted checking on them every day.

Seated on the cold, faded linoleum floor in the vestibule, she pulled on her quilted boots. "I'll be right back," she called through the open kitchen door. "Just going to check the vines."

"You don't have to," Rick yelled, his words loud enough to shake the trees outside. He finished pouring himself his coffee. "I told you, it's just snow. The wind-chill only makes you nervous. It doesn't have any effect on the vines."

"Yeah, but it was freezing last night." Liz wouldn't let her voice rise to his decibels. Sure, the snow was fluffy but Matt had warned them that ice could destroy their tender vines.

"Well, I gotta leave soon. I'll shovel when I get home."

"I know. This won't take long. Just give the kids some Cheerios, please."

"Since when did this become my job?" Rick mumbled. The hairs on the back of her neck stood straight up. Liz swallowed a retort and zipped her jacket. Just once in a while she'd like him not to make a snarky comment when she asked for help, which she'd been doing more readily since her conversation with Kristin. He never did see her point, though, so why say anything now? Liz pulled her knit hat down around her ears and tried not to slam the door behind her.

Clean white snow, peaked like meringue, covered the stone path. Rick had constructed it himself last summer after they planted the vines. It circled around the back of the house and ended at the gravel road at the base of the hillside. "This way, on wet days, we won't have to trudge through mud," he'd said. At the time, she warmed to those words, thinking it was so sweet of him, and she was proud of the arduous work her husband had done. Okay, she thought now. What about snow? He could have gotten up earlier to shovel. Her dad always did that so she and her brother and sister had a clean sidewalk when they left for school. But Rick wasn't Lou and she knew she shouldn't compare them. She tried hard not to.

Breathing in the clean, crisp January air should have been invigorating. It should have relaxed Liz, but her tight shoulders would not loosen. She lifted her knees high, her boots making deep footprints in the crunchy snowdrifts as she made her way up the hill.

Liz walked along the first row of vines, every muscle tense. The early morning sun glared off the alabaster landscape, and, combined with the deep snow encircling the plants, all she could manage was a cursory look. She knelt, getting her knees soaked, and brushed the white stuff away. When she peered in, a shaky laugh escaped her lips. With eyes closed, she raised her head to the cloudless sky and nodded a thank you. Four shoots were growing from the mother vine. Matt had explained that's all there would be this first year. "And when they grow about six to ten inches high," he'd said, "it's time to pick the strongest one and train it up the stake." She scrambled along the row, soaking her denim-clad legs and gloved hands, brushing snow from several more plants, her quick, worried breaths the only sound.

At the end of the row, still on her wet knees, Liz dropped her head back and let out a deep, thankful breath. These vines were growing just as they should be. She checked her watch. Only ten more minutes until Rick left for school, and there were four more rows to check. Not enough time. Liz stood, whisked the white fluffs from her legs and rushed over to row two. She bent down, brushing the snow away from the base of those plants and checked their shoots. All good. She thanked Mother Nature again, hoping she had protected the rest of the babies, then ran back to the house kicking snow along the way.

In two months, in late March when the earth was brown and moist, Matt would come back. He would show them how to choose the strongest shoot and teach them to train it to the stake. Their infant vines were well on their way to becoming tall, vibrant adults, and Liz would keep checking on them, no matter what the weather or what Rick said.

CHAPTER 20

On a breezy Saturday morning when the air was filled with the earthy scent of spring, Liz left the kids with her father, who had come to babysit, and met Rick and Matt in the vineyard. It was time to prune the vines.

"See this vertical shoot here," Matt said, looking at Liz. "As I was telling Rick, this shoot – cane is the proper term – is what you want to keep. It's got to be between six and ten inches long and straight up. That means it's vigorous. All the others get pruned."

"But we're supposed to tie the vines," Rick said, leaning over his wife's shoulder for a closer look at the tender cane in Matt's fingers.

Liz rolled her eyes. When they called Matt earlier in the week, letting him know they were ready for their next lesson, he explained they had to cut back most of the green shoots before tying them. "Next year you'll keep more, two or three, but not now," he'd said. "You want the vines to establish themselves, to create a good root system and develop a strong, woody trunk."

Liz took a step closer and lifted another delicate shoot. She looked at Matt. "I hate to lose it. Do we really have to cut them all back?"

"All except one," he said, handing her a clipper. "The plant will grow stronger that way." Matt tapped her on the shoulder. "Don't be nervous."

Liz grasped the secateur tightly, looked at the pointy blades then up at the sky. "Please don't let me kill these babies," she whispered. She wasn't a religious woman, didn't go to church, but hoped someone or something was listening. Matt gave her a little nudge. She placed the clipper around the delicate cane and snipped.

"See, that wasn't so bad, was it?" Matt's eyes creased, with a warm smile forming gentle quotation marks around them. He turned and focused on Rick who stood a few paces behind them with a scowl on his face. "After you're done with this," he told him, "I'll show you how to tie them."

Rick nudged his chin toward the cane Liz had just pruned. "It looks like a stick with a green leaf. If I didn't know better, I'd pull it, thinkin' it's a weed."

Matt laughed. "Well, don't go pulling anything out of these rows or you won't have a vineyard. My wife almost did that our first year — figured she was helping me." Smiling, Matt shook his head. "She learned fast. She's good."

Liz felt her mouth turn up just a little then said, "It's the buds, right, that form on these canes that'll make the fruit?" She needed to make sure she'd understood what Matt had explained earlier.

"Yes, but remember, you have to scrape off any you see this year. You're not going to have plump, juicy wine grapes for three or four years. You've got to let them mature."

Liz handed the clipper to Rick. "Come on, hon, you give it a try." Rick took the tool from her hand, and pulled the next cane to him. Liz winced. "Easy, they're babies," she said.

Rick cut a quick look her way. His glare told her not to interfere. He found the base of the tender green shoot and cut it off, then moved on to the next cane. After pruning three more, he handed the clipper back to his wife. "Your turn. Like you originally agreed," he said with a shrug, "this is a joint effort."

Liz planted a sweet smile on her face, though every nerve in her body twitched. She took the shears from her husband, as if all was perfect with the world. Joint effort, she thought. That's a laugh. Sure, it's what it's supposed to be, so why's he annoyed? She walked to the next cane hoping now that he sees they actually have grapevines, Rick would join in the effort more often.

With the blades placed exactly where Matt had shown her, Liz snipped the weaker shoot from its strong mama, wishing she didn't have to wait so long for the vines to bear fruit. She was ready to go into business *now*. Matt had given them the name of the buyer he used, and the man agreed to purchase their Seyval when it was ready. If the grapes were viable.

Several hours later, Matt walked over from where he was working and suggested they stop. "You can finish another day," he said, "Or days actually. It takes a long time to get a whole acre pruned, and I'm happy to have helped, but you don't need me anymore for this."

Liz was sorry Matt wasn't going to continue. She hadn't realized what a time-consuming job pruning was. How was she ever going to get it all done?

"So," Matt continued. "I've got to get my boys to their baseball games, but I'll give you a quick lesson on tying the vines." Liz called Rick over and, like two serious students, they followed their teacher to an already pruned vine and paid close attention to his every word.

"The goal here is to form strong, straight shoots to develop the trunk, so we've got to secure it to the stake to keep it from drooping or breaking once the heavy grape bunches develop." He picked up a ball of twine he'd left on the ground earlier. "Tie it tight enough to secure it," he said, handing the thin rope to Rick, "but not too tight. We don't want to cut into the trunk. And as this cane grows, we'll train it bilaterally making a cordon. It'll look like arms reaching right and left grasping the wires, eventually holding up big beautiful bunches of grapes." He pointed to the wire above, the one that Liz had strung across the rows last summer with the help of her neighbor.

Rick tied one vine and handed the twine to his wife. "I'll do one," she said, "but I think we better call it a day. Matt's gotta get home and my dad's been with the kids all day."

As the three tired workers walked down the hill, Matt glanced up at the newly formed heavy clouds. "Looks like we're gonna get some rain. Hopefully, tomorrow you can finish pruning." He turned to Rick. "You've both got a good grasp on what's got to be done, so you don't need me for that. And after you get everything tied, you can start digging out the next rows. You're going to plant Cab Franc, aren't you?"

"Yes," Liz said, thinking about all the work they'd have over the next few months. "Cornell is sending a thousand plants. It'll cover two more acres, like you said." Matt nodded. "And if we keep having success, we'll plant more. Some Cayuga and Vidal."

"Yeah. We're gonna cover all thirteen acres with fruit," Rick said. His chest puffed out.

"We've got our work cut out for us, but I love it. And it's what we wanted." Liz looked up at Rick. "Right?" He gave her a thumbs-up.

They reached the bottom of the hill and walked together to Matt's truck. As he slipped into the driver's seat, he turned to them. "Today was great. You're well on your way to an outstanding vineyard." And then, with his eyes directly on Liz he said, "I'm impressed. You've got the hang of this. Good work." His uplifted brow seemed to say he was surprised. After all, she was a woman.

CHAPTER 21

The next morning, Liz woke to rain battering the window panes. She slid up onto her side, leaned on her elbow, and gazed out the window on Rick's side of the bed. He was tucked under the covers, snoring. Well, sleep as long as you want, she thought. It doesn't look like we're going to be doing any work today. She slipped out of bed, grabbed a robe, and padded off into the kitchen in bare feet. Maybe she'd be able to have a quiet cup of coffee before everyone woke and read some of *The Handbook on Wine* Matt had given her. She wanted to learn every single thing there was to know about planting and harvesting.

The soaking rain kept the Bergens indoors all day. Liz managed to get through two chapters of the handbook after breakfast while the kids played on their own until Noah nagged her to play blocks with him and Bethany needed help with a jigsaw puzzle. Although she would have loved being in the vineyard working alongside Rick, it was a cozy indoor family day. In the afternoon, Liz took out her box of art supplies and finger painted with the kids on the kitchen table. Rick watched basketball until his mouth dropped open and the snoring began again. Schlitz was a wonderful sleeping pill.

Later, after the children were asleep, Liz sat on the couch curled up under an afghan. Rick turned on the television and, just like when they were newlyweds, put his arm around her shoulders and drew her close. Liz let out a quiet, contented sigh, and they settled in to watch *Bonanza*. Happy to be with her husband, Liz didn't complain about how cold it was in the house. She would cope with his refusing to set the thermostat any higher than sixty-two as long as he was home with her and sober. He hadn't had a drink since the two beers in the afternoon, and she was glad to have his warm body next to hers.

"If it's not raining tomorrow," Rick said as the Cartwrights rode their horses across the TV screen, "I'll meet you in the vineyard around four o'clock."

Calm seeped through her body. Liz laid her head on her husband's shoulder and stared at the TV, but instead of the vast expanse of the Nevada ranch, her eyes saw rows of tall green grapevines reaching toward the sun, its rays nourishing the roots, canes, and ultimately, the fruit. Then Rick withdrew his arm, stood, and went to the kitchen for another beer.

CHAPTER 22

The sun was low in the sky. There was only about an hour, maybe an hour and a half more of daylight, and Liz couldn't wait any longer. She checked her watch again. Four fifteen. Where was Rick? He was supposed to be here already. Instead of her secateur, she grabbed the ball of twine and scissors from the golf cart and stormed off to the first row of grapevines. She'd rather tie them and get them going. Rick could prune, and she'd be right behind him ready with the twine.

"If you see Daddy coming up the hill, let me know," she told the kids who were already seated on the army blanket. "And Noah," she pointed her finger toward her adorable little guy in his hooded Mickey Mouse sweatshirt, "you stay right there on the blanket with Bethany. Play with your cars. She's got homework to do."

Her back to her children, Liz focused on the first cane. Taking care not to break it, she tied it to the stake about four inches from the ground, then stuck her finger between the shoot and the twine making sure the rope was loose enough that it wouldn't strangle the baby vine. Since the cane was already about eight inches long, she tied it again, higher, keeping the line straight. She'd read that the straighter you tie the growing shoots to the stake, the more uniform and upright the trunks will be on the mature vines. Then she stepped back and checked her work. Pretty good, she thought, and moved on to the next vine doing the same, even rubbing off a few swelling buds. "You're not supposed to grow yet," she told them in apology. With two vines tied, she checked her watch again. It was four twenty and still no Rick. Damn it. He promised. Liz continued along the row, listening for her husband's tires on the gravel road, but the only sound she heard came from her children. She swallowed her anger and continued working, letting the vineyard calm her. Despite Rick's absence, being on her hillside vineyard taking care of her vines, Liz felt a lightness in her body, as if she was weightless, floating through the flora.

After working another row, she stood and rubbed the small of her back. She couldn't help it. Aggravation crept back in. Where the hell was Rick? Staying late for a student again? Or out with the guys for a beer because they insisted? And I'm just supposed to smile and say, "That's okay, honey. I understand." Understand my ass.

Later that evening, dinner dishes done, an exhausted Liz ambled into the living room. Her children were playing quietly on the floor while their father relaxed with his feet on the cocktail table, the newspaper open on his lap.

"Come on, Noah, put your cars away. It's bath time," she said, a little more harshly than usual.

"No! Not now," he whined.

Liz grabbed a little metal car from his fingers. "Yes, now!" she yelled and lifted him off the floor. Bethany's head shot up, her mouth wide open. Liz rarely yelled at her kids, especially not little Noah. In a sing-song tone, she tried to make amends. "Come on, honey, I'll make you a bubble bath and you can sail your boats. Then I'll read you a story." Rick looked up from the newspaper and grumbled, "Don't waste water. I need a shower too," and the hair on Liz's arms stood on end. Without a word, she carried her son across the room.

After a warm bath and a story about Curious George the monkey, she kissed her son good night and went to make herself a cup of tea. Rick was in Bethany's room reading her *Peter Pan and the Pirates*, a classic Golden Book Liz had borrowed from the nursery school figuring Noah would love the story of the little boy who didn't want to grow up. She was surprised her daughter asked Daddy to read it to her, and so glad he agreed. Maybe he identified with Peter? He sure acted it sometimes, expecting her to do everything, as if she was his mother, or the mother he wished he'd had. Rick's mother barely made dinner; they were always at "The Club." She knew that was why he hated frozen dinners and why he expected her to cook every night. And okay, she did it, most of the time, even if she barely had time to buy the roast beef much less make it perfectly medium rare with all the trimmings. Isn't that what wives were supposed to do? She'd always thought so. That's the life she had wanted – once upon a time.

Standing at the kitchen counter, staring at the tea bag as it changed the water from clear to a toasty brown, Liz considered ways to approach her husband.

"Where the hell were you this afternoon?" No, that wouldn't be good, though that's exactly what she wanted to say. Rick hadn't even apologized when he walked through the door at six thirty expecting dinner, as if he'd never promised to help her in the vineyard. Liz had let it go, not wanting to argue in front of the kids, but she was busting inside. If he wasn't going to be part of this vineyard and do the work that needed to get done, well . . . Liz didn't know what she would do. Those little babies growing in their soil were precious. Each tender shoot was a new life, not just a plant but a beautiful vision, first Rick's alone, then theirs together, and now it seemed more and more to be hers alone. Again, she envisioned rows of tall vines with clusters of fruit dangling from their outspread arms all across their hillside. She couldn't get this picture out of her mind, and how they'd gather and sell the plump, juicy fruit, and live off the land as Rick had wanted. If he was too busy to help, well then, Liz decided, she would do the work herself, no matter how long it took. She never dreamt she'd take to the land as she had. She loved working in the vineyard with sweat dripping down her face and dirt under her nails, though she preferred it when Rick was with her. Maybe his teaching job really did take up a great deal of time. Back in college, when he first mentioned he wanted to live off the land, Liz had told him farming and teaching school at the same time wouldn't be as easy as he thought. Yet he swore he'd do whatever it took, that he would take care of her. What had happened to that pledge?

Liz picked up her mug and carried it to the living room. As much as she tried to squash it, to understand his career and give him a pass, she was furious Rick hadn't shown as promised. And she still had no idea how to approach him about it to keep him from losing his temper. Maybe there really *were* answers in tea leaves.

Rick walked into the living room, beer in hand, directly to the television.

"Honey," Liz said from her seat on the couch, "would you mind not turning that on now?

He flicked his head toward her, a pinched expression on his face. "Why?"

"I just want to talk to you awhile. We never get a chance anymore."

"Yeah, well you're so busy with the kids, every night a bath and homework, then reading stories." He swatted the air in front of him.

No, don't say it, Liz told herself. Go easy. Make nice. But why is he jealous? They're his kids for god sakes. She forced down the furor rising inside her body, heating to a frenzy.

"Okay. What do you want to talk about?" Rick said as he sat back in the arm chair across from her, his right ankle on his opposite knee, his foot shaking up and down. He took a swig of beer. "So, what is it?"

"Nothing special. I just want to be with you, like last night." She took an Oreo from the plate on the coffee table and pulled apart the two chocolate cookies. "I know you're really busy at school," she said, picking at the white filler with her fingernail. "And you're right." She licked the frosting from her nail then continued, eyes still on her fingers. "Between your working late and me busy in the vineyard, then dinner and . . ."

"So that's it. The vineyard."

"No, it's okay." Liz scraped the white off the cookie with her teeth. "I know school takes up lots of time. I got a lot of the work done today. I'm making headway on tying the vines, and I know you'll help me tomorrow or the next day. Whenever . . ."

"Yeah, I'm sorry, honey, but I had two kids in detention and I had to be there." From Rick's sweet tone, her shoulders relaxed. That was the voice she knew and loved. "And," Rick continued, "remember that boy I almost failed? Well, he asked me to give him some extra help. What was I supposed to do? Not give it?"

Liz knew extra help didn't last until six o'clock but all she said was, "Of course you had to stay and help him." She gobbled down the two chocolate halves and pulled another Oreo from the plate.

"I'm really busy after school, Liz, but I'll be in the vineyard with you all weekend." He took another gulp of beer and, as quick as a bee sting, his gruff voice returned. "Anyway, you're doin' a fine job yourself. You obviously don't need me."

"Yes, I do," she said, her voice full of saccharine. She thought she should get an Oscar for her performance. "I always need you."

Rick jutted his chin at her. "You're doin' the man's job, Lizzy, but never forget," he said pointing his finger in her face, "you are a woman."

"What's that supposed to mean?"

"Work as hard as you want in the vineyard, tie the vines, prune, whatever, but don't skimp on the house or the kids . . . or me."

No matter how much she didn't want them to, tears clouded her eyes. She blinked hard, chomped down on the cookie, and grabbed another. As much as she told herself she wouldn't let him get to her, that she'd be strong, she couldn't help it. *And skimping on him? What the hell does that mean? He's never around. What does he want from me?*

"Oh, don't cry, sweetheart," Rick said as he stood and walked over to the couch. He sat next to her and took a cookie himself. "These are good," he said, splitting it in two. "See, that's what I mean. Thanks for putting these out." He smiled at her, sugar *and* saccharine tinged his words. "You always know my favorite foods."

A few minutes later, cookies and beer consumed, Liz suggested they watch TV. "Yeah," Rick agreed, looking at his watch. "It's 9:30. *Peyton Place* is on." He walked over and turned the television on, then came back and sat next to his wife, his feet on the coffee table. Together they relaxed against the sofa cushions watching Rodney, Norman, Connie, and all the others of the soap opera town.

"Is that a new cologne you're wearing?" Liz asked as the first commercial came on.

Rick drew back. "I'm not wearing cologne."

CHAPTER 23

Liz was used to working solo, but she'd had it with Rick's excuses. Over the past year and a half, there were more and more. He seemed to always have to be somewhere else, even the occasional weekend fishing trips with his buddies when he never came home with a catch. And to top it off, she was disgusted with the outcome of yesterday's presidential election. Even the brilliant autumn sunshine couldn't ease her aggravation. There was a sour tang in her mouth. She wanted to spit. This was not the life she'd planned and Richard Nixon was not the man she wanted in office. Influenced by her father's distrust of Tricky Dick, she supported Humphrey while Rick, who proclaimed Nixon was a law and order man, not a hippy protestor, strutted around all morning as if he was in the White House himself. Liz didn't believe him for a minute. Hadn't Rick professed to wanting to live off the land, not be tied to a nine-to-five job like his father, who had been obsessed with the mighty dollar? How could he not see he was the direct opposite of the Republican Party? Was he doing this just to get her goat? She let out a disgusted breath and looked at the four rows of vines she'd already raked. Then, with her hands tight around the rake's handle, she took in the remaining eleven. Dead leaves surrounded her tender vines. Damn it. Does the wind really need to bring me every leaf from the whole damn county? Isn't it enough we've got our own forest?

Liz loved the shade from the maple and oak trees that lined their gravel road and the intoxicating earthy scent they emitted, especially on a damp day like today. And that ancient sycamore in front of the house brought a smile to her face every time she drove up the road. As gorgeous as they were, they caused an enormous amount of work. "At least last summer he mowed the lawn," she grumbled, remembering how she had to beg Rick to give her a hand and not go off for another weekend.

Although Liz loved working in the vineyard, running between it and nursery school, in addition to taking care of the house and the children, was exhausting. She was glad her dad was visiting again, keeping the kids busy so she could get the raking done. She could always depend on him. But *I need some time for myself,* she thought pulling crisp leaves into a pile. *Something's gotta change. If it doesn't, I'm going to collapse.*

Every season there was something to do, whether pruning, mulching, raking, or tying. She'd hoped after their talk last summer that Rick would be better, but it was over two years since they'd planted their first vines, and still, she was the one doing practically all the work. She wiggled her shoulders. "We're living off the land," she said, mimicking her husband's voice. Liz shook her head hard. "Oh, why am I being so negative?" She kept talking to herself. "Maybe because I barely got any sleep last night watching the election returns? No. It's because I'm freakin' exhausted all the time." Silently, she continued pulling leaves from around the base of the plants, thinking. *I am proud of Rick. He's so dedicated to his students. I just wish he was more devoted to our land. And our family.*

Liz bent down, lifted a pile of leaves onto the bamboo tines, then dumped them into the bag waiting on the grass. *This is ridiculous. There's got to be a better way.* She decided she'd talk to Rick about it, or maybe Matt. He'd know better if there was another way to keep them from crowding the vines. She had other things she needed to talk to Rick about.

Later that night, after the kids were tucked in bed, Liz gathered her confidence, thinking it was a good time to make her plea. Rick might be more amenable to her quitting work at the nursery school, now that he had some alcohol in him. She couldn't wait much longer though. He was already popping the top of a second can, and with another twelve ounces in his bloodstream, he'd probably lose his temper. He'd done that too many times and too many things had been thrown at her: shoes, spoons, even toothbrushes like on the night she stupidly got out of bed and met him in the bathroom. She shouldn't have yelled at him about doing his share of the work, not when he was obviously wasted. Now, she would take it slow and easy.

"Honey, you know how tired I've been every night," Liz said as she leaned against a kitchen chair watching her husband take a slug of beer. She saw his back straighten and knew she had to be careful, not mention anything about needing his help. "And I know I haven't been very responsive in bed," she added apologetically. That ought to get him, even though he hadn't made any advances the past several weeks, but who's counting? Put the onus on me, she figured. Play to his precious dick. "I think if I didn't have to work at the nursery school, I wouldn't be as exhausted." She forced a flirtatious smile with upturned eyes and a little lift of the shoulder. When they were first married, it worked. "I'd have more time to do everything in the vineyard." She emphasized the word everything rather than focusing on his doing his share. "It's the only way this experiment will succeed, especially now that we've got three acres planted. And come spring, we're putting in another."

Rick scowled and turned away. He strode into the living room. Liz followed right behind. He sat on the tweed sofa opposite the picture window that framed their land and propped his feet on the pine coffee table with all its dings and scratches. She stood facing him. Her shoulders squared but her hands behind her back were picking her cuticles.

"If you don't work, money's gonna be really tight." Rick downed a mouthful of beer and continued. "It's not like you make a ton, but we need it. This isn't a good idea."

Rick's brow furrowed. He seemed to be thinking. She gave him time. When the silence began to scream, Liz could no longer hold it in. "We'll make it back," she said, realizing she needed a more solicitous tone if she was going to get anywhere with him. This was a big change. Originally, she'd argued to go back to work. Now she was telling him she wanted to quit, though that wasn't saying she didn't want to work. Would he, *could* he understand that? "We'll probably make even more money when we sell the crop. Think of how much more I can do, how many more hours I'll have to devote to the vineyard." She thought she had him there. He'd probably figure, if she had more hours at home, she wouldn't nag him to help.

"And what about before we sell it?" Rick growled. "We've got another two years before the grapes are ready."

"I know. But if I don't quit now, I won't have the strength to do what's needed when they are."

Rick stared at the aluminum can as if it were speaking to him. He didn't say a word. Things were going her way. She sat next to him but kept her back straight, invoking a posture of power, and placed her hands on her lap, leaving her cuticles alone. Rick turned and looked her in the eye.

"Why now? Winter's coming. There's not that much to do. Not every day at least."

"You're right. I didn't mean I'd quit immediately." Feed his ego, she thought. Let him think this was his idea. "I wouldn't want to leave the school high and dry anyway. By spring though, when there's hours of work in the vineyard, it would be good if I had more time." And if I had your help, she thought, but swallowed the words. She had no idea how she'd get it all done herself. "Plus," she added, "if I didn't have to be concerned with the kids – worked while they're in school – I'd have more hours to do it all and get more done."

"You like having them there with you." Rick's emphatic tone was mixed with a bit of confusion.

"I do, but you're right. They do get in the way sometimes." Liz did like having them in the vineyard with her – when Rick was there too. A family affair working the land together. Rick let out a huge wet burp then nodded slow and easy as if he was still considering his answer. "All right," he said. "We'll give it a try. But not 'til the spring." Then, with that damn finger pointed at her eye, just short of poking it, he added, "But we gotta cut back, Liz. No more frozen food. You'll have to really cook." He turned his face from hers, swallowed another mouthful of beer, and, with a curled lip uttered, "Since you'll have more time."

CHAPTER 24

"You want your student, a young woman with two babies at home, who happens to be majoring in horticulture, to assist me in the vineyard?" Liz was stunned by her husband's proposal. She looked at him as if through a fog and continued slipping her arm into her pajama top's sleeve. "What are you thinking? Where does she have the time?" She stood with her back to her dresser with the notched-collar shirt unbuttoned, unable to do anything but stare at Rick. "And where's the two bucks an hour you want to pay her coming from? Minimum wage is only a dollar sixty."

Rick shrugged a shoulder, as if saying, so what's your point? Liz didn't know where he was going with this. Then he issued his curt response, "You keep workin' at nursery school and we can swing it."

Every muscle in her body tensed, but Liz knew there was no sense in shouting. It wouldn't get her anywhere if she went on the attack. Calm down, she told herself, as she buttoned her pajamas and forced her voice to a lower, sweeter decibel. All her previous hopes of sex on this bitter cold late November night were thrown out like trash.

"I appreciate you wanting to get me some help," she said. "But Rick, please understand, I am going to give up teaching this spring. My mind is made up. I need the time to devote to the vineyard. And, if this Bobbi wants to help out now and then, well that's fine. I could use it."

Annoyed that she couldn't keep those last few words from spilling out, Liz waited for Rick's anger to burst. She hadn't meant to bring up the fact that he hardly did his share. Fortunately, though, Rick was focused on her damn job. After a few more minutes of terse discussion, with Liz standing her ground, Rick huffed out of the bedroom. "We'll see how it works out," he grumbled, his parting remark, always having to have the last say. "Nothing is definite here."

Liz let Rick think he'd won this round, but there was no way she'd go back to teaching once she left – or any other job, for that matter. She couldn't believe she'd actually said the words, "my mind is made up" and that he hadn't thrown anything at her. She pulled the blanket back and climbed into her side of the bed. The bare branches of the trees scraped the windows.

Three months later, after Rick wouldn't let go of the idea of asking Bobbi to help, Liz gave in. Figuring she'd better get to know this young woman before they started the late-winter work, Liz invited her over for coffee and told her she could bring her six-month-old twins.

"As much as I adore my boys," Bobbi said, seated across from Liz at the kitchen table, her skin creamy, her scent as fresh as Ivory soap, "a few hours a day without Mickey and Minnie will be a welcome relief." She looked down at her two little guys sleeping on the quilt on the floor, curled up on their bellies, lips pursing on pacifiers.

"Doesn't school bring you that?" Liz asked.

"Yes, in a way, it did."

"Did?"

Bobbi ran her thumb over the gold band on the fourth finger of her left hand. "I'm sorry," she said. "I didn't tell Mr. Bergen. I dropped out." She glanced down at her kids again, then back at Liz with hunched shoulders. "I was afraid you wouldn't want me to work here, you know, since I'm not studying hort anymore."

"Oh, no. Not at all. That doesn't matter." How could it, Liz thought, when I never studied it either. I was nineteen, too, when I dropped out. Liz's index finger found the rough cuticle around her thumb and picked.

"When Mr. Bergen told me about your vineyard," Bobbi said, sitting straighter, "just thinking about being on your hillside nurturing vines, my skin prickled. And when I asked my mom if she'd mind watching the kids more often, she said it was fine, that I should go for it. She knows it's better for me to be busy. I need to keep my mind off . . . well, everything."

Liz gave her a puzzled look.

"Oh, you don't know that either," Bobbi said. "Glen, my husband, is MIA."

"He left you?"

"No. MIA like . . ." her voice broke. She swallowed hard. "Like Missing In Action. He's in Viet Nam." She sniffed back a tear. "Sorry," she said, wiping it from her eye. "His plane got shot down Christmas Eve. He hasn't been found yet."

Liz fumbled for words, but all she managed was a heavy nod. This poor girl, she thought. How can she function?

Bobbi gave a little lift of her shoulders. "Yeah. It was a shitty Christmas present. That's why I'm so glad to help you out. I need to dig in and make something good. Make something come alive."

Liz reached across the table and softly tapped Bobbi's hand that was wrapped around the coffee mug, as if its warmth could change things. And that two dollars an hour Rick wants to pay her, she thought, well . . . I guess my husband is a softy. But, come June, I don't know what we'll do. I won't have a salary anymore.

CHAPTER 25

On Bobbi's official first day of work at Riverview Vineyard, Liz handed her a shiny new secateur, her very own vine clipper. Almost a head taller and almost ten years younger than Liz, she bent down to get a better look at the spot on the cane where Liz was pointing, then clipped it off as instructed.

"And we do this because the fruit is only produced on one-year old canes," Bobbi said, confirming what Liz had explained.

With the waning sun casting its glow over the vineyard, Liz snipped off a weak shoot with her own secateur and told Bobbi she was right. "You're a fast learner," she said. "I'm impressed."

"I took some books out of the library," Bobbi explained, looking to where Liz was clipping. "If I'm going to work here, even just part-time, I've got to learn everything."

Liz wondered how Bobbi had the desire to study anything with her husband missing, somewhere in the jungles of Viet Nam. After all, she quit college. How can she focus on grapevines? It was enough she had two babies to take care of.

"And," Bobbi continued, "you prune annually, before bud break in the spring. Right?"

Liz nodded. Wow! She even has the terminology down.

"So you think next year you'll have your first harvest?"

"Yeah, we should. Maybe even this autumn. It depends when they flower. At least that's what Matt said. You have to have the flowers to set the fruit." Liz explained Matt was the grape grower teaching them the ropes. "He even found us a buyer for the grapes," Liz said. "He'll be back in a few months to check on the vines and let us know if they're ready to harvest." She looked up, hearing squeals coming from across the hillside where her kids were jumping off the stone bench, and longed for the day when she'd be able to work while they were in school. Bobbi's twins, wrapped in wool caps and quilted jackets, were lying on the old army blanket, babbling and kicking their little feet in the air. To Liz, their baby talk was as joyful as the first flowers in spring.

"I'm really looking forward to that," Bobbi said. "Maybe we could make some wine of our own. I know you're going to sell the grapes, but why not make a few bottles?"

Liz chuckled. "It's a thought. But really, we've got to make money and I'm not so sure selling my own vintage is going to do that."

Liz liked Bobbi's gumption – that she was already thinking ahead. But *"wine of our own"*? *First day on the job and insinuating herself into the business?*

The women continued going down the row, vine by vine, pruning where needed with Liz giving instructions on exactly where to cut each shoot. She soon realized Bobbi was quite adept and didn't need her hovering, so Liz stood and stretched the creaks out of her back. "How about we each take a row?" she said. "No need to keep doing this together."

"Exactly what I was going to suggest," Bobbi said with a smile as bright as her blonde curls. She checked her watch. "We'll get a lot more accomplished that way. We've only got about an hour more of sunlight."

Liz walked around to the next row and got to work. Every few minutes, she peered over the tops of the vines to where Bobbi was diligently working, immersed in the greenery, as if she was actually a part of the plants herself. The coo from the mourning doves, off in the distance, brought a sense of serenity, and with the soft chatter of the children playing nearby – all felt right with the world.

As the sun dropped behind the mountains, Liz, carrying one twin, and Bobbi the other, followed Bethany and Noah as they ran down the hill back to the house. They stopped in front of Bobbi's Ford.

"You're terrific," Liz said, surprising herself how much she appreciated Bobbi being there. "We got so much done today, much more than I would have on my own. Thank you so much."

"No, Liz," Bobbi said, as she buckled the baby in his car seat. "I've got to thank you. This was fabulous." She backed out of the car and reached for her other child. "These have been the best two hours I've had in months. All I thought about were grapevines." Tears pooled her eyes. "Your vineyard . . ." she took a deep breath, ". . .well, it's been the best medicine for me. Even when I cuddle my kids," she said, kissing the top of the baby's head, "as sweet as they are, I can't get Glen out of my mind. I'm always wondering where he is, picturing . . . oh God, just imagining the worst, the most horrible things." She swallowed a hard lump in her throat. "I'm sorry," she said, sniffing back tears. "I didn't mean to . . ."

Liz reached out her arms and wrapped her new assistant, along with baby, in a warm hug. *Somehow, I will find a way to keep paying her.*

CHAPTER 26

Liz kissed Bethany good night, then, after reading Noah a story she bent over, kissed his head, and walked out of his bedroom leaving the door slightly open. Just like on all other Friday nights when Rick was out playing poker, she turned on the television in the living room, settled into her favorite wing chair next to the window, and watched a movie. A late summer breeze blew softly through the café curtains, soothing her tired bones. And as usual, at eleven, expecting Rick at any moment, she turned the TV off, undressed, and climbed into bed. The clock ticked. Liz punched the pillow, forming a bigger indentation to lay her head. She waited. No Rick. At eleven thirty, Liz tossed the covers aside and ran into the kitchen, grabbed a bag of Wise, and took them back to bed. Sitting straight up, listening for the sound of truck tires, she chomped on salty potato chips and checked the clock every few minutes. Midnight was not exactly what Liz thought he'd meant when he said, "The game might go longer tonight, so don't wait up." She stared straight ahead, envisioning cars piled on top of each other, windshields smashed, and Rick lying in the street with his blood pouring over the macadam. But someone would have called her, she kept telling herself. It didn't help. She shoved more chips in her mouth. Salty crumbs sprinkled the sheets. How dare he do this to me! She was used to Rick coming home late, but never this late. There was one time though, the night after Bobbi came for coffee with her twins. Liz had wanted to ask Rick if he knew her husband was MIA, but he never came home. Looking down at her expanding waistline, she remembered how infuriated she'd been. That night Oreos were her comfort. She'd consumed half a box when he finally called to say he was staying over at his friend's, that he'd had too much to drink and would see her in the morning.

The side door squeaked. Liz quickly got out of bed and stashed the half-eaten bag of potato chips in a dresser drawer. She didn't want to hear Rick say anything, again, about her getting fat. Even if it was all his fault. If he hadn't come home so late, she wouldn't have been stuffing her face.

Hearing him opening and closing kitchen cabinets, Liz shoved the drawer closed and hurried back to bed, brushed the crumbs onto the floor, and grabbed the latest issue of *Life* magazine from the night table to read, as if she'd been engrossed in it all night.

Rick walked into the bedroom, one hand holding a glass of water, the other pulling his shirttail from the waistband on his pants. "Still awake?" he said, his face scrunched in annoyance.

Forget the magazine. Liz couldn't keep the anger out of her voice. "Yes, I am. Where've you been? It's really late."

"What? I'm in high school? You givin' me a curfew?"

The stench of scotch or bourbon or whatever the hell he was drinking permeated the air with each word, his face just inches from hers.

"No, of course not," she said, backing away, forcing her anger aside. It wasn't worth it with him like this. She mustered as much sweetness as possible. "It's just that I was really worried. And I've got good news."

"Yeah?" Rick turned, put the glass on the dresser – once again without a coaster, which drove Liz batty – and emptied his pants pockets. He put a bunch of coins on top of the pine chest of drawers, then his silver money clip.

At least he hasn't lost it all, she thought. The clip appeared to be about the same thickness as always, a few bucks, nothing bulging though not empty.

"Matt was here today," she said. "He told me it looks like the Seyval will be ready for harvest soon. Isn't that great?" And we'll sell those grapes, she said silently, and your money clip will expand. Then maybe you won't drink so much.

"And Cab Franc?"

"No. They won't be ready for a year or two. But that's what we expected. Having this one is a gift from Mother Nature. I'm really excited about it."

Rick unbuckled his belt and tossed it on the floor, then stepped one leg out of his jeans, wobbled, righted himself, and kicked off the other leg. He left them where they fell. "So, we got ourselves a vineyard," he said, his chest puffed out with pride. "I'll call that guy in Warwick, let him know we're ready."

"Almost ready," Liz said. "You're right, though. It's a good idea." Liz was glad Rick was finally going to take some responsibility with this experiment, as he continued to call it. "And we should let Cornell know too."

"Yup. I'll take care of that."

"Thanks."

He drew his head back and scowled at her as if saying "What are you thanking me for?" Rick continued to undress, dropping socks and shirt on the floor alongside his pants, as if that's exactly where they belonged. "I'm doing my part. You got what you wanted." He climbed into bed clad in his white Jockey shorts with the waist band pressed below a growing beer paunch. "You do all the work when you shove the kids off to that playground camp." His lip curled. "Making useless pot holders."

Every muscle in her body quivered. No, keep quiet, she told herself. There was absolutely no reason to tell him, again, how proud the kids were when they came home with their hand made lanyards and pot holders and Bethany getting the first-baseman spot on the softball team.

"And," Rick said, "don't forget, I dug out that new acre."

Liz fought back words that wanted to spring out of the gates of her teeth. She reminded herself to just be glad he'd at least done that, even though she and Bobbi had planted all the new vines and dug the poles and strung the wire.

"I'll be there for the harvest," he said, pulling the blanket toward his side. "You need a man for that." He slid farther under the covers and mumbled, as if half asleep already. "Any news on her husband?" Liz shook her head. "That's shitty."

Rick turned over and in just a few seconds was snoring as loud as the train that used to pass by their garden apartment when they were first married and everything seemed so promising. She turned her engagement ring round and round on her finger remembering, wishing he was that same guy, sober, hardly ever angry, and so affectionate. She let out a frustrated breath and got out of bed. Let it wait 'til morning she always told herself, but no, she couldn't. She hated disarray. Twitching with irritation, she snatched his pants off the floor. Just because he had a maid growing up, he thinks he can do this. Or maybe he just doesn't think. Jeez. She lifted his shirt and a familiar scent filled her nose. The same one she'd smelled the last time. Now she knew it. Shalimar. The perfume she used to wear in college. Her stomach hardened. Her world teetered. She crumpled the shirt in a tight fist, dumped it in the hamper, then slammed the bedroom door behind her.

CHAPTER 27

On a mid-September morning Liz, needing some time alone, told Rick she was going to check on the vines, to see if they were ready for harvest. "Go ahead. Let me know," he said and kissed the tip of her nose, like he'd always done when things were perfect.

Liz closed the side door behind her and strolled up to the vineyard, lifting her head toward the brilliant sun. She drank in the crisp scent of autumn, a welcome aroma from the perfume she could not get out of her nose these past four weeks. She got sick to her stomach every time the memory of the scent on her husband's shirt came to her, even though each day when she picked another off the floor and buried her nose in the cotton, she only smelled smoke. Liz prayed she was wrong, that maybe there was a woman in their poker game who'd bathed herself in Shalimar that night. Rick smoked and she was sure all the other guys did too, so that smell wasn't a surprise. But perfume? Twice? She was too frightened of what Rick would say, so she never mentioned the shirt. Or was it that she didn't want to know? As much as she told herself not to be, she was jealous, always wondering what was wrong with her. Why would he need another woman? Wasn't she good in bed? Liz couldn't help it; she still loved that guy she married nine years ago, the one who had smiled up at her from his seat in the college library the first time she entered the building. But Rick was not that guy anymore and she didn't know what to do about it. She wanted him back. Pulling her flannel shirt tighter across her chest, Liz dug her heels into the grass and continued up the hill remembering that day.

* * * * *

Liz stood at the door to the stacks taking it all in. The scent of old books. Oblong tables in front of rows and rows of metal bookshelves. Students in practically all of the chairs, their heads buried in study. How much knowledge must there be in this room, she wondered. Spotting an empty chair at the end of the far table, she made a beeline for it, only to discover a pile of books stacked in front of it. "This seat taken?" she asked the guy in the next chair.

"It's yours, if you want it," he said, his voice as sexy as Montgomery Clift's in *The Young Lions*. "Make yourself at home." Liz liked his smile and the way the corners of his eyes crinkled. He oozed sex. "I'm Rick . . . Rick Bergen." He introduced himself, looking her up and down. When he added, "I've never seen you before. I'm sure I would've remembered," her cheeks heated. Obviously an upperclassman, he wore a V-neck sweater with the sleeves pushed up to midarm, exposing soft, sandy-colored hair. And he'd noticed her, a mere freshman. She was smitten.

* * * * *

"We're beating you, Mommy," five-year-old Noah called from the golf cart as they zipped by. Rick waved from the driver's seat, as if all was normal and this was a fun day with the family. Liz waved back trying to hide her surprise.

For the past few weeks, Liz had tried hard to keep up the pretense of a happy family. She wanted her marriage to work and wondered, as Rick zipped by, if maybe he did too. He was all smiles with their children beaming alongside him, racing to the vineyard. Maybe I *am* nuts, she thought and picked up her pace.

By the time Liz arrived at the top where the hill plateaued and the glorious green vineyard stretched out in front of her, Noah's face was already covered by cascading vines. Liz kneeled next to him and together they inspected the grapes. She took a clump in her hand and felt for firmness. Plump and juicy, ready to burst, just as they should be. "Only a few more days," she told her son, "and then we can pick them."

From further down the vineyard, Rick's voice boomed. "The Cab Franc are nowhere near ready."

Liz stiffened. Of course not, she thought, we only planted them two years ago, and, on the night of the Shalimar shirt, she had told Rick they wouldn't be ready this year. Obviously, he hadn't been listening. He was too drunk. Or maybe too guilty.

"Go play with Bethany," Liz said to Noah. With a heavy chest, she continued down the row trying to shake off that night . . . again. She focused on each cluster of grapes, making sure insects or birds hadn't bruised the fruit. Rick seemed to be doing the same thing on his side. Let him, she reasoned, and concentrated on the grapes that were ready.

"Mommy, mommy," Noah's voice cut through the quiet, a whine Liz knew meant he had some kind of complaint about his sister. "Befany ate a grape!"

Even though she was in no mood to referee, Liz couldn't help but smile. She adored Noah's lisp. Then, as usual, Bethany chimed in. "I'm not the only one, Noah ate one, too."

"No eating grapes," Liz called out over the tops of the green vines. "Remember, we have to sell them."

With thick juice dripping down his chin, Noah ran over to his mother. "Why? Why can't we keep them?" A little tongue swiped a lower lip.

"Sweetie, I told you before – when we sell the grapes, we'll get money, and then we can buy you a new big-boy bike." She swallowed the other words she was thinking – *and Daddy can buy more vodka.* She forced a smile as she wiped the sweet juice dripping down her son's chin and told herself to relax, that Rick was obviously trying.

CHAPTER 28

"That was Mother on the phone," Rick said as he walked into the living room.

"Your *mother?*" Liz was stunned. They hadn't heard from the woman since last Christmas. "Where's she been all this time? And how come she never answered your letter?"

Rick plopped on the couch opposite Liz, seated in her favorite chair with her bare feet splayed out on the ottoman. The kids were Ivory-soap clean and tucked in their beds, fast asleep, and the television was on low so as not to wake them. This was the kind of night Liz loved. She and Rick together, a steaming cup of tea for her, one well deserved beer for him after a busy day working the vineyard and his vegetable garden, with the TV casting a soft glow on the tranquil room.

Rick took a big gulp of the Schlitz. His Adam's apple bobbed as he swallowed. "She's been sick," he said. "That's why she never wrote – probably why she didn't send the kids their birthday presents."

"How sick? I mean, it's been a long time – not that we hear from her very often. You did write to her, though, and called, didn't you?"

"Yeah, but she never answered or called back. I guess I should have pursued it. I just figured she was her old self, all caught up in her fancy Florida life, no time for me." He shrugged, his face blank. "Turns out I was wrong. She's got cancer."

Liz's mouth dropped open. A sudden coldness hit deep in her core. The voices on the TV irritated. She stood, shut it off, and sat next to him. Liz might not be a fan of her mother-in-law; the woman had never come to visit them – not once in the nine years she'd been living in Florida. She hadn't even come for Bethany or Noah's birth. And it was far too expensive for the four of them to have flown to her. With Mrs. Bergen's money, she could have paid for them to come down. That would have been a nice Christmas present one year, but no, she'd never have thought of it. In spite of it all, Liz never wished her to be ill.

"Oh, Rick," she said, reaching for his hand. "I'm so sorry. How bad?"

"She says she's home now and doing better." He pulled his hand away and took a slug of beer, swallowing hard. "They had to remove a lung a few months ago and she's still having chemo. Says it makes her real sick. She's got an aide living with her."

Liz remembered the long months when her mother was going through chemo, how ill she had been and how her father was always right there by her side through it all, cleaning her mess, wiping her brow, helping her to the bathroom, bringing her broth and jello, the only foods she could get down. It was an awful time and it must be especially lousy having a stranger do all that for you.

"You need to go see her," Liz said.

"What for? She doesn't want me to — said she doesn't want me to see her like this."

Liz felt sorry for Rick. He was never wrapped in a mother's love like she had been. "No, hon. You'll regret it if you don't. Believe me. I hated seeing my mother so sick, and I used to run away to friends' houses as if I could erase it, but actually, I am glad I was there." She picked up her tone, trying to sound positive. "You know, she might just beat it."

"Lung cancer? Doubtful."

Liz sighed. "I know, but there's always a chance." She remembered trying to believe the same thing as her mother lost more and more weight and got weaker with each passing day. The sour stench of death came back to her. She shook it away with a force so strong it rattled her ears.

"I don't believe your mother means it. I think she'd be glad to see you, even if she doesn't admit it."

"We've got harvest next week. I can't go."

"That'll take two days, Rick. Go right after."

"It's expensive. I'm not gonna spend that kind of money."

"This is your mother, Rick. She may not be the most loving, but she's still your mother."

Rick stared straight ahead squinting, as if a decision was written in the air in front of him and he couldn't quite make it out. Then, as if some great idea dawned on him, his eyes opened wide. "Okay. I will." He kept nodding. "I'll go right after harvest." A grin slowly spread across his cheeks. Liz wondered what made him change his mind so quickly and why he suddenly seemed to be happy. And, with an even brighter smile, he added, "Get this, Liz. She wants to give you her diamond."

"What? Why?" Oh God, Liz thought, she must really be near the end if she's thinking like that.

"She called yours an itty-bitty stone." Liz could practically feel the bile fill Rick's throat, the disgust in each word. "She said I should have taken the money my father offered and bought you something substantial, not that spit of a thing." He jutted his chin toward her hand. "Those were her exact words."

Liz studied the ring on her fourth finger. "This is not some itty-bitty spit of a thing. How dare she?" She looked up at her husband. "I love my ring and the fact that you paid for it all by yourself. I . . . I don't want her diamond."

"Three carats, Liz. Think what it can buy."

"Oh, Rick, please. This is not the time to talk about stuff like that."

CHAPTER 29

Liz bent over Bethany's bed, swept her daughter's soft hair from her brow and kissed her warm, sleepy head. "Time to get up," she said, breathing in the sweet scent of an eight-year-old fresh from a good night's sleep. "Grandpa's going to take you guys to the school bus this morning."

"I know, you're picking grapes," Bethany said from the cocoon of her pink comforter. "And you got to start real early."

"That's right. And I probably won't be here when you get home from school, either. I've got to bring the crates filled with all those grapes to the man who's buying them. Daddy will be here though, at least 'til after dinner, and Grandpa's staying." She pulled the covers off her daughter and tickled her belly. Bethany giggled and wiggled. Liz kissed her nose and said, "Rise and shine, sleepy head," then headed downstairs.

The scent of pancakes sizzling on the griddle wafted through the house. As much as Liz would love to have them, there was no time for a big breakfast. She and Rick were meeting Bobbi in the vineyard at seven. Harvesting even half an acre, as they planned to do on this first day, would take hours, and morning was the best time, before the sun was high in the sky.

"Here, I made you one," her dad said, handing Liz a silver dollar sized banana pancake, the kind she always ate as a kid. Love wrapped up in flour, eggs, and milk.

Noah, who always woke before the sun, was seated at the kitchen table watching Grandpa Lou. Liz walked by, ran her fingers through his wavy brown hair, and kissed his cheek. "Have a good day at school," she said as she gobbled up the savory breakfast treat.

"I don't wanna go," he whined. "I wanna pick grapes with you."

"Not today, honey, you've got school. But tomorrow, bright and early, you can come to the vineyard and help."

Liz was glad Noah wanted to help. She wanted her kids to get used to the work, even if they were only able to do a little, so that when they were older, they'd join in and love the land as she did. She and Rick had been living on the farm since they bought it in 1963, but the land hadn't crawled under her skin until they planted the vines in '66. Now, three years later, the rich loamy soil producing lush succulent fruit was as much a part of her as her arms and legs.

She ruffled her son's hair one more time, then walked over and opened the kitchen door. "See you later, Dad," she said as she stepped out. "The vines will be waiting for you."

"As soon as I get the kids off and pack the cooler, I'll be there."

"Thanks, you're the best." Liz closed the door behind her and smiled, picturing the four of them together at her very first harvest: she, Rick, Bobbi, and Lou. They'd pick grapes for a few hours, then flop down on the grass and eat the ham and cheese sandwiches her dad was going to make and whatever other treats he'd surprise them with, and after that, pick some more. It was a glorious day; even the damp morning mist was wonderful. She trotted up the hill, her face blazing with joy.

Over the next several hours, with painstaking precision, the four pickers clipped two and a half tons of green grapes. They placed the clusters into the orange-colored crates Liz had laid out the day before. Music filled the air. Bobbi's voice sang out accompanying the Beatles from the transistor radio resting on the ground. Rick joined in from his row, belting out the chorus about needing someone to love. Liz looked over at Bobbi, expecting to see a sad expression but the words didn't seem to bother her. The sun shone on her smiling face. She was simply singing along. Or hiding her emotions really well. Liz shook off her own thoughts and joined the vineyard choir when the tune changed to one from that new singer, James Taylor, singing about going to Carolina. When the day's harvest was complete, Liz sat high in the cabin of their very own used tractor. She drove it up and down the rows while the others hefted their bounty onto the attached wagon.

Bone weary despite being exhilarated from a job well done, Bobbi, Rick, and Lou climbed aboard after the last crate was placed. Rick pushed Liz over to the passenger's side and took his place as driver. The other two found a space in the wagon for the short ride back to the house.

"We're not done yet," Bobbi told Lou who was resting against the crates opposite her. She was crouched in the only empty corner available. "Now we've got to load these onto the truck. You know, Liz was really lucky when Mr. Franklin offered to loan his. Until then she was really stressed how she was gonna get the fruit to the buyer in Rick's little pickup."

"Hey," Liz called from up front. "You two talking about me?" She had heard the words but wouldn't admit it. She wanted to hear what her father would say. Was he proud of her yet?

"No," Bobbi called back. "Mr. Franklin."

"He's a good guy," Lou said. "A little quiet, keeps to himself, but a good neighbor."

"Sure is," Liz called back thinking how generous he had been. "But now we've got our own tractor. Pretty cool, isn't it?" she said, tapping the side panel.

Rick pulled the tractor to a stop alongside the green pickup parked in front of their house.

"I'm bushed," Lou said climbing off the wagon. "I don't think I can lift another box." He looked at his daughter. "Good job today, Lizzy."

Liz was all warm inside, and Rick gave him a friendly slap on the back. "No worries, old man. You go rest. I'll do it." And to Bobbi, he added, "You should get home. It's been a long day."

"No, I'll help load, and then I'm gonna drive with Liz. She shouldn't go alone."

Bobbi cares more about my welfare than my husband does, Liz thought. We don't know this guy and what he might try to pull. I'm glad she'll be there with me.

"Whatever," Rick said. "I'm gonna load the truck, and if you two ladies want to go together, be my guest. I'm sure it'll all go nice and smooth."

Liz and Bobbi hefted a few crates onto the truck, then Liz nudged Bobbi. "Let him finish," she whispered. "All he's gonna do later is play cards." They went into the house, used the bathroom, grabbed a soda each, and then took their seats in the truck, waiting for Rick to be done.

"Whew! That was a lot of work," Rick said, wiping his brow. He looked through the driver's open window. "Should bring us a nice penny."

"Yeah. Hopefully, he'll buy them all." Liz pulled the sweaty red bandana from her head, tossed it on the floor, and, as Rick patted the driver's door, drove away. No worries, she silently said, in an imagined conversation with her husband. I wouldn't want to keep you from your poker game. My dad can stay with the kids. No problem, dear.

She turned onto Route 9 with a bitter taste in her mouth, the one that had lodged there the moment Rick had told her that she'd be doing the delivery alone. He had his Friday night poker game. *Well, I've got Bobbi.*

CHAPTER 30

"I really don't want to try it," Liz said from her comfortable chair in the living room. Rick stood in front of her, waving a joint in her face.

"Ah, come on, hon. It's cold and blustery out. We can get all nice and warm together. The kids are asleep . . ." *Sgt. Pepper* was playing on the stereo, and Rick tried to entice her with his sexy wink, the one that usually made her hot.

"No. And I'm not so sure Beth is."

"Oh, come on. You have no idea how great you'll feel." He leaned in closer and whispered, "And sex will be incredible."

Liz drew back. "How do you know?"

"Ooh," he teased, lifting his brows a few times, then sat really close to her on the couch. His musky scent was like a hug. "The guys told me." He shrugged, "How else would I know?" He offered her the lit joint, gave her a nudge, and Liz succumbed.

Rick was right. The sex was fabulous. Liz had never once felt such an intense orgasm and that night she'd had three.

A few weeks later, when she was at the kitchen sink washing the dinner dishes, Rick walked in from the bedroom with a plastic bag. "What's that?" she asked.

"A really good half ounce." Rick pulled out a kitchen chair and sat. Liz turned and eagerly watched him roll a joint, then sat next to him. He handed it to her and she took a long drag, held it in her lungs, then slowly exhaled. Rick took a toke and she had another. After two more, her heart raced. Her skin felt raw. She was completely spaced. Liz got up and grabbed the Oreos from the pantry. Rick laughed as she ripped the box open and grabbed a handful. Together they ate through the package and, as a chaser, devoured a bag of chips.

The next morning, her throat raw, Liz rolled out of bed swearing, "Never again."

"Yeah, you say that now," Rick said. "You'll change your mind."

"No. Last night was the absolute last time. I don't like feeling out of control. And I sure don't want to get fat."

Rick glanced down at her flabby belly and lifted his eyes.

"Oh, shut up." She knew what he was thinking. "I'm trying. It's just hard."

"Okay, suit yourself. I'm still gonna smoke."

Liz wished he wouldn't, but she knew she had to pick her battles. This marriage had to work. Already she had failed at one thing – college. She refused to be a two-time failure.

Over the next year, Liz desperately tried to lose the twelve pounds she'd put on since their wedding. She never took another toke. She didn't need any more excuses to gobble Oreos. Those cookies, or anything else she could get her hands on, were her best friends on the nights Rick didn't make it home, which was happening more and more since she had sworn off marijuana.

"Rick, please. Stop smoking grass," Liz said one morning when he walked in after being out all night. This wasn't her first plea, but his answer was always the same.

"You don't want me driving when I'm drunk or stoned, do you? I might have an accident or get arrested."

What could she say to that? "Well, then at least call and let me know you're not coming home so I don't have to worry all night." Sometimes he did call. And then there were those nights when she gorged on junk food.

Work in the vineyard went on as usual, whether Rick was stoned or not. Season after season, Liz and Bobbi worked in the vines during the week, and on weekends, when Rick was sober or not on a fishing trip, he joined his wife. Liz sucked it up and forged ahead, not wanting to argue. Besides, she liked the work, even alone. And, she thought, at least the scent of Shalimar hadn't infected their home again.

A few weeks before their third harvest in 1971, Rick walked into the house one Saturday morning after being out all night. Liz was at the kitchen sink rinsing her coffee cup. She was relieved he'd made it home in one piece and vowed to herself she wouldn't mention pot or that he was out all night again. Plus, it was too pretty a day to ruin it with a fight. But when she turned and saw his bloodshot eyes, she couldn't help herself. Her nose wrinkled in disgust.

"Oh, Rick," she said, "you're a mess. You look like you just rolled out of bed." He stood in the doorway across the room, his shirt and pants wrinkled, as if he'd slept in them or they had lain crumpled in a pile on some floor. His leather belt with the big brass buckle hung from his hand. Liz turned back to the sink, shaking her head, muttering. "That must have been some strong grass. I wish you'd stop smoking that stuff." Her eyebrows pulled together making deep creases in her forehead. "And," she said, looking over her shoulder, "why isn't your belt on your pants?"

"'Cause I didn't feel like puttin' it on," he yelled. "That okay with you?" The buckle flew through the air. It smacked the mug in her hand. Shards of porcelain flew everywhere. With a jagged chunk still in her fingers, Liz cocked her elbow like a pitcher about to fling a fastball.

As fast as lightning, Rick was across the room. He grabbed Liz by the arm. Shoved her. She stumbled. The broken piece fell to the floor. Her back slammed into the edge of the counter. She doubled over. And Rick kept yelling. "Who the hell . . .? Don't you ever . . ."

"Daddy," Bethany screamed, running into the kitchen, cutting him off. Her head shot from her father to her mother, who'd righted herself the moment she saw her daughter. "What's going on?"

"It's okay, honey," Liz said catching her breath. She sat on a kitchen chair trying to look normal. "I dropped a mug and daddy bumped into me when he picked it up." She forced her heart rate down. No ten-year-old should have to witness this.

Bethany's scrunched face told Liz she wasn't buying the story. Continuing the cover-up, Liz asked Beth to get the broom. "Be a sweetheart, please. I need to clean this up." There was a great deal more that Liz needed to clean up. That smirk Rick had on his face when he shoved her was one. If only her nails were longer, she'd have loved scraping them down his cheeks. Though where would that get her? Rick had never touched her before. Sure, he'd yelled and thrown things at her, but this was the first time he'd gotten physical. It was never going to happen again.

With Bethany out of earshot, Liz peered at Rick. All the anger she felt spewed out as she growled, "Go! Sleep it off. We'll talk later."

"I'm . . . I'm sorry, Liz . . . I don't know why . . . But how dare you throw a cup at me?"

She held up her hand to keep him from coming closer. "Stop. Go! Leave . . . me . . . alone." Each word more acidic than the last.

Several hours later, Liz and the children were walking up and down the rows inspecting the fruit when Rick appeared, looking well-rested and smelling of soap, hair tonic, and aftershave. He was smiling, as if nothing had happened earlier.

"Whatcha doin', bud?" he asked Noah, whose seven-year-old fingers were around a plump blue-black grape.

"Testing if it's ready."

"And?" Rick asked, appearing very interested. Liz stopped and watched her son and husband, who looked like two serious grape growers discussing their crop. If she wasn't so angry, her heart would have warmed.

"Almost," Noah said. "Maybe one more week."

"Get a load of him," Rick said with a laugh. "Our own little vintner."

Liz nodded and forced a smile. Rick tussled Noah's head then walked down the row, over to the next where Liz stood alone. He put his arm around her shoulders. She stiffened. "Really, I'm sorry," he said, removing his arm, looking at her with apologetic eyes. "You're right. It was heavy duty grass and I shouldn't have smoked again this morning. I promise, I won't do that ever again."

Liz didn't know exactly what Rick was promising. That he'd never shove her again? Or smoke marijuana in the morning? Or not all? Whichever it was, she decided not to press it. This was the first time Rick truly seemed ashamed.

CHAPTER 31

After an entire day spent picking with the October sun warming their shoulders, Rick loaded the last crate of grapes into the truck, a dented orange one they'd bought a year ago, rust spots speckled across the hood. That, together with their own tractor, made Liz feel like a real farmer.

"I'll document the yield when I get back from Warwick," she told Rick as he stepped away from the Ford.

"Why don't you wait 'til we complete the whole harvest?"

"It's easier if I do it after each pick. Then I won't have so much work at the end, and Cornell will get the results faster." It was already six o'clock and the slanted autumn light was darkening. Liz and Bobbi wanted to get on their way. Between the long ride to Warwick, and Hank Scanlon, the buyer, always making them hang around while he inspected the fruit, it would be a long night. Liz didn't want to waste any time discussing the way she handled the paper work.

"Okay, see you later," Rick said. "I'll probably be asleep when you get back. Gotta work tomorrow."

Unfortunately, Rick's dream of living off the land wasn't working out. The amount they made per crate had only gone up seventy cents from when they sold their first yield two years ago. If her arithmetic was correct, Rick's salary was twice what they'd get this year from Mr. Scanlon. And she refused to sell Rick's mother's ring, no matter how often he mentioned it. For the past two years, the flawless marquise had sat in a safe deposit box waiting for Bethany to inherit. Liz refused to wear such a huge rock, no matter how gorgeous. It was too glitzy, aside from the fact that she feared losing it among the vines or in the dirt or in the leaves. Or anywhere.

"Leave it in the bank for now," Rick had said the last time they argued over selling the gem. "But don't tell Beth. It may never be hers."

As she drove down their long road, Liz recalled how Rick had growled when he spit those words and how she'd screamed inside. She would never let Rick sell that ring. That's not why her mother-in-law had given it to her. It was to stay in the family, be an heirloom – not pay for her son to buy weed or live off the profit, as long as it lasted. White knuckled and teeth clenched, Liz completed the mile up their lane and turned onto Hill Valley Road, heading off to sell her grapes.

A few minutes later, she turned onto Route 9, the whoosh of passing traffic the only sound in the truck. Finally Bobbi broke the silence. "Why are you strangling that steering wheel? Whose neck is it?"

"Oh, it's nothing," Liz said, shaken from her contemplations. She reached over and turned on the radio. It was better to listen to Cousin Brucie than to pour her heart out to Bobbi who, after four years, still didn't know for certain if her husband was dead or alive. Without a body or any remains, the army continued to classify him as Missing in Action.

"Liz, I've been with you long enough to know when you're happy and when you're not. And right now, you seem miserable – not to mention majorly pissed. So it's not nothing. What's going on? Is it that Rick's not bringing the fruit to Scanlon?"

"No. Not at all. I'm okay with that now. Really, forget it."

Liz switched the station to WNEW and listened to Allison Steel's sultry calming voice. She glanced at Bobbi whose eyes were fixed on the windshield as if studying words written across the glass. She wanted to tell Bobbi, but how could she when her husband was MIA? Instead, she focused on the curving road, telling herself she really was all right with Rick not bringing the grapes to the seller. They passed an Esso station and Friendly's Ice Cream Parlor, an A&P where Liz sometimes shopped, and, farther down the road, a turnoff to another farm where huge, stately trees stood with yellow ribbons tied around the trunks.

"You know," Bobbi finally said, her eyes still looking out the windshield. "I thought we were friends. That I wasn't just your assistant."

"We are friends. It's . . ."

"It's that you don't want to talk to me about Rick. I get it." Bobbi shifted in her seat and faced Liz directly. "Really, I can deal with it," she said. "What I don't know is . . ." She pressed her lips together and turned back to the windshield. "No. Never mind."

"What? Tell me."

"Nothing. Forget it."

The hum of the tires filled the silent air. A few quiet moments later, Liz took her eyes off the road. She looked directly at the side of Bobbi's face. "Come on, what were you going to say?"

Bobbi licked her lips. Her head shook like a nervous twitch. "I shouldn't put my two cents in."

Liz tapped a finger on the steering wheel, over and over again.

"Okay, if you insist." Bobbi turned to face Liz, who gave her a little nod encouraging her to go on. "You're not going to like what I have to say, but . . . I know Rick drinks. His eyes are glassy more times than not, and you've told me you don't like him smoking so much grass, that you've asked him to stop and he won't. Right?" Liz nodded, small up and down movements. It was hard to admit the truth. "Well, remember those Saturday mornings when I stopped at the house for coffee before we went up to the vineyard? The three of us were supposed to work together, and," she shrugged, "too many times Rick was nowhere around. You made excuses for him, but I knew better. Rick is not the guy to go grocery shopping early in the morning, and how often can someone go fishing? But I kept quiet. I didn't want to embarrass you. Your red eyes – they told it all."

"What do you mean?"

"Oh Liz, I'm sorry but, come on. Rick hadn't even come home, had he? And you were up all night crying."

Liz took a deep breath and, on the slow exhale, nodded. "I don't want to bother you with my troubles," she said, her voice full of compassion. "You've got enough of your own." Relieved, though, that she could finally let it all out, Liz straightened her spine, attempting to be stoic. "You are right," she said and went on to tell Bobbi about all the times Rick hadn't come home. "And he did it again a few nights ago. We fought like crazy." As much as she tried to hold it together, her self-control waned. She sniffed back tears and recounted the story of the shirt that reeked of Shalimar. "As hard as I try, I can't let it go."

"What did he say? How'd he defend himself?"

Liz kept quiet, her eyes on the road.

"You didn't call him on it." It was a simple statement with annoyance and a tinge of sympathy mixed in.

Liz felt her friend's eyes on her, pressing hard. Still, she didn't say a word. She refused to admit she was petrified of what Rick's answer would have been. And she hated the doubt that kept creeping back at her every night he didn't make it home for bed even though she told herself that yes, the rural roads were pitch black, he could miss a curve and land in a ditch. She didn't want him driving them stoned.

Bobbi let out a long, frustrated breath and turned away, Allison Steel's subdued voice in the background. Liz stopped at a red light, continued when it turned green, pressed on her high beams to see better, then made a left off the dark road and paid the toll for the Thruway. Bobbi, eyes peeled on the car in front, kept biting her lower lip. She fiddled with the top button on her shirt.

"What? What is it?" Liz said, sliding into the traffic.

Bobbi shook her head. "No. I'm afraid . . . I don't want to overstep my bounds."

"Come on."

Bobbi sighed. She clasped her hands and held them tight in front of her chest. "All right," she said, gathering her words together. "I'm sorry, but my father . . . well, he was a cheater and I saw what it did to my mother." Liz bristled at the word. Bobbi reached one hand across the seat and with a touch so light and full of compassion, patted her friend's arm. "She didn't deserve it, Liz. And neither do you."

"The Way We Were" played on the radio. Memories lit the corners of Liz's mind.

CHAPTER 32

Liz parked the truck in front of the dilapidated building that should have been somewhere in the Wild West with horses tied up to a post outside. "I can't believe he still hasn't painted this place," Bobbi said, as they climbed down from the truck. "And the front porch . . . the shingles look like they're about to break off the house and crumble."

"Step lightly," Liz said as they walked up the broken boards. She pulled the string on the cowbell hanging above the wooden door. Two minutes passed. No answer. She rang again. A loud clang resonated through the air. Still no one came. "Damn. Rick said he confirmed with him yesterday. He knows we're coming." She stepped off the front porch, leaving Bobbi waiting at the door, and walked around to the back. Maybe Hank was there.

A metal crusher sat on a cement slab. Liz walked over to it, stood on tiptoe, and peered into the open cylinder on top. Spots of red stained the gray-colored steel. He must be crushing some red varietal, she thought. Damn, if he's in his winery, he'll never hear us. She pictured him in his underground room filled with oak barrels sitting on a cold cement floor. When he'd shown it to the women the first time they came to sell their bounty three years ago, Bobbi almost swooned. "Wow, wouldn't it be great to have something like this," she'd said. Liz reminded her it was not in their plans. "We're grape growers and sellers," she'd said. "Not winemakers."

Disgusted, Liz walked around to the front of the building. She called out to Bobbi as she rounded the corner. "I don't think Rick ever called him. He's not here. Or he's just being his ornery old self again." Every time Liz brought him their grapes, Hank Scanlon made her wait. She often wondered if he would treat Rick the same, if Rick was the one doing the delivery. Somehow, she thought not – that Scanlon just didn't like dealing with women.

"Give him some more time," Bobbi said. "You know what he's like."

"Yeah, a real prick. At least he buys." Five minutes later, Liz had had enough. She wished she could go home, but what would she do with three tons of grapes? And how would she handle Rick's anger? He'd be furious. She paced up and down the dilapidated old porch, fuming.

A moment later, a gray-haired man with a long beard to match and a stomach bulging over his dirty dungarees opened the door.

"Sorry," Hank Scanlon said. "I was down in the winery. Couldn't stop what I was doing. So, where're the grapes?"

Liz pasted a smile on her face, as much as it irked her to do so, and pointed to her orange pickup truck.

"OK, you know the drill," he said. "I'll be back soon."

Liz and Bobbi stepped inside to Hank's makeshift office while he and his assistant, just as scrappy looking, unloaded all the crates onto his wagon and drove it around back where he'd make sure the fruit wasn't damaged, like he always said.

Liz wanted to spit. Every time she envisioned his dirty fingers on her solid crop, a sour, bitter taste filled her mouth.

An hour passed with Liz getting more aggravated by the minute. She and Bobbi were seated on the only two chairs in the grimy room, Liz on an orange vinyl she always had to wipe down before putting her bottom on it and Bobbi on the torn black vinyl ready for the garbage heap.

"Are your sister and her husband coming back next week?" Bobbi asked, referring to when they'd harvest the remaining two acres.

"I think so."

"You know, next year, we might need more pickers," Bobbi said. "By then, we should have eight acres producing, maybe more."

"We'll see how it goes. So far, we've managed. It's a lot of work, but we get it done." Liz thought how she and Bobbi carried out practically all the work in the vineyard, all year long, but if it wasn't for Rick, she didn't know how they'd get all the crates onto the wagon and then again onto the truck. There were so many.

Another hour passed. Liz paced. "He does this every time," she said, walking from window to door for the umpteenth time, ignoring the huge girly calendar hanging on the wall. "I swear, he wouldn't treat a man this way." She sat, grumbling about Mr. Scanlon, then kept quiet, and the conversation she and

Bobbi had in the car came back to her. Although Bobbi hadn't said another word about Rick's possible cheating, the idea of it gripped Liz like a choke hold. What would she do if she smelled perfume on his clothes again? Would she be able to confront him this time? Giving Rick an ultimatum was not an option. That was like being on the edge of a cliff. Once you threw yourself over, there was no going back. And how could she face her father if her marriage failed? He'd be so disappointed in her. First college, then marriage? And how would she keep the farm? She'd have to sell and then . . . No! There was no way in hell she would allow that to happen. Elizabeth Bergen would not be a failure.

Bobbi lifted an outdated newspaper from a pile on the desk with the headline, "Women Strike For Equality." A picture on the front page showed a woman holding a sign. "Sisterhood is Powerful." She flipped through the pages as Liz stood and walked across the room to the open window.

Liz gazed at the darkness outside. Her mind drifted to a thousand places. Her mother's face, her dad's crestfallen expression when she told him she was quitting school, the grapes in Scanlon's hands, her bank book . . .

"What?" Bobbi said. "You look really intense. What are you thinking about?"

"My grapes."

"Yeah?"

"They're like my children," she said, still staring out the window, her voice soft and dreamy. "And I don't want Hank Scanlon, or anyone else, taking care of them. She turned to face Bobbi. "They're mine. They need nurturing, tender loving care."

"Yeah, and you do that," Bobbi said.

Liz stood with hands on her hips. "Yes, I do. And I want to see them grow up." She lifted her chin, thrust her chest out, and announced, "No more selling. *I'm* going to make the wine."

CHAPTER 33

The quiet hum of the refrigerator greeted Liz as she walked through the dark house. She flipped the light switch, illuminating the narrow staircase, and climbed. Bethany's bedroom door was slightly open, the way she liked it, not wanting to be closed off from her parents who slept downstairs. Liz tiptoed in and stood at the side of her daughter's bed watching her budding chest rise and fall with each quiet breath. Childhood is so wonderful, she thought. Not a care in the world. Liz tucked in the blanket around her sleeping daughter and walked across the hall to Noah's room. His feet, as usual, were tangled in the fluffy blue comforter that he'd thrown off as he did every night. Careful not to wake him, Liz gently slipped the cover from under his feet and pulled it to his shoulders. The house was downright chilly since Rick insisted on keeping the heat low during the night, just warm enough so the pipes wouldn't burst. He paid the bills and their electricity was not going to be high. Liz kissed her son's forehead and then quietly closed the door behind her. She hurried down the steps bursting to tell Rick her plan.

There wasn't a hint of light coming from beneath their bedroom door. Damn, she was so fired-up, ready to become a vintner, that she wanted to sing out her plan to Rick that very minute, and now he was obviously asleep. Liz had talked incessantly about it on the ride home with Bobbi, how she was going to learn everything there was to know about wine making. Crestfallen, she opened the door slowly, stepped inside without making a sound, and walked over to her dresser.

"Oh, you're up," she said, the bounce back in her step when she spotted the reflection of Rick sitting in bed.

"Yup. So how'd it go with Scanlon?"

Rick lifted something to his mouth. A glass, Liz realized, hearing ice cubes tinkle. The giddiness drained right out of her. "Fine," she said, aware now that Rick might not take to her plan as eagerly as she imagined, depending on how much he'd already imbibed. She'd have to go slow – warm him up.

"Really well," she answered pulling off her jeans and sweater. She felt Rick's eyes float over her as she unhooked her bra, not in the lustful way of their early married years which had always aroused her. No, this was more an examination, as if he was comparing her body to something or, as Bobbi's words came back, to someone. Her insides twisted. She turned and opened her dresser drawer. Her fingers ran over the soft cotton of a night shirt. No, she thought, and moved it aside then dug under more nightwear – cotton and flannel – and pulled out the silky black nightgown buried underneath. She turned again toward Rick and slipped it over her head slowly, sensually, then sat on the edge of the bed, her bare back exposed. She stared out the window to where the vines, now nestled in darkness, grew and then swept her legs up onto the soft sheet letting one fall open. As it rested on her husband's long lean thigh, skin to skin, she settled back against the pillows purposely making no mention of his drinking at midnight.

"What's the matter, hon? Why can't you sleep? It's not like you," she said, playing the concerned wife.

"Stuff on my mind." The malty scent of Scotch drifted from his lips, reminding Liz of the smell of Band-Aids.

"Wanna talk about it?" She hoped her sweet, solicitous tone would be the wound care they needed and the adhesion to her plan.

"No. I'll figure it out." Rick took a swallow of the toasty-colored liquid. "Tell me about tonight. Did he buy all of it?"

"Yes."

"Give me the check."

Liz sighed. "It's in my wallet."

"So?"

"It's in the kitchen, hon. Can't it wait 'til morning?" Liz didn't want anything to cut into her plan.

Rick let out a disgusted grunt. She ignored it and told him how Hank had made them wait, and then, as her hand stroked his bare thigh, she carefully rolled out her blueprint to becoming vintners, making sure she used the word we instead of I.

"Interesting," Rick said. "Something to think about, despite the fact that we don't know what a good wine even tastes like."

Liz laughed, delighted he seemed intrigued. "Right, remember how I thought Boone's Farm was nice until Matt told me that fruity drink shouldn't be called wine?" Liz wanted the memory to evoke more loving times between them, when everything seemed to have promise. "That shouldn't stop us, though. We can learn."

Rick put the glass on the night table and reached out to her. "Come here," he said, his voice deep, insistent. She leaned in, letting her head rest against his chest, heat radiating through hers. It all seemed to be going her way. The nightgown's thin spaghetti strap fell from her shoulder. He pulled her closer, dropped the other and kissed her neck, then, with an unexpected force, flipped over and mounted her. With strong, firm hands he pressed her shoulders into the mattress and didn't let go. His manhood pushed hard against her. His wet tongue slithered between her breasts, made feverish circles around her navel, then slid down to her mound. He drove it inside and out and up again, bit hard on her nipple, and thrust his member deep inside. It pounded against her wetness. In a fevered pitch, her teeth clamped her lower lip stifling shouts until she couldn't hold back any longer. One last assault. One loud grunt. And Rick collapsed, rolled off, and turned away.

Liz lay on the crumpled sheet barely breathing. The damp between her legs was as sticky as her thoughts. Never before had Rick nailed her to the bed, taking her body with such fury, like a beast to a bloody chunk of meat. The occasional times they did have sex he was sensual, slowly bringing her to a pitch that made her beg for more. What was this? She thought she had the control until he slapped her hands to the bed. Not ready to give up, she turned on her side and spooned him. Rick tossed her arm off and rolled onto his back.

"Okay," he said, staring at the ceiling, hands clasped behind his head like the mighty king of the jungle. "No more selling. It's a fine idea." He sat, tall and straight, and turned to her. "That said, my dear, it is not a woman's job. *I* will be Riverview Vineyard's winemaker."

CHAPTER 34

The storm door banged shut. Rick stepped over two little pairs of muddy boots strewn across the worn linoleum and slipped out of his jacket.

"You're home early," Liz called from the kitchen, just a step up from the vestibule where Rick was hanging his parka. She sat at the table with the library book she'd taken out earlier in the day open to the first chapter.

"Surprised?" he said, as he tossed his book bag on a kitchen chair and kissed her hello. His stubble chafed her soft cheek.

Yes, Liz thought, I am. It was a rare occurrence when Rick got home before the sun set and even rarer when he kissed her without expecting sex. She dog-eared the page and closed the large hardbound book.

Rick pointed to the title, *The Chemistry of Wine.* His brow furrowed. "What are you reading that for? I told you last night. I am the winemaker." He pointed his finger at her. "The grapes are your baby. Putting them into a bottle is mine."

"I know, but I figured I should understand the procedure. We're a team. I can help."

"I don't need your help. Winemaking is my realm. Mine," he said, pointing to himself. "I'm the winemaker. Remember?"

Liz certainly did, and just like last night when he'd made that announcement and then turned his back to her, every muscle in her entire body tensed. Acids and bases might not have been her forte in school, but, no matter what he said, Liz was going to learn all about them. How to adjust the acidity to get a dry white wine or a sweet rosé. While he, the satisfied king, had snored next to her, she'd wrestled with her thoughts. *Rick barely does anything with the vineyard, so why should he be the winemaker? Maybe he needs something that's all his – that he needs to be The Man.*

Am I being emasculating? It's his fault I took the reins. The flutter in her gut came back hard, twisting, turning, squeezing her inside out. *Oh my God, is that why he went to other women?* Like a wet rag, that wiped away all her denying. All right, she'd told herself as the gray dawn broke. It's his. If it means he'll stay in my bed. That I can keep the land. And my marriage. However, she would learn every detail of the winemaking process anyway. Liz wanted to pick those grapes and see them through to the final sip.

"And," Rick announced, "I'm gonna quit my job. Be a full-time vintner."

"What?" Her head jerked back. "Are you nuts? What are we going to live on?" Her pitch grew louder. "You do know it takes quite a while 'til a bottle of wine is ready to be sold."

Rick shot her a look that would make a Rottweiler cower. "We'll get a farm loan," he said. "I went to the bank today. There's no problem."

"Even if we don't have an income?"

"You can go back to work."

"Right," Liz yelled, unable to control herself any longer. "And you're going to do everything in the vineyard plus make the wine? I don't think so."

"Oh," he said with disgust. "Go prune your grapes and keep 'em nice and clean. Don't let the birds get 'em. Just leave everything else to me."

"Really? And what happens if the wine doesn't sell? Did you ever think of that? How do we pay back the loan then?"

"The land's collateral."

The words sucked the air right out of her. The land. The rich, brown earth she loved. That was frightening. Liz definitely wanted to stop selling their grapes. She couldn't help trembling with excitement at the very idea of making their own vintage and selling cases of bold, beautiful wine. Talk about experiments. Growing grapes for Cornell was nothing compared to doing this, especially with no other money coming in.

"Matt told me that out of just one of our acres," Rick continued, his chest all puffed out, "we could yield seven hundred twenty bottles of wine. Think about it, Liz. Next year we'll have eight acres producing. And soon, all thirteen. That'll bring us over nine thousand bottles. At maybe six bucks a bottle, that's not bad, huh?"

Liz did some quick calculations in her mind. Her fingers twitched. Then reality hit. "Don't forget we'll have plenty of expenses," she said. "Not to mention paying back the loan."

"Yeah, but the net should be very pretty. I don't need to teach anymore. I'm gonna live off the land." He walked over to the refrigerator and pulled out a beer.

A breeze blew through the open window above the sink, ruffling the curtains. Liz felt the chill. Her thoughts in a jumble, she walked over, closed it, and stood gazing out at the ridge of hog-backed mountains in the distance, their trees covered in bronze and gold. She had to admit, she was glad Rick was finally going to have his dream. Would it keep him home now, she wondered? No . . . she hoped. Would he stay sober, now that he had what he really wanted — thanks to her and Bobbi? Maybe this was the new start they needed. She practically smelled the heady scent of grapes fermenting in their own oak barrels and could almost feel the velvety red coating her tongue. Rick tapped her shoulder as he passed by on his way to the living room. She stayed, contemplating. As the soil nurtured her vines, Liz prayed it would do the same for her marriage; however, her chest tightened at the uncertainty of it all.

CHAPTER 35

The snow, falling in drifts, carpeted the land in a pure white blanket and kept the Bergens inside all day. From his spot on the living room couch, Rick yelled at the Boston Celtics like an NBA coach while Bethany and Noah sipped hot chocolate at the kitchen table. "Don't spill," Liz said, moving the farm catalogues she'd ordered closer. She was busy comparing prices of the equipment they'd need the following autumn when it was time for Rick to make the wine.

"Make sure it's stainless steel," Rick shouted from the living room. "And has a motor." Liz pressed her hands on the table, hard. She knew the type of de-stemmer they'd need. It was one that separated the stems from the grapes and crushed them. Then she shook her head and corrected herself once again. It wasn't they. It was he. Yet she couldn't help thinking in the plural. All winter and spring, when not in the vineyard or canning vegetables from Rick's garden, Liz secretly researched winemaking at the library.

"I need a press too," Rick said, taking big strides into the kitchen. "Let me see what you're looking at." He stood behind Liz and pointed to the picture on the page. "That's a good one. See those paddles? They beat the grapes, separate them from their stems, and spit them out here." He showed Liz where the grapes would fall. "Then the must – that's the juice, seeds, and skins that are left after the stems come off – gets crushed." He flipped some pages and stopped at another piece of equipment and the teacher in him pointed. "Here, this is a press. It's for making white wine. After the grapes are crushed, they're . . ." He stepped back and waved his hand in the air. "Forget it. You don't need to know all that. Just order the machines. You're doin' great, Lizzy."

Liz knew the press extracted the juice from the crushed grapes. She knew all the words that rolled off Rick's tongue, and she even knew the Latin term for must, *vinum mustum*. She wasn't about to tell him, though. After all, winemaking was his realm, even if she would have gotten an A in the course from her clandestine study.

"What about oak barrels?" she asked, looking up at him, trying to appear innocent. "Don't we need them?"

"Of course we do. Just get these first. I have to figure out how many barrels I'll need and build some strong shelves to house them. There's not enough floor space in the barn."

"You're going to stack them? How will you get to the top to . . . to do whatever you need to do with the juice that's fermenting in those barrels?"

"A really tall ladder. That's what Scanlon does, and some other vintners."

Liz was glad Rick had seriously taken to learning the art of winemaking, and she loved how he sparkled every time he came home from a lesson. He had that same excitement in his eyes that she fell in love with thirteen years ago when he was a college senior with the world at his fingertips. Yet she hated that Hank Scanlon was now his teacher. Of all the winemakers in the Hudson River Valley, why that misogynist? He'd even told Rick he was right to be the vintner – that men would not accept women in that fraternity. Liz fumed when Rick had told her about their conversation when he first visited the old codger. Scanlon had said it was enough that she had acted as the seller, but Rick should absolutely not let her have a hand in making the wine. There were only three women winemakers in the country, he'd said, all in California. As if a woman's hormones would disturb the fermentation.

"Those barrels are about three feet high," Liz said. "And leaving enough space between each to lift the lids and get inside you could stack maybe four, if I'm right. The ceiling's about seventeen feet high isn't it? That's a mighty tall ladder."

"Yup. Don't worry. You're not the one climbing it." He bent and kissed the top of her head, then went back to the game.

It was a long winter. Finally, the snow melted, the earth warmed, and the vines swelled with tiny buds. By June, the flowers bloomed. Mother Nature pollinated and fertilized the blossoms, setting the fruit, and Liz was hopeful. It looked like 1972 would bring them a good yield. At the end of the month, Rick retired his teaching degree and walked out of Hudson Tech for the last time.

"Why are you going?" Liz asked when he came home later that night and announced he'd be joining the senior class on their annual summer field trip.

"They needed another teacher to fill the chaperone requirement, so I figured why not? It'll be fun being out in the wilderness learning survival techniques. We have to find our own food, cook it over open fire, bathe in the river . . ."

"And that interests you? Be my guest. I just don't get it. Are they paying you?"

"No. I'm a volunteer," he said, the yeasty smell of beer on his breath. "I've got the time now, so why not? Come fall, I'll be very busy, deep into winemaking."

And you won't be busy all summer, Liz said silently. Of course not, with Bobbi and me doing all the work. Liz wondered how Rick would react if she announced she'd be going away for a week. He hadn't asked if she minded. He hadn't even consulted her about the poker tournament he joined that would take him away several weekends over the summer. Oh, how she would have loved to go along and get to know the other wives, have a lazy afternoon by the hotel pool, and dress for dinner in a dining room with table cloths and china, without children. She knew her father would stay with Bethany and Noah, but when she broached the subject the other night, Rick cut her short. "This is a guy thing," he said. "No women."

Although she loved her life that revolved around the vineyard and wouldn't want to change it, Liz wished she had a group of girlfriends that she could take off with. Other than Bobbi, she really only had her high school friends who she saw from time to time when she went back to New Jersey or if they came to the farm to visit. Plus, her work in the vineyard left her little time to make connections with the local women. Sure, she knew some of the mothers of Bethany and Noah's friends. They were all active in PTA, played tennis, and whatever else they did with their days. Liz didn't have time for any of that. Besides, she lived miles from town. If only they knew she had grown up just like them. She wasn't a hippy, like they surmised. She was merely a woman who fell in love with her land and was looking forward to seeing her own bold red in a crystal glass. And to sharing it with friends. The first part of that dream was about to come true. The second brought an ache to her chest.

CHAPTER 36

"Come on Beth, I'll race you to the raft," Rick called out over the happy squealing voices of children splashing in the swimming hole. Beach blankets, striped and flowered umbrellas, coolers filled with sandwiches and snacks covered the tiny sandy beach where the locals spent their summer Sundays.

"You're on!" Bethany shouted, dropping her beach bag on the sand. At eleven, she was an accomplished swimmer and one of the best on the town's swim team. Having climbed trees since she was able to stand, Beth wasn't even afraid of the fifteen-foot-high diving board that made older kids shudder. She kicked off her flip flops and ran into the cool water, avoiding a toddler making sand castles at the edge. She dove under the rope separating the deep end from the shallow, and took off with her father following close behind.

Watching from the sand, Liz couldn't contain the grin that spread across her cheeks. It was so great having her whole family together on this glorious afternoon, the air mixed with lemonade and Coppertone. Usually the kids went with their friends, riding their bikes down the narrow roads and coming home in time for dinner, all sandy and sunburned. With Rick leaving the next day for Survival Week, after some coercing on their mother's part, they agreed to Family Time. A warmth radiated through Liz stronger than the blazing sun. She laid out the beach blanket and cooler filled with Noah's beloved bologna sandwiches on store-bought bread and Bethany's orange Cheez Doodles instead of Rick's preferred potato chips, then raced into the water to have a catch with her son.

An hour later the four Bergens, tired and hungry, flopped down on the blanket, and Liz divvied up the sandwiches. Rick cracked open a beer and leaned back against the old maple tree that created a wide span of shade over the small sandy beach. "This is nice," he said. "Looks like everyone and their cousins came out today."

Liz took a sip of Coke and nodded. She couldn't be happier, especially when, after gobbling down lunch, the kids ran off to swim with their friends. She and Rick lay on the blanket, the brilliant summer sun seeping into their skin while a soft breeze washed over them, helping Liz blow away her doubts and fears. Lying there together reminded her of the picnics they used to go on that one year they were in college together when she fell hard for that cool senior with the red Impala convertible. She reached for Rick's hand, intertwining their fingers just as they used to. If only there weren't crowds around them and he could unclasp his hand and stroke her body as he did all those times they snuck behind the soccer field. His sensual touch, mixed with the thrill of sneaking, and making out on the scratchy army blanket, brought her nineteen-year-old self to an incredible fevered pitch. She sighed, reveling in that memory. Oh, how she wanted that again! A soft giggle escaped her throat as she realized it was the same blanket their kids had played on when they planted their first vines. *That old, green, scratchy thing sure can tell lots of stories. Maybe we will have more. Maybe after today, things will change.*

"Hey, Rick, is that you?" A tall, tanned man peered down at them.

Rick opened his eyes. "Hey, man," he said scooting up to lean on his elbows. "I didn't know you came here. Don't you live in the burbs?"

"Yeah, but the kids like this place better." He looked over at Liz and introduced himself. "Rick and I used to play poker together." He turned to Rick. "Haven't seen you in a long time. Not playing anymore?"

Liz's eyes flicked from one man to the other. Suddenly she felt hot, and it wasn't from the sun.

"Umm, no, yeah," Rick stammered. "I'm still playin'."

"Oh . . . right."

"Yeah, I'm with . . . with that other group."

"Yeah, yeah, sure. I remember."

Rick turned away. He grabbed another beer from the cooler.

"Well," the tanned man said, "it was good seeing you." He smiled at Liz. "It was nice meeting you too. Enjoy the day."

Liz watched him walk along the beach to his family. Despite the breeze, the air felt still.

CHAPTER 37

On a rainy, humid August afternoon, Liz sat on her daughter's bed looking through old photo albums with her. There were pictures of Liz as a baby, a little girl with blonde curls, and of her sister and brother also growing up. The ones of her parents as newlyweds and those holding their newborn children made Liz feel warm all over. From their bright eyes and smiles, she could almost feel the love between them. Sadly, the sensation was bittersweet. Would photos of their family, of Rick and Liz, Bethany and Noah, evoke the same warmth in her children someday when they were older looking through their own family albums? The heavy ache in her chest said she wasn't so sure.

Bethany sat back and leaned against the pillows propped on the oak headboard. She cocked her head, like a puppy. "How come I never met Daddy's mother? Didn't she want to know me? And Noah? We were her only grandchildren."

"Oh, honey, she wasn't very maternal, but I'm sure she bragged about you to her friends. We sent her pictures of you every month when you were a baby."

"But she never came to visit. Not even for Christmas."

"No. She wouldn't get on a plane. And it was much too expensive for the four of us to fly there." Besides the fact, Liz thought, she never invited us. "We do have pictures of her," she added, "and your grandfather. Want to see them?"

"I have," Bethany said, all self-assured. "They're on a shelf in the barn in that box Daddy got when his mother died."

Liz remembered the big package that arrived a few weeks after her mother-in-law's death. Rick had relegated it to the barn. "There's not enough closet space in the house," he'd said. "One of these days I'll go through it. Probably nothing in there worth keeping." Liz had forgotten all about the box until now.

"There was other stuff in there too. A baggie filled with some kind of spice or something, like you use when you make spaghetti sauce. Why's it there?"

Liz had to close her mouth fast before her daughter asked why she was so surprised. "I don't know, sweetie. I'll take a look. Maybe Daddy dropped it by accident."

Bethany was not buying that explanation. Liz saw it in her eyes. She's too grown up for eleven, Liz thought.

"Did Grandma Bergen like you?" Bethany asked.

Where did that come from? Her daughter's question surprised her and not only because it was asked. "You know," she answered. "I'm not sure. She did give me her diamond."

"What diamond? I never saw it."

"I know. We put it away in the bank – for someday." Liz smiled at her daughter imagining her all grown up wearing that ring on her finger. Then she shook her head thinking of her mother-in-law. "You know, Grandma Bergen and I really didn't have much to do with each other. She was very controlling."

"Like Daddy," Bethany said.

Again, Liz's mouth fell open. "Daddy isn't like his mother." Or is he, Liz wondered silently. I never knew if she was genuine or playing me. And no matter what I wanted, even planning my own wedding, she always got her way.

"Mommy, Daddy's always telling you what to do. And, well . . . the kids at school say he takes drugs. That boy from down the road, the one with the long hair and dirty fingernails, he told me Daddy buys weed from his father." Bethany lifted a shoulder. "That's marijuana, isn't it?"

Liz squeezed her eyes shut. How does Bethany know that? And how the hell am I going to answer her? Liz's breath hitched. She bit her fist to control herself and to bury her shame. Like fever, anger heated her chest. "I'll be back in a minute," Liz said and hurried out the bedroom door. She flew through the house. The side door slammed behind her.

Rick had already built the shelving for the oak barrels that would arrive in a few weeks. Liz glanced around looking for the box. It was cold in the barn, although temperature didn't register with her at that moment. She stretched her neck to see all the way to the back of the first shelf and stood on her toes to try to see higher. The box wasn't on any shelf she could view from floor level. "Damn it."

She grabbed the ladder from the opposite wall and slid it over, centering it in front of the shelves, then climbed. It wasn't on the second shelf or the third. "Seriously, Richard," she mumbled. "What the hell are you hiding?" Her heartbeat kicked up, then as quick as a finger snap it slowed and she calmed along with it. Okay, maybe he was being smart. He put it high so the kids wouldn't find the grass. Liz understood that and frankly was glad Rick had thought of it. She wasn't happy that he was still smoking the stuff, but what if the kids had found it and lit up? Oh, she wanted to smack him. Bethany had found it. So, Rick, your plan didn't work after all.

Times were changing too fast for Liz and she was having trouble keeping up. Jeez, when she was Beth's age, she was listening to love songs by Perry Como not Jimi Hendrix and his psychedelic shit.

With a tight grip on the ladder, Liz climbed a few more steps. She focused on the shelving in front of her, too petrified to look down. She had to be at least twelve feet off the ground by now. Her heart pounded. How the hell did Beth do this and why does she have to be such an explorer? Couldn't she keep to trees? A little higher, and she'd have a clear look at the entire top shelf. Carefully, Liz placed her foot on each rung and there, shoved as far back as possible, was a brown corrugated box. She leaned forward and reached in. Not enough. She had to go up one more rung. Barely breathing, she climbed, stretched her arm, and grabbed onto a corner. She maneuvered the box a little closer, let out a huge breath of relief, and slid the box toward her.

There's no way I can get down carrying this, she told herself. And I don't really want to have to climb back up either to put it away. Liz gathered her nerve and centered herself on the ladder with the box directly in front of her. With one hand on the shelf, steadying herself, she leaned over and flipped the box onto its side. There was the bag of grass, half full, and the photo album Bethany mentioned. It fell forward. Before it could topple to the floor, Liz grabbed it. Loose pictures tumbled out. She scooped them into her fist and had to put them on the shelf in order to right the box, so Rick wouldn't know she was snooping. Even though he'd probably hid the box all the way on top so the kids wouldn't find it, Liz knew her husband would not want her to be going through his things either.

All in order, Liz gathered the loose photos in her right hand to put them in the box and shove it back where it had been. Okay, so she saw the bag of grass. She was satisfied. Yet how could she tell her daughter that she was correct, her daddy was taking drugs? At least now she would tell Rick his hiding place had been discovered, and demand he stop smoking.

With the pile of pictures clutched in her fingers, and with her left hand still holding tight to the edge of the shelf, Liz loosened her grip on the photos ready to toss them into the box. "No!" she cried as they all tumbled to the floor. Her breath burst in and out. Her shoulders tightened.

Liz forced herself to calm down. She had to retrieve all the pictures and get them back into the box. With one deep bolstering breath, she crept down the ladder and, with clammy hands, made it to solid ground. She took a moment to gather some bravura, then scooped up the pictures and squared her shoulders, ready to climb back up and return them. She glanced at the top image, expecting to see baby Rick or big boy Rick. Instead, her eyes opened wide. It was a picture of Rick. Adult Rick. But who was the woman in a flowered sundress standing with him under a palm tree, his arm around her waist?

CHAPTER 38

"Where did you find that?" Rick said, looking at the photo Liz had just shoved in his face. He was seated in the wing chair in the living room with his feet on the ottoman, beer in hand, relaxing after what he'd complained was a grueling week at Survival Camp. Liz stood next to him with a strong grip on the picture. He reached to take it from her. She pulled her arm back and held it tight to her chest. Her husband's rapid blinking, as if he was totally confused by what he'd seen, didn't fool her one bit.

"In the box you hid in the barn," Liz answered, staring him straight in the eyes. Thunder rumbled outside. Rain poured. Liz held the photograph out again. "Who is she?"

Rick lowered his head, averting her gaze, then up again laying his eyes directly on her. He shrugged his shoulders. "I don't even remember her name – just some girl I met when I visited my mother. Remember, you insisted I go?"

"Yes, and I also remember you didn't want to go and then all of a sudden you changed your mind, like it was a great idea. So, Richard," she said, shaking the picture at him. "Who is she?"

"Honestly, hon. I didn't even know I had that picture. You say it was in the box?" He lifted a shoulder again, so nonchalantly it made Liz's blood boil. "My mother's aide must have thought it was important and put it in with all the stuff she sent me. I don't even remember the photo being taken. There were so many times the women at the condo wanted a picture with me." He looked like a peacock strutting its feathers. "They claimed my mother would love it."

"Right," Liz said. "Sure." A quiver ran through her stomach. "And you expect me to believe that?"

"Sweetheart. Please. It was all flirtatious. All those ladies loved having me around."

"And all those ladies would be seventy, Richard. Your mother lived in a senior community. This one," she said, pushing her finger against the woman's face several times, "isn't even thirty." A flash of lightning streamed through the window, illuminating the image.

"She must have been someone's daughter," Rick said. "Yeah . . . yeah, I remember now. Mom's neighbor had her daughter living with her. Right. That's who she is. And she wanted a picture under that palm tree. It was a real pretty tree right alongside the pool. And I remember her taking the photo out of the Polaroid. I thought she kept it." He shrugged again. "Guess not."

With a sour, bitter tang in her mouth, Liz turned her back to Rick. She had to walk away, had to regain her composure, or, like Vesuvius, she'd blow. She went into the bedroom. Rick's sneakers were on the floor smack in her way. She kicked the right one, then the left. It hit the wall. She left his sweatshirt where it lay crumpled on the oval braided rug on his side of the bed and looked out the window. The rain was so fierce she barely made out the vineyard.

"How could you?" Liz grumbled. She meant that question for Rick, although it smacked her in the face. "And how could I have been so blind?" It felt like time stood still. She picked her cuticles, worrying the dead skin around the thumbnail. She moved backward and sat on the edge of the bed still mumbling. "Harvest is next month. I need him here." Liz stood, straight and tall. "Or do I?" She clenched her jaw, tightened her fists, and swung around. With long, determined strides, she raced back into the living room. Rick wasn't there.

"Where the hell are you?" she yelled.

"In here," Rick called from the kitchen. "Stop yelling. You'll wake the kids."

Like he ever cared. She found him standing by the open refrigerator popping the top off another beer can. Liz walked right over and slammed the door. "You took that floozy in the flowered dress to Florida, you shit! And if she's your so-called Friday night poker game, then you can get the hell out right now."

"Lizzy, please." Rick took a swig of the Schlitz then put the can on the countertop. He shoved his hands in his pockets. "I swear she's nobody. Like I said, I didn't even know that picture was there. Just let it go."

Liz felt shaky. Her breath quivered. She closed her eyes and blew breaths from her nose, in and out, in and out. She nodded, not able to utter a word. Rick put his arms around her. "Come on, sweetheart. Sit. Let's talk about good things, our harvest next month, the wine we're gonna make." He gave her the smile and wink that always made her tingle. This time, she felt nothing.

CHAPTER 39

Curled up tight on the edge of the bed, Liz woke in the same exact spot she'd gone to sleep the night before. The gray dawn peeked through the window. Dust motes danced in the air. She rubbed her eyes and lifted her head to see the clock on her bedside table. Seven thirty. The house was quiet, which meant the kids were still asleep, and Rick, all the way across the vast wasteland of mattress, was on his back, snoring. Good. She slipped out of bed, quietly opened a drawer and grabbed some clean underwear, jeans, and a tank top and went into the bathroom to bathe and dress. Liz didn't want to wake him, since there was absolutely no way she could talk to him right now. No matter what he might say, she knew she couldn't be civil. It would take her time. Liz wanted to believe him, but all night she wondered why he had saved that picture. She'd barely slept a wink. Did he really not know it was in the box?

After a steaming hot shower, as if she could wash away her questions, Liz dressed, then put the coffee up and went into the laundry room. Rick's clothes from his week at survival camp were waiting for her. She dumped the dirty lot into the washing machine. Where's his sweatshirt? I told him to pick it up last night and put it in the basket. With an aggravated huff, she marched back into the bedroom. There it was, still in a heap on the floor. Liz grabbed it, gave his sleeping form a disgusted look, and walked back out. That pernicious, suffocating smell caught her again. Shalimar. It was all over his sweatshirt. It permeated the walls, strangled her. Liz raced back into the bedroom, threw it at him. "You fucking liar," she screamed. "Get up. Get the hell out of my house."

"Wh . . . what?" Rick said, shaking himself awake. He raked a hand through his hair and, with a foggy expression, innocently asked, "What the hell are you yelling about?"

"This!" She shoved the sweatshirt down on his face. "Tell me, how many of the boys on that so-called survival trip wore perfume? Huh?" She grabbed the blanket off him and yanked his arm, trying to pull him off the bed."

"Hey, get your damn paws off me!" He shoved her away. Wobbling, Liz grabbed onto the night table, then righted herself, her muscles quivering.

"I want you out," she screamed. "Now! I'm done with your lies."

Liz bounded over to the dresser, grabbed their framed wedding picture, and flung it across the room. It shattered against the wall – silver and glass sprayed everywhere. Rick jumped out of bed, grabbed her bare arm, and twisted it behind her back, screaming, "If you weren't such an emasculating bitch . . ."

"What? You wouldn't have fucked other women?" Her veins pulsed. "Let go of me!"

Bethany rushed into the room "Mommy, Daddy," she screeched. "Stop!"

Rick untangled Liz's arm and pushed her aside. He shook his fist over and over, his forearms rigid, muscles flexed. Red-faced, he jerked his head back and forth, from his wife to his daughter. "Your mother's gonna tell you a pack of lies. Don't believe a word." Then he glared at Liz. "You want me out? Well, you better run back to daddy 'cause I'm sure not gonna support you."

"Go to hell," Liz grumbled. She looked at her daughter who stood frozen to the spot with her lips and chin trembling. "Beth," she said quietly, trying to control herself. "Go back to your room. Please."

"But Mommy . . ."

"Not now." Liz turned and pulled out a drawer from Rick's armoire. She stared at the clothes inside. "Go!" she said, her voice more forceful now.

"No," Rick said, "let her see what you're doin'." Venom spewed with each word.

Liz grabbed her head and folded over herself. She didn't want Bethany seeing this. It would be difficult enough explaining everything to the kids later – plus she needed them on her side. Liz lifted her head and stared at the ceiling. Then, with the ferocity of a hungry animal, she dug into his dresser drawer. She tossed out underwear and socks, opened another, and chucked out a pile of shirts.

"You better get a good lawyer," Rick said with a guttural roar. He scooped up his clothes and shot a look at his daughter. "Your mother's demented." Then he stormed out and slammed the door behind him. The walls shook.

Liz slumped to the floor, her head bowed, a palm pressed to her chest. Bethany rushed over. "What's going on?" she said, sitting next to her mom. "What happened?"

Liz couldn't form the words that were needed. All the built-up tension suddenly released. Tears poured.

"Mommy," Beth cried and wrapped her arms around her mother. Liz pulled her close and together, with quaking shoulders, they held tight to each other, their heavy breaths the only sound in the room.

CHAPTER 40

"Good riddance to him," Bobbi called out as she stepped through the back door into Liz's kitchen. She'd come over as soon as Liz had called. "It's about time."

Head down, Liz mumbled into the Formica counter. "Yeah, but what am I going to do?" She swished a cinnamon stick into her coffee, watching the dark brown liquid flow back and forth.

"You're going to be fine. You're going to soar!" Bobbi's voice sang out, cheery like the yellow walls around them.

"With harvest in just a few weeks?" Cupping the mug in her hands, Liz turned and met Bobbi's gaze. "And who's going to help pick?"

"Rick wasn't doing that anyway," Bobbi reminded her. "Not when he was going to do the crush."

"Yeah, but he had all his buddies coming. I can't call them now. It's just us regulars. You, me, my dad, and maybe Kristin and her husband on the weekend." Liz leaned back against the speckled counter and took a sip of the steaming blend, hoping the cinnamon would soothe her nerves. "And if I'm going to make the wine now, I'll need you to drive the filled crates to me. We just don't have enough pickers." Liz placed the coffee cup on the counter. Her fingernail found the hardened cuticle around her thumb. "To top it off, I have no idea where the money's coming from."

"That's the same situation you were in anyway. Rick wasn't teaching anymore."

"Right. And that scared the hell out of me. But now it seems even worse. First thing I need is to pay for the licenses – New York State and Federal. And they're not cheap!" Liz grabbed the cup and took another swallow, as if the coffee would give her courage. Holding it tight in both hands, she uttered the thought that had kept her insides twisting all night. "It kills me to say this, but . . . I'm scared and . . . oh jeez, as much as I don't want to," she let out a deep sigh and plunked the mug on the counter. "I *have* to sell the grapes."

"Oh, no you don't." Bobbi took Liz's hand in hers and, eyeball to eyeball, said, "Do *not* make Rick the reason you give up your dream."

Liz's chin trembled. Her chest shook. Her hands flew to her eyes and she broke down. Sniffing hard, swallowing the hard knot in her throat, she tried to stop the tears, but they kept pouring. "Why did he need her?" she cried. "What's wrong with me?"

"Oh, sweety, nothing's wrong with you." Bobbi drew Liz into a hug and held her until the heaving in her chest eased.

"It was supposed to be so good," Liz said, pulling back and swiping her drippy nose. "We had all this land and the fruit . . ." With her knuckles, she wiped her eyes and collapsed into a kitchen chair. "And it all turned to shit. And now I have to go back to selling." Bobbi shook her head, giving Liz a fierce negative, then sat. "How can I not?" Liz whined. "I have to feed my kids. I don't want to go back to my father."

"Your father?" Bobbi's brow creased.

Liz told her what Rick had said.

"That's just mean," Bobbi's lip curled. "We'll figure this out. And, you know, I do appreciate it, but you don't have to pay me. I get Glen's salary."

Liz lowered her head. Her heart felt like it was shrinking. "I might have to take you up on that. But I still need money. I can't wait for the wine to sell."

"You'll get money from Rick. He has to pay alimony."

"Yeah, right. If I'm lucky." Liz lifted her cigarettes from the table, extracted one, and held it between her fingers, unlit. "I'm just so scared. What if I don't get anything from him? What if this winery thing doesn't work out? I always thought – really, was always told – that my husband would take care of me. That's what my mother said. Divorce was not in her realm of thinking. And it for sure was never in mine, at least not when I dreamt of marriage. I don't know how you go on, Bobbi, not knowing at all if Glen is ever coming back."

"Liz, I know he's not. After all this time . . ." She shook her head. "MIA is just a term they use. It doesn't only mean missing in action – for me, it's never found. I used to think he was captured, maybe a POW, but by now, I'd know that." Bobbi shrugged. "And scared – hell that's not a strong enough word for how I felt, how

I feel even now. But I don't let it strangle me. I won't. I have to go on. For my kids. Hell, for me! What good would it do if I crumbled? Not to say I didn't crumble, and for several months. But I got myself together. I had to. And you do too. You will."

Liz struck a match and lit the Winston. She took a deep drag and slowly blew it from her lips, watching the smoke swirl making waves and circles in the air. "You're right," she said. "Rick cannot win. Whatever it takes, I will make this work. I will not sell." Like a first-place winner with a trophy, she held her cigarette high in the air. "I will have a winery – a damn successful one. And Rick is not going to have one cent of it."

CHAPTER 41

Through the fog of a sleepless night, an idea formed in Liz's mind – a feasible one. Finally. The 1972 harvest season was less than a week away, and for far too many weeks she'd sat in bed smoking, picking at her cuticles until they bled, playing with one idea after another. Now she had it! She sat up straight, grabbed the pillow from behind her head and held it close to her chest. Yes, the words were as clear as a first-grade teacher's writing on a blackboard. It's crazy, she thought, but what the hell – I need help. Liz tossed the squashed pillow aside, threw off the covers, and bolted out of bed.

After a hot shower, she dressed in black cotton pants and a long sleeve T-shirt of the same color – it made her look thinner. She left it untucked. In the kitchen, she made her children's favorite toast. The warm cinnamon scent of the bread mixed with the nutty aroma of perked coffee gave her the extra lift she needed. The kids bolted into the room, grabbed the toast, threw Mom a kiss, and, yelling "bye," raced out the door. Clutching her coffee mug and cigarette, Liz followed. She stood at the edge of her front porch and watched Bethany and Noah run off to the school bus stop at the end of their road.

With the early morning sun warming her shoulders, Liz felt ready. Energized. Then she looked down at the Winston in her fingers, its grey smoke swirling in the clean air, and grimaced. She tossed it to the ground, stepped off the porch, and drove her foot hard into the burning tip twisting it back and forth, again and again. "He's out of my life," she said, burying the tobacco deep in the dirt. "I do not need these anymore." One more hard stomp on the filter and she was ready.

Arms pumping, Liz walked around to the side of the house and, using her sleeve, wiped the morning dew from the golf cart's windshield, then hopped in and headed up the lane, avoiding pot holes and divots, as the green carpeted valley rolled out behind her. The soft twitter of robins and blue jays, the morning's music. Her vineyard, its rows of grapevines as straight and tall as soldiers in formation. The lush rolling hills of the Hudson River Valley, a sight she never tired of, and desperately wanted to keep. The September sky, its bright blue the same as her children's eyes. But the empty feeling in the pit of her stomach was back. "Please," she prayed softly. "This has to work."

Liz drove on. She felt the strain of the past month on her face. There were new lines around her eyes, and her usual fluffy blonde waves fell limp. Off in the distance, she spied her neighbor's silo, and a few moments later, her heart racing in nervous anticipation, she reached Hill Valley Road, turned right, and stopped at the first house. A deep breath to calm her nerves. A quick pep talk. "I can do this. I can. I *have* to." She stepped out of the cart and headed up the walkway.

Liz raised her hand and knocked quickly on the red door before her courage evaporated. A moment later, a tall woman – probably in her fifties – with a flour-dusted apron wrapped around her shirtwaist dress opened the door. "Hello," she said, with a quizzical look in her eye. "Can I help you?"

"Yes, hi, I'm your neighbor . . . Liz . . . Liz Bergen. We've never met before, and I wanted to introduce myself. I live just up the road at Riverview Vineyard." Her upbeat approach could have won an Oscar. Before the woman could say a word, Liz continued. "I was wondering . . . if you've got any time to spare, I really need help picking grapes."

"Slow down," the neighbor said. "I don't understand."

"Oh," Liz cleared her throat. "I'm sorry." Then, not able to stop herself, needing to get the speech out that she'd rehearsed all morning, she blurted out the words. "As you probably know, it's harvest season, and I've got eight acres to pick, only I don't have enough help this year to get it all done."

Liz omitted the reason her help was absent. She didn't want anyone feeling sorry for her. Or any gossip. She cleared her throat again and continued. "I was hoping you and some other neighbors might be willing to give me a hand. I'm offering fifty cents a crate, and it really doesn't take long to fill one up." She stopped to catch her breath and smile. The woman's brow creased, though she nodded, as if telling Liz to go on. "You could make some extra money," Liz said. "Buy yourself something pretty." She lowered her voice a bit and continued, like a conspirator. "It's beautiful in the vineyard, and I won't even mind if you slip a grape or two into your mouth. It's tempting. As long as we fill all the crates."

"That's a lot of acres," the woman said, brushing pie crust from her hands.

"Oh, I'm sorry," Liz laughed. "I don't mean we harvest them all at once. They're not all ready at the same time. It'll take several weeks."

"Weeks?"

"Well," Liz tried hard not to pick her cuticles. "Whatever time you can give me will be greatly appreciated." Liz hoped she was hiding the tension that made her muscles feel like cement.

"I don't know the first thing about picking grapes," the lady said. "What would I need to bring?"

"Nothing. Just your hands. It's really an easy task. I supply all the tools and will show you just what to do."

"How long will it take?"

"We start at 8 a.m.," Liz said, "and should be done before noon. You'll still have the whole afternoon to yourself."

The woman looked at her rough hands then back at Liz. "I don't mind hard work," she said. "Makes you feel alive, doesn't it?" With a sweet smile, she added, "Why not? I'll give it a try. It'll be nice being out in the morning air."

Liz felt her cheeks pull into a big grin and was careful to tame the nod, not to look overly excited, especially when the woman added, "It actually sounds like fun. If you don't mind, I'll ask some of the ladies from church too."

Liz felt her knees go weak. "Oh, that would be wonderful! Thank you." Then she tilted her head. "Which church do you go to?" she asked. "I haven't been in a long time and . . . and would like to start going again." Liz needed girlfriends and church might just be the answer. Her mother had had a large group of lady friends from St. Anne's. If only Liz could find the time.

After a short discussion on the Unitarian Church in nearby Highridge – which Liz was not quite sure she understood, having grown up Catholic – she said good-bye. She turned and practically skipped down the woman's flagstone pathway. As soon as her feet hit the sidewalk, she thrust her fist to the sky and shouted, "Yes!"

Leaving the golf cart in its spot, Liz hurried up the street. Hill Valley Road was nothing like the block she grew up on, where she could practically touch her neighbor's house. Liz passed an open field filled with end-of-the-summer wild flowers and finally turned onto a stone walk to another front door. She hoped this neighbor would be as agreeable as the last, then realized she didn't even know the aproned lady's name. Now, that wasn't friendly, she told herself. Too caught up in your own problems, huh? She pressed her index finger to the doorbell and heard footsteps from inside. A tall, heavy-set, middle-aged woman answered, her eye glasses hanging from a beaded chain around her neck, her finger keeping place in the Readers Digest she was holding.

"What do you want?" she said, holding the door halfway open.

Liz stepped back a bit, even her head retracted. She introduced herself and this time asked the woman's name.

"Mrs. Wilcox," the woman answered. "What can I do for you?"

Liz rattled off her speech, but before she could invite the woman to taste the grapes, the door shut in her face. "Don't think so."

Not wanting to take the time to go back for the golf cart, Liz trudged along and knocked on the door of the next house. An elderly man answered and after Liz blurted out her speech he said, "Maybe. Depends how I feel that day."

Liz walked away, biting her lower lip. She almost turned around to head home, but the grapes formed a picture in the morning air, and she forced herself to go on. "If I don't get them picked," she muttered, "I could lose everything, and wouldn't that make Rick happy?! That bastard." She carried on to the next house refusing to think about that now. She'd deal with Rick and the lawyers later. Harvest came first. And making the wine. And selling it.

Liz knocked. No one answered, but she was sure she saw a curtain move. Feeling totally dejected, she retraced her steps, then stopped. "No," she said aloud. "I refuse to give up. I will not lose my land." She crossed the road and knocked on the first door she came to on that side of the street. Though she heard footsteps inside, no one answered. She ambled on to the next and, again, no answer. She turned and lumbered down the walk hoping Bobbi was having more luck at the school bus stop. While Liz was knocking on neighbors' doors, Bobbi was at her corner asking the stay-at-home moms to come and give them a hand picking grapes. They needed some young strong women. Harvest didn't wait for the weekend when men were home.

Liz walked on down the street. There was only one more house to try.

A tall woman with short, brown hair in a nylon warm-up suit answered. "And I'm Nancy," she said as Liz introduced herself. When she heard Liz's plea, her face lit up. "Yes, I would *love* that! I'm so bored staying home. Before my kids were born, I was a florist. Now I'm just a mommy." Liz smiled. She certainly knew what that was like. Thinking she might have a new friend here, she said, "I've got two of my own" and answered "eight and eleven" when the perky woman asked their ages. "Oh," Nancy said, "mine are younger. They wouldn't know each other."

Drained, feeling like time was slowing down, Liz made her way back home. Out of all the houses she'd stopped at, only two women were definite. That sunny hopeful feeling she'd had when she woke had vanished.

CHAPTER 42

Three days later, when the Indian summer sun was barely awake and long, flat shadows stretched across dew-covered grass, Liz, with Bobbi at her side, stood in front of her winery that had been refashioned from the old gray barn. Rick had started the renovation last summer when he installed the shelving to house the oak barrels, and her father and brother-in-law had completed the job, installing a modern electrical system with the necessary climate controls and new foundation. All was ready for Liz to make wine. First, though, she needed to get the grapes picked.

"Where are they?" Liz asked, looking at her watch for the third time. "The school bus left a half hour ago, and the one on your corner probably longer than that. Are you sure they know it's today?"

"Yes," Bobbi said. "Stop asking. Give them time."

Liz wondered about the woman in the apron with her friends from church. And where was Nancy? She said she'd come – if her kids were in school. Damn, maybe they're sick. This isn't good. Liz was depending on them and on the women Bobbi had talked to. They said they'd come. Bobbi believed they were sincere. Yet all was quiet – as silent as every other morning on the farm. No sound of an engine coming up the road.

Lou made his way along the path. "You know, Lizzy," he said, "maybe these women have other kids at home and can't get away." He stood alongside his daughter with his signature pipe clamped in his lips. The subtle aroma of pipe tobacco filled the moist morning air.

"Thanks for coming, Daddy," Liz said, looking at his gently wrinkled face. "And thanks again for this." She pointed to the winery, newly sided with rough-hewn oak sourced from a local hotel undergoing its own renovation. That this building had once housed cows was not at all obvious. "At least I can depend on you," she said. He gave her shoulder a little squeeze.

"There, look!" Bobbi shouted. She pointed to a brown station wagon in the distance. Behind that more Chevrolets, Pontiacs, and Fords made their way up the gravel lane. Liz bounced on her toes, as excited as a little kid at the circus.

"Oh my God, Bobbi!" she shrieked. "What did you do? Go to every school bus stop in town?"

"Just about."

The cars parked along the side of the road. Engines shut, and women emerged from the drivers' doors, some from the passenger doors, and some even from the back seats. "Come on," yelled Bobbi, looking over her shoulder at Liz and Lou. "Let's go give 'em the clippers and get started."

The three of them ran over to greet their pickers, buckets full of harvest scissors clutched in their hands. The clink of the blades banging against their metal pails reminded Liz she'd have to teach these women exactly how to clip a clump of grapes. She hoped she wouldn't lose any. She needed every single oval-shaped piece of fruit.

Liz practically skipped as she led everyone up the hill, the occasional "Gorgeous," "Wow," and "Beautiful" comments adding to her euphoria. At the top, one woman turned and announced, "Gee, you can see all the way to the Hudson!"

Bobbi organized the women so each one had a separate area to harvest while Liz danced from row to row, meeting everyone and demonstrating how to clip to get the whole cluster. "Here," she said to the woman with the floppy brimmed hat. "Clip it right here and you won't damage the vine." She caught the look of fear on the lady's face and gave her arm a light pat. "Don't worry, sweetie," she said. "If I can do it, so can you."

A little farther down the row, Liz bent and stuck her head under the bounteous clumps of grapes hanging from the cordon. The two predominant arms reaching out from the six-foot tall grapevine spread out to the right and left, forming a T around their wire supports that kept the mouth-watering, pulpy fruit from crawling on the ground. They looked like a mother holding out her arms, welcoming her children.

"Hi," she said, peeking through the grapes, then realized this was the neighbor in the apron whose door she'd knocked on first. Liz was glad she'd left the apron home today, but would have preferred if the woman wore pants instead of a dress. *Well, she did say she didn't know anything about picking grapes.* Ignoring the woman's couture and surer of herself now with her feet grounded in the rich soil of her vineyard, Liz said, "I'm sorry. I don't even know your name, but I do want to thank you for coming to help today. I really appreciate it."

"It's Dotty," the woman said. "I'm glad to be here." She pulled herself out of the canopy of fruit and wiped a patina of sweat from her brow as she straightened. "Your vineyard is magnificent, Liz. I can't believe I never knew you were just up the road."

Dotty had more questions and Liz answered them all, explaining that this varietal – the Seyval Blanc – was the first they'd planted. "They're kind of like my first-born," she laughed then explained that it would take several months for these grapes to actually become a bottle of wine. "You'll have to come back and taste it," Liz said, then thanked her again and continued on down the row.

She spotted a young woman who appeared to be wearing a grape hat, her head completely covered with the succulent fruit. "Hi," Liz said. "Thanks so much for coming to help. What's your name?"

"Sandra," answered the woman, pulling her head out of the abundant clumps and standing. She was tall and slender and brushed her manicured hands on her jeans. "My friend over there," Sandra said, pointing to a physically fit woman who Liz realized was Nancy, the neighbor she'd met the other day. "She told me you needed some help picking grapes and since I love being out in my garden, I figured, why not?" Waving her hands as if she were conducting the Philharmonic, she added, "This place is unbelievable. So beautiful."

"You're not from around here, are you?" laughed Liz, noticing the way Sandra dropped the "r" in her speech. "I'd know that accent anywhere. I'm originally from north Jersey, not far from the city."

"Actually," Sandra said, adjusting her tortoise shell glasses. "I'm from Brooklyn. We moved here a couple years ago, right before my daughter was born. First, we lived really rural, like you, but I missed having a neighborhood and stores nearby, so we went suburban."

"I know what you mean," Liz said. "How old's your daughter?"

"Three. She's with my aunt today, and my son's in school, in kindergarten. I love being in your vineyard, Liz, but I'm glad we only pick in the morning. I want to be home when he gets there."

"How far do you live from here?"

"About fifteen minutes, but you know, the kids around here all go to the same school. That's how I heard about your needing help." Sandra smiled. "My son is in the same class as Nancy's. Sandra lowered her voice. "You know," she continued. "Nancy's great, even if she jogs, which I don't understand at all." She laughed. "She's not like everyone else in these parts." She waved her hand, palm up, taking in the farm and surrounding land. "When I lived out here, it was hard. You know, living around families who'd been here for generations. I wasn't an insider." She pushed her glasses up a bit and leaned in. "I hope you don't mind my asking. I'm really not one to pry, but did you ever feel like that?"

"Yeah, I did. Still do sometimes. But Bobbi's different too, and look at all this," she said, thrusting out her hand at the passel of people, some standing, some crouching or kneeling under the cordon, all picking her fruit. "Most of them, I suppose, are just good ole' country folks lending a hand." Liz reached up and gently pulled a sun-kissed Cab Franc off the vine. "Here, taste this." She handed Sandra the lush red grape, surprising herself that she was actually giving one away for free. She shook it off and, with the depth of a mother's love, added, "There's nothing better."

Bees swarmed around Liz as she continued along the row. Ignoring the insects, she stopped for a moment, tipped her head back and let the warmth of the sun seep into her closed, grateful eyes. Then with a long sweep of her hand she pushed the honey bees away and spotted an elderly woman in the next row wearing a pair of red high heels. Her hand flew up, covering her mouth like a clamp, suppressing a laugh. *Where did she think she was going?* Not wanting to startle the lady, Liz gingerly approached. "Honey, do you have another pair of shoes with you?" Then she realized this was the same woman who always smiled at her in the supermarket, the only one who ever did. Now it was Liz's turn to be friendly, and not just with a shy smile. "I'm afraid your feet are going to hurt in those," she said. "I can get you a chair, if you'd like."

The gray-haired senior looked at Liz, as if nothing was out of the ordinary, and simply answered, "No, dear, don't bother. I wear these all the time. I wouldn't feel dressed without 'em."

Liz smiled. "Okay, but if you change your mind, if you get tired, just let me know." To herself, she added, "And please keep filling those crates." She patted the woman on her shoulder. "Thanks so much for coming to help today. I hope I can call on you again."

"Absolutely, dear. My name's Rose. Just ask Dotty, or anyone, for my number. They all know me."

There was a constant murmur reverberating throughout the vineyard. She overheard snippets of conversations including, "This is paradise" and "Look how plump these are. I bet they'll make a great wine," which made her hopeful. But there were also complaints. Lower backs hurt, shoulders ached, and necks felt stiff. Liz was afraid the pickers wouldn't come back in two weeks when the Vidal Blanc and Cayuga White had to be harvested. But she couldn't help laughing to herself at the outfits some of the women wore. Where did they think they were working today, in a bank? Then she spotted a woman in jeans, appropriate attire for picking, except all she had on top was a bra! Her eyes shot open. No shirt! Oh, what the hell. Just get me through harvest. It was time for her to get to the winery and start the crush.

As Liz headed downhill, she heard singing coming from the vineyard. The tune was familiar, a catchy one. She joined in the chorus of "This Land Is Your Land." It sure is, she told herself looking around at all the women. Several were friends who came together "just to enjoy a morning out together doing something different," as they had told her, singing as if they were at a hootenanny. She remembered singing with her friends back in high school on street corners or in paneled basements, and that ache crept back into her chest. Liz had loads of girlfriends in high school and even when she and Rick were first married living in the garden apartment. On sunny afternoons, they'd meet outside with their lawn chairs, their babies napping in carriages, preschoolers playing tag and Giant Step. Now those friends were scattered. Letters, phone calls, and birthday cards brought them together, but it wasn't the same. A vintner's life didn't leave time for long chats on the phone or over coffee in the afternoons.

Halfway down the hill, Liz heard Sandra's voice calling her. "Liz, come here for a minute, please," and thought, I don't have time now. Bobbi can take care of it. But Sandra persisted. She ran over to the edge of the vineyard, her hand waving in the air, calling out, "Liz, wait, I've got to ask you something."

Liz turned around and climbed back up. What is so important? I've got to start the crush. Before she even got to the top of the hill, Sandra called out. "Nancy and I were wondering; besides picking grapes, do you need any other help?"

The unexpected offer, like summer rain after a long drought, made Liz giddy and light.

CHAPTER 43

"Tired?" Liz asked. She and Bobbi, having just finished the crush, were plopped on the cool ground in front of the winery, their weary backs leaning against the old wood. The late afternoon sun cast shadows on the barn door. All the pickers had left hours ago, and Bethany and Noah were in the house with Grandpa Lou.

"I'm exhausted," Bobbi said. "But we did good today, didn't we?"

"Yes. We did." Liz stood. "Come with me." She reached for Bobbi's hand.

With a grunt, Bobbi got up. "What now? I thought we were done for the day."

"We are. Just humor me." Liz led Bobbi around the side of the winery building where they'd have a better view of the vineyard. Just as the vines draped their extended arms over their own supports, Liz placed one of hers on Bobbi. "That's really something," she said pointing a finger toward the hillside. "Sometimes I can't believe it's mine." She sighed, a contented, tired sound. "I never could have done it without you, ya' know." With their heads tilted toward each other and soft smiles on their faces, they were like two proud parents looking at their children under the wedding canopy.

Then, with a glimmer in her eye, Liz stepped out of their half embrace and waved her hands in the air as if she'd just crossed the finish line in first place. "Two of the women offered to come back! To help with whatever we need."

"Really? Not just picking?"

"Yup. Whatever."

"Who?"

"Sandra, the one with the New York accent . . ."

"And that part in the middle of her head. She looks like Kathryn Ross." Bobbi said, taking a seat on the grass. "Except with glasses."

Liz joined her and crossed her legs. "Who's that?" A chilly breeze reminded her summer was over.

"The actress – from *Butch Cassidy and the Sundance Kid*."

"Oh, right. She was in *The Graduate* too." Liz shuddered, remembering the night she and Rick drove to Poughkeepsie to see it. "Rick hated that movie. He wanted to walk out, but I wasn't having it. We finally had a date night and I was *not* going to let anything ruin it, so I slid my hand up and down his inner thigh and begged him to stay." She chuckled. "He figured he'd get a hand job. Between that disappointment and the movie, he grumbled the rest of the time."

"Why? It was a great movie."

"I think because the parents reminded him of his, and the whole thing about the father and his friend pressuring the Dustin Hoffman character. Rick's father wanted him to go into business. Not plastics, necessarily. Just something where he could make a ton of money. He wasn't thrilled with his son becoming a teacher. Mr. Bergen was very successful, made gobs of money – and always smelled of Scotch." She quieted for a moment thinking how Rick swore he'd never drink like his parents. "Anyway, Rick wouldn't take a penny from him, and I was actually proud of him wanting to make it on his own." She shook her head slowly. "What a mistake. I can only imagine what his father would think of him now." With a wave of her hand, Liz erased the thoughts that tried to creep in. "No! Today was too perfect. I will not go down that road." She stood and smiled at Bobbi. With hands clasped overhead, she stretched right and then left saying, "So we've got two women coming back . . ."

"Who's the other? Her friend with the Hanoi Jane hairdo?"

"Whoa!" Liz dropped her arms, drew her head back. "What's with you and the hairdos?"

Bobbi laughed and twirled her ponytail. "You could never tell with this dirty-blonde mess," she said. "But she does remind me of Jane Fonda. You know, those pictures of her sitting next to the antiaircraft gun in Viet Nam."

"I don't see it . . . well . . . maybe those long wispy bangs. So what?"

"No. It's the whole style. The way the top looks like a helmet and the length, all uneven." Bobbi flipped her hands up. "I know, everyone says she's antiwar. I thought so too. So why so buddy-buddy with the Viet Cong?"

Dumbstruck, her mouth agape, Liz was unable to form even one word. Since those photos, some people assumed Fonda was pro Viet Cong, hence the nickname. But she wasn't. Liz understood how Bobbi might feel. Hell, it was the

VC that killed her husband – or captured him. They still didn't know for sure after almost four years. Liz hoped Bobbi wouldn't hold this against Nancy. It was *just* a hair style.

"You know what," Bobbi said getting up. "Forget it. I'm just very touchy. It's late. I've got to get home." She walked a few steps, stopped, and turned back. Liz was still standing in the same spot, stunned.

"Oh, Nancy's probably nice," Bobbi added matter-of-factly. "Why else would she volunteer to help?" Zipping her sweatshirt, she headed to her car calling out, "See you tomorrow."

Liz watched her cross the grass. She worried the cuticle on her left thumb, thinking she'd never seen Bobbi like this. A chill ran through her. "No," she muttered to herself. "It's just a haircut. And, anyway, Fonda's against the war." Liz realized many military families hated the actress. If Nancy rubbed Bobbi the wrong way, for whatever reason, well, she'd have to keep the women apart. But how? "Oh jeez," she mumbled as she checked the lock on the winery door. "I hope there's no trouble."

CHAPTER 44

The following week, carloads of women showed up again, eager to pick the Cayuga White grapes. Orange plastic bins, scattered throughout the rows, waited for the greenish-white clumps of fruit. The women, layered in turtle necks, flannel shirts, and sweatshirts to ward off the early morning chill, spread out along the rows, each with her own secateur. Even Dotty had shed her dress for slacks and a quilted jacket though Rose's feet were still clad in heels. Just like my mom, Liz thought, looking at the red pumps. She never felt dressed in flat-soled shoes.

As the morning went on, Liz noticed Bobbi avoiding Nancy by keeping herself two rows away. "This is ridiculous," she mumbled, then silently kept talking to herself. "If Nancy is actually going to help us out after harvest is over, these women are going to have to talk to each other. And get along." Liz knew she needed Bobbi. But I also need Nancy and Sandra, she thought. There's so much to do. If they're willing to pitch in, well, hell, I'm going to let them no matter what their feelings are on the war or who they're going to vote for next month. Liz hoped McGovern would win. She'd had enough of Nixon, and Bobbi certainly felt the same. Liz would not allow politics to sour her wine.

"Would you please finish this vine?" Liz asked the stay-at-home mom picking next to her. "I've got to get to the winery soon and first have to check how the others are doing."

"Absolutely. Go do your stuff."

Liz meandered down the row, checking with each picker, hoping she didn't look like she was rushing, and eventually made it to the section where Nancy and Sandra were harvesting. Someway, she wasn't sure how, she was going to find out if Nancy was a hawk or a dove. As she approached, she overheard Nancy say, "Unless she needs us."

"Are you referring to me?" Liz asked.

"Yeah," Nancy said. "Will we be picking tomorrow?"

"Possibly. Depends how much we get done today. Why?"

"I'm going to canvass for McGovern. Just trying to figure out which day. I can do Saturday when my husband's . . ."

Liz didn't hear the rest of what Nancy was saying. She felt so giddy learning Nancy was a Democrat. "That's fabulous!" she said throwing her hands in the air, waving them about trying to get Bobbi's attention. Sandra looked at her askance. "Oh. I know," Liz said sheepishly. "I must sound crazy. It's just that . . . well . . . I want Bobbi to hear what you just said." She peered over the vines, caught Bobbi's eye, and motioned her over. "You see," she practically whispered, not wanting others to know Bobbi's business though it was important that Nancy and Sandra did. "Her husband is MIA and with your hair . . . well, it's like Jane Fonda's." She gave an embarrassed shrug. "Bobbi was afraid you're for the war."

Nancy's mouth fell open. Sandra squeezed her eyes shut saying "Oh my God."

"What's going on?" Bobbi said approaching the three of them. "Need some help?"

Liz shook her head. Nancy jumped in before she could utter a word. "Bobbi, please. I am *so* sorry if my hairstyle offended you. I am totally against the war."

Bobbi's brows met in the middle. Drawing her head back, she glared at Liz.

"Sorry," Liz said. "After I heard what Nancy's planning, I had to tell her."

"What's she planning?"

Nancy gave Bobbi an apologetic smile. "I'm going door to door asking people to vote for George McGovern."

"And she's protested against the war," Sandra added. "She marched in Washington and—"

"Please, Bobbi," Nancy said, cutting off her friend. "I feel awful. Don't be angry at Liz for telling us. I understand how you felt though I . . . I never imagined my hair would . . ."

"Yeah. Okay," Bobbi said. "Fine."

"I hope it honestly is," Nancy said. "Because I am *so* not a hawk. I want this war over fast." She shook her head. "And I sincerely hope your husband is found. Alive."

CHAPTER 45

Several weeks later, Liz stood outside the winery, tenting her eyes from the afternoon sun as she looked toward the vineyard for her father and Noah. The tractor came into view, its gears grinding. "Here they come," she yelled to Bobbi, who was inside fiddling with the motor on the press. Yesterday, when they'd used the machine, it had given them some trouble. Nancy, who knew a little about car motors from her husband, had stayed after the other pickers left. Together, she and Bobbi, with their minimal knowledge, tried to fix it. Now, Bobbi wanted to make sure that this batch of grapes, ready to be pressed today, would thin out more easily.

"That sounds awful," Bobbi said, coming outside, looking at the tractor in the distance, its gears squealing. "Almost as bad as the press." Spotting Noah sitting high next to his grandpa, she tapped Liz on the shoulder. "You know, you made a good decision. What's one day of school – especially when it's the end of harvest – after all he's been through."

"Yeah. Look at my little guy. He's been smiling all day."

The past three months had been very hard on the eight-year-old. Liz couldn't fathom how a father would not want to see his kids. Lou had always been her rock, and her heart cried for Noah and Bethany who would never have that from their own father. She knew Lou was a better role model for them than Rick ever was, and was so glad he'd moved to the valley, but still . . .

"Come on," Liz said. "They'll be here in a minute." The women rounded the building. Liz leaned against the wall letting the autumn sun warm her tired shoulders. Bobbi sat on the concrete. Her neck creaked as she rolled out the kinks. "I think the machine's ready," she said. "First, we'll crush the grapes picked today, once we get 'em off the tractor, then we'll press the batch from last week. Honestly, Liz, I don't know if I've ever seen a woman work harder than you."

"Well, you're no slouch. Look at all you did yesterday, my Miss Fix-It lady. Plus, you crushed two tons this morning, and we've got another two coming now."

The tractor pulled up alongside the building, and Lou stepped down from the driver's seat. Noah jumped to the ground. "Wow, that was something," Lou said, walking around to the attached wagon. "Noah's quite the wingman. He knows how to work the clutch." He gave Liz a wink as he ruffled the mass of hair on his grandson's head. "Quite the farmer you have here, Lizzy."

Liz smiled at her little guy. "We can take it from here, Dad. Why don't you and Noah get some lunch."

"What about you?"

"No, too much work to do. We'll eat later."

"I want to crush," Noah said, hands on hips, his lower lip jutting out.

"Okay, honey. But just one batch."

With his chest puffed up and with his mom's help, Noah lifted a crate full of red grapes, lumbered over to where the stainless-steel cylinder stood on the cement block, and dumped it in. Then he turned the knob and, with his mother at his side and Bobbi and Grandpa standing opposite, he watched the drum rotate, spit out the stems, and squish the plump grapes into must.

"Good job," Liz said, "now lunch."

"One more," Noah whined.

"No, honey, enough. Bobbi and I have a lot to do."

Noah slumped off.

With the men gone, Liz and Bobbi completed the crush then went inside. They ran the press, then after several batches Liz wrinkled her brow. "The skins are still too thick," she said. "You sure it's okay?"

"Yes. Just don't put your hands in. Let the machine do the work." Bobbi looked at Liz as she would one of her twins and pointed a finger, the hot-pink nail jabbing the air with every word.

"This is frustrating," Liz said. "The skins are just as thick as last week's. Why's it taking so long now?" She stood, not moving a muscle, watching the knife-edged blades grab the load from the bottom and carry them up and over and around in a circular motion, like folding a cake batter. With each cycle, the red grapes squeezed down farther, pressing against the metal blades. More juice oozed from the skins, and with each repeated cycle, more and more filled the tank.

"It's still like sludge," Bobbi said and turned off the machine. She pulled out some of the skins, thinning the juice, then turned it back on.

The blades whirred, the grapes squished. Liz shook her head, keeping her eyes peeled on the fruit. "The consistency is still not right."

"Should I stop it?" Bobbi asked.

"No, wait . . . maybe it'll sort itself out. Give it a little more time."

The door opened. Liz heard its usual squeak but kept her focus.

"Hi, girls," Dotty called over the din of the press. "I brought you lunch."

"That's so nice of you," Bobbi said as she turned away from the machine. "Come on in and watch. See what happens to the grapes you picked this morning."

Not able to pull her eyes off the juice in the tank, Liz merely waved her hand. "This is all wrong," she told herself. "It looks like syrup." She called Bobbi over to take a look.

"Just a sec. I'll be right there."

Liz heard the women, their voices a murmur. All that resonated was the motor working overtime. She kept her eye on it, watching every fold and squeeze. *Okay. It looks like it's clearing up . . . No. It's not . . . It's not right.* She dipped her fingertips into the liquid, then slowly, carefully, slid more of her hand in, just below the cuff on her denim shirt. Between the whirring blades, she swished her fingers, picking out a few skins. Then, a blade grabbed the edge of her shirt – pulled her hand in – flipped it up – up, over, out like a dolphin jumping out of the water. The press sliced through skin, ripped it open. Liz screamed. "Shut it off. Shut it off!"

Bobbi ran over. "Oh my God," she screamed and quickly stopped the machine.

Gasping for breath, Liz grabbed her blood-soaked arm. She pressed it against her chest, her heart banging, the metallic smell of iron in the air.

Dotty whipped off her sweater, ran over, and wrapped it around the lacerated arm.

"I'll call 911," Bobbi yelled.

"No!" Liz screamed.

Dotty pressed hard trying to stop the gushing blood. "You're going to be okay, honey," she said in a calm voice. "But we've got to get to the hospital."

"No ambulance. Please." Liz howled like a wounded animal.

"You're gushing," Bobbi pleaded. "We have to—"

"No!"

Dotty and Bobbi locked eyes. "Okay, I'll drive," Dotty said. With one arm around Liz's back, the other pressing hard on the wounded arm, she quickly led Liz out of the building.

"Wait, I'm coming," Bobbi yelled, running after them.

"Stay," Liz cried. "Finish." With mucus and tears pouring down her face, the words blubbered from her lips. She gulped, trying to suck in some air. Another gulp and she crumbled. Dotty's strong arms held her upright.

CHAPTER 46

A sudden sharp wind whipped around the community hospital's brick exterior. Dotty held Liz close and rushed her through the Emergency Room door. A pungent, antiseptic odor hit Liz in the face. She grimaced. This was not where she wanted to be and, coming from a suburb of New York City with enormous medical centers, this one-story building was certainly not her idea of a hospital.

"Sit," Dotty said, hurrying Liz to the only vacant seat. "I'll get help."

Perched on the edge of a green vinyl chair with her arm clutched to her chest, Liz watched Dotty race to the desk and push her way in front of a gray-haired man in overalls. "Help," she said. "My friend's going to lose her arm!"

"Ma'am, calm down," the receptionist said. "Where's your friend?"

"There." Dotty spun around and pointed toward Liz. "The blonde with the bloody arm. She needs a doctor. Now."

The receptionist stood, peered over the desk and called out, "Nurse!" A few seconds later, while Dotty incessantly tapped her heel, a woman in a white uniform hurried out from behind a swinging door. "Over there," the receptionist pointed out Liz."

The nurse swiftly crossed the room and knelt in front of a pale-faced Liz. "Let me see, honey."

With her good hand, Liz reached over and tried to grasp a piece of the bloodied sweater from her shoulder. "No, I'll do that," the nurse said, her tone tender. With deft fingers, she slowly pulled off Dotty's red-stained cardigan. "Well, the bleeding has stopped," she said examining the exposed arm, its skin ripped apart, raw. The nurse held the limb in both her hands and gently turned it from side to side. Like an archeologist, she inspected the gash. Liz's stomach clenched as she imagined the depth of the wound. Would she lose the use of her arm? Would she need surgery? Oh my God, what if they had to amputate? Afraid she'd faint, she looked away. With the tip of her forefinger, the nurse softly prodded the edges and asked if that hurt. Liz nodded, her arm throbbing, pain shooting from wrist to shoulder. She winced with every tap.

The nurse stood and gave Liz a sympathetic smile. "I know it's scary, but you're going to be okay," she said. "The cut is ragged so you'll probably need stitches, but it's not very deep. Doctor will see you soon."

"Soon?" Dotty said. "She needs him now!"

"Please, give us a few minutes." The nurse gave Liz's shoulder a little pat and turned to Dotty. "As you can see, we're very busy today and, thankfully, this doesn't appear to be serious."

"Not serious? The machine almost ripped her arm off!"

"What machine?"

Dotty explained.

"So, you've got a winery?"

Liz nodded and the nurse responded in kind. "Impressive," she said. "I didn't know we had women winemakers around here."

"Liz is the first," Dotty said, her chin held high.

Raised eyebrows from the nurse told Liz, again, that she was impressed. That's nice, Liz thought, but my career might be over before it ever begins.

"You will need a tetanus shot," the nurse said. "But don't worry. We'll get you back to work soon. Your arm is intact."

"Thank goodness," Dotty said, looking at the ceiling.

"Can you come and fill out some forms?" the nurse asked Liz.

"I'll do it. Let her rest," Dotty said as she picked up Liz's bag. "Your cards are in here?"

Liz dropped her head and gave a tiny nod. "Just my license," she whispered. *Shit, how am I going to pay for this? I don't have health insurance anymore.* She sat back, letting her head rest against the cold wall. Maybe the nurse was right, but Liz felt like she was drowning and it wasn't only from the pain. Her confidence had crashed all the way down to the basement. Slumped against the stiff chair, she stared at the blank ceiling lit by cold white fluorescent lights and replayed the last six weeks in her mind. Everything had been going so well. All the grapes had been picked and until today, all they'd lost were two crates worth – both to bunch rot. Liz had thanked her lucky stars the day they picked the Vidal. If she hadn't recognized the fungus, those grapes would have contaminated the tank and she'd have lost that entire day's harvest. That was four weeks ago and her good fortune had continued. It was one thing to book-learn winemaking she thought, but to actually do it – without any hands-on training? All had been going so smoothly. She'd been so proud of herself – until now. "What the hell was I thinking," she mumbled. "What the hell *am* I thinking? I can't even run the press."

"Liz Bergen," a voice called, shaking Liz from her negativity. She looked up and saw a large woman in pink scrubs holding a door open. "Doctor is ready," the woman said. "Come with me."

Liz, with Dotty at her side, followed the aide into a curtained cubicle. The crisp white paper crinkled as she sat on the gurney. At her side, sharp objects sat atop a metal table along with gauze pads and plastic bottles filled with unknown liquids. Liz cringed, imagining what the doctor would do to her arm. The nurse had made her feel a little better. But what if she was wrong and it was deep? It sure hurt like hell. Maybe she *would* lose the use of her arm. The world was spinning away. She was losing her grasp. Fear sat deep in her marrow. Her limbs shook. The nurse came over and placed a warm blanket over Liz, gently laying her arm on top. Then she stood at the head of the bed. Her strong, comforting hands pressed on Liz's shoulders, partially abating the anxiety. The hum from the fluorescent lights above soothed her further. In her mind's eye, Liz saw Bobbi standing in the winery, finishing the press. And Bobbi will help with everything else, she thought, feeling her tight chest ease. She'll add the yeast, adjust the acidity . . . "Oh no!" she cried, her stomach roiling again. "What if my blood got in the juice? I'll lose it all. I can't afford that."

CHAPTER 47

Over the next two weeks, night after night, Liz huddled under her blankets cradling her healing arm, picking her cuticles, as if she could tear her worries away. The skin around her thumbnail bled. With puckered lips, she sucked the wound, then threw her hand aside and kicked her legs free of the covers only to grab them again and pull them to her chest. She desperately wanted to sleep. If only she could erase everything gnawing her, eating her up. Would she get alimony from Rick? Child support? Would her attorney live up to Bobbi's recommendation? After all, she wasn't some shark from Manhattan. What could she actually get Liz? Rick wasn't working.

Liz sat, counting figures in her head. Numbers she'd need to buy supplies, to feed her kids, to pay the electricity bill and phone and . . . Hell! To keep her land. Last night she again thought she'd give it all up. Go back to selling grapes. Winemaking was just too difficult. So far, she'd been lucky. Even without her blood infecting the batch, it was so much trouble. They could not get the right color. And what if something else went wrong and she had to dump it all? What would she do then? The hour hand on the clock crawled from midnight to 1 a.m., then 2 and 3. Finally, absolutely exhausted, she dropped onto her pillow and fell asleep. She woke at six to birds chirping outside her window, calling to her.

She got out of bed and padded over, pushed the bright yellow curtains aside, lifted the scalloped shade, and opened the window to breathe in the fresh autumn air. She stared out to her vineyard, all thirteen acres, then looked at her hands, the same hands that dug into its rich, brown soil. She rubbed her fingers together and brought them to her nose. The earthy scent lingered. Liz thought of how she nurtured her vines through bitter cold winters covering the plants with old sheets, protecting them from cracking ice, and how she prayed for rain through summer dry spells and worked to keep pecking birds and pesky insects away, as any mother would to protect her young. Now, in the gray of dawn, the harvested vines entwined on their stakes reached to the sun, and Liz pictured next year's fruit, plump and juicy, growing on their arms. She was certain she could never give up her dream. "I will get through this," she told her bedroom walls, then shouted it out, letting the whole world know as she went into the bathroom to get ready for the day's work.

With her wounded arm pressed against her side, Liz gingerly made her way down the ladder one slow step at a time. Though she was no longer in pain and therefore able to work, she had to be careful. She didn't want to bang the twenty-two stitches holding the skin together.

"I don't know what's wrong with this batch," she called over to Bobbi, who was perched on top of another tall ladder checking the sugar levels in the other juices already aging in the oak barrels. "It looks like milk, not wine."

"It's freezing in here," Bobbi said. "Maybe that's the problem. What's the temp?"

Taking her last step and placing her foot firmly on the cement floor, Liz finally dropped her shoulders. She walked over to the thermostat on the side wall. "It's sixty," she yelled. "Right where it should be," and buttoned her burgundy colored flannel shirt over her thick cotton turtleneck.

Liz walked over to the tasting table where an empty wine glass awaited its turn to hold a few ounces of her first batch of wine. She picked it up and stared at it, as if it held all the answers, then plunked it down and picked up a test tube, then an eye dropper, all empty, ready and waiting to be used. Not one was able to offer a solution. Even though she was aware of that, Liz mumbled under her breath. Her brow furrowed. She knew she was carving worry lines between her eyes in addition to the dark circles under them. Most of the barrels had beautiful colored juice fermenting into wine – bold reds and golden whites. What was wrong with this one? Why couldn't she fix it?

"There's got to be an easier way to do this," Bobbi called as she descended the ladder, her eyes focused on every rung. Once she was safely down, she walked toward Liz. "I've been reading about using oak chips instead of these barrels," she said. "It's supposed to be less expensive and a hell of a lot safer."

"I don't understand. What would we put the chips in?"

"Steel barrels. They hold a lot more juice, plus it only takes nine days for the chips to infuse the wine rather than nine months soaking in an oak barrel."

"That's incredible."

"Yup. And it's safer. You know, oak barrels can contaminate the juice. Steel is cleaner. We should look into it for next year. In the meantime," Bobbi added, "I think I can fix the milky batch. I'm pretty sure I screwed it up."

"How?"

"After you went to the hospital that day, I cleared out a lot of the skins."

"Why? The more skins, the more intense the color."

"Yeah, but it's all I could think of. I had to get the juice thinner. I'm really sorry."

"Don't be ridiculous. Nothing to be sorry about. We're learning this together – by the seat of our pants – and my arm." She laughed and lifted her sutured limb. "We'll get there. I have faith."

Even with those positive words, Liz felt her throat constrict, her mouth go dry. If all went as planned, the white wines would be ready in about six months, for Easter. Liz wondered, will that be a happy holiday?

CHAPTER 48

November finally arrived. Between her arm being in the wrong place, weeks of harvest, and making their very own first batch of wine, Liz hadn't talked about this day with anyone other than her lawyer, no matter how much she worried about it. Winemaking had been their primary focus. The election, with its disappointing result, a close second. McGovern may have lost. Liz was not about to.

She was seated on a tweed sofa in her lawyer's office picking the cuticle on her left thumb, pushing the hard skin back as if she could push back the past several years. Adele Samuels, Attorney at Law, sat opposite, her slender legs crossed at the ankles, her red-varnished nails clicking as she tapped on the chrome arms of a black leather chair.

"I can't believe he's doing this again," Liz said. She looked at the clock centered on the teak bookcase stuffed with leather-bound volumes of *McKinney's New York Statutes* and copies of *Child and Family Law*. It was ten past two. The appointment had been scheduled to begin on the hour, the same time as last week.

"If they don't show in the next five minutes," Adele said, "I'll have to reschedule."

"Are they coming together?" Liz asked. "Or are they both totally unreliable?"

Before Adele could answer, the door opened and Rick's lawyer walked in. "So sorry," he said. "We were caught in traffic." Liz wondered how much traffic there could be on these rural roads on a bright sunny November day without a drop of rain in sight. Her lawyer sat with upturned brows. Then Rick sauntered in. He glanced at Liz, as if he didn't even know her, and took a seat on the opposite sofa leaving the glass coffee table, like an island of ice, between them.

148

"Hello, Rick," Liz said, taking the higher road. She couldn't believe he'd come for an important meeting dressed in worn-out, dirty jeans. Whatever happened to the preppy guy she met in college? Even that sweep of hair across his brow that she used to love to touch looked like it had been drenched in oil. It hurt to see what had become of the man she once loved. Yet that was not going to influence her in any way in the day's proceedings. She was ready to fight.

"So, Mr. Bergen," Ms. Samuels began. "Your lawyer has informed me that you are not working right now, though you are a teacher. Do you have—"

"That's right. I'm done with all that."

The lawyer let the words hang in the air as she tapped her manicured nails. She studied his snide expression. "So then, you have no income," she stated.

"Correct."

Ms. Samuels looked at Liz, then at Rick's lawyer. "Well," she said, in the tone of someone who'd just won the round. "This leaves us at an interesting place. As we discussed previously, Mr. Bergen is giving full custody of the children, Bethany and Noah, to their mother." Rick's lawyer nodded in agreement. "Since Mr. Bergen hasn't any income," Samuels continued, "it is obvious he won't be able to pay any child support or alimony . . ."

"That's right," Rick cut her off, grabbing the trophy.

"Well, we have an offer for you, sir," Samuels said, giving Rick a condescending smile. "And under the circumstances, it is best if you seriously consider it." She nodded to Rick's lawyer, then stood, commanding the room in her crisp tailored navy-blue blazer and pencil skirt. Rick, still seated in his man-spread, seemed to curl into himself as the attorney focused her eyes on him. "Mrs. Bergen will continue to live in the house. The deed will be in her name alone."

"What? I own that property."

"Sir, you own only half of the property. Now, with this agreement, you will deed that portion to Mrs. Bergen."

"No, I won't."

"Rick, listen to her," his lawyer said. "You don't want to fight this."

Right, Liz thought, because if you do, if you even try, I can prove you're an adulterer. Don't push me.

"Sir," Liz's lawyer continued. "You will have a lien on the property. On the property alone."

Liz could tell from the way Rick narrowed his eyes and the way his head flinched back that he was totally confused. Obviously, her lawyer also understood.

"You will not profit from the land, Mr. Bergen."

"I get nothing?"

"No. You will get your share of what the land is worth."

"What the hell's that mean? What's the land worth?"

"A survey was done," Liz's attorney said, looking directly into his large pupils. Liz realized he was stoned, as wasted as when he'd come home to collect the rest of his things that day in September, when the kids were in school. It had been the first time she'd laid eyes on him since she threw him out the month before.

"The land is worth two hundred thousand dollars," Ms. Samuels stated.

"So she pays me half. When do I get it?"

"Mr. Bergen, you must realize that your wife does not have that amount of money available to her right now."

"She's got a three-carat diamond," Rick growled.

Adele looked over at Liz who shook her head.

"I know all about the ring, sir. It was a gift from your mother. Mrs. Bergen is not required to sell it at any time."

Rick's head jerked. His nostrils flared.

"Mr. Bergen." Ms. Samuels put her hand up. "We will work out a fair figure. Elizabeth will send it to you on a monthly basis, until the lien is satisfied."

"I want it weekly."

Liz shot up straight, her eyes wide open.

"That's unheard of," Samuels said.

"Rick, don't," his lawyer added. "Monthly is fine."

"Nah," he said, pulling his thighs in and standing straight. He took two steps toward Samuels and pointed his finger in her face. "It's that or I keep the land."

Adele Samuels did not move. She planted her feet wider and shook her head. "Oh, sir," she said, "you are barking up the wrong tree. Basically, you do not have a leg to stand on." She turned her back to Rick and walked toward her desk. "Take what's offered. You're lucky to get that."

"What the hell! The whole idea of buying the farm was mine."

"And the whole idea of cheating on me for years was yours too," Liz grumbled from her seat on the sofa. She wanted to spit. She'd love to see the saliva drip down his face and wipe off that cocky look.

"Okay. Enough," Rick's lawyer said. He stood and put a strong hand on his client's shoulder. "Make it weekly," he stated, eyes directly on Samuels, "and he'll sign."

Adele turned to Liz, with raised brows. Liz didn't want to give him an inch, yet she wanted this whole damn thing over. Weekly, monthly, what's the difference, she thought. I don't have any money now anyway. She gave her lawyer a slight nod and swallowed the putrid taste in her mouth.

"Then I'll have to write an addendum," Ms. Samuels said. "You'll both have to initial it. I will then have the final document typed and ready for your signatures by the end of the week."

"I gotta come back?" Rick said. His attorney placed a hand on his client's shoulder and muttered, "One more time. Then you can go." Liz wondered where he was going.

Ms. Samuels walked across the room and opened the top drawer of her large rosewood desk. She pulled out a legal size manila folder, took the official document out and with a silent, questioning expression stared at Liz, offering her another chance to disagree. Again, Liz nodded. Samuels sat and, with her Mont Blanc pen, adjusted the terms. "If you'll both come here," she said, her eyes and voice serious, "I need your initials."

Liz stood and looked at Rick with an upturned palm, as if saying, "are you coming?" He grunted. Avoiding the side of the room where his ex-wife stood, he strolled to the lawyer's desk.

"I'm goin' to California, where the real wineries are," he mumbled as he picked up the pen. He looked at Liz, waiting on the opposite side of the desk. "You can have the farm," he said. "Try all you want. You'll never make it."

As Liz watched him initial the addendum, the smirk on his face made her blood boil though grief sat deep in her bones. Oh, how she wanted to make him eat his words! No matter what it took, she would be a success. She pictured bottles of her wines standing proud on store shelves all dressed up in beautifully sketched labels. First, though, she had to figure out how to pay for it all. And how to feed her kids.

CHAPTER 49

Liz snatched the ringing phone from her night table. The morning sun peeked through the bedroom blinds lighting up the polished floor, its wooden planks looking brand new. "Yes," she shouted, hearing her sister's voice on the other end. She sat up tall. "You were right. I got it!"

"Jeez, Liz, would you get with the program already?" Kristin said. "It's a farm loan, and you own the farm. Honestly, I don't understand why you assumed you wouldn't get it. Women are allowed to support themselves. You know, we won. Congress passed the Equal Rights Amendment. And we'll get it ratified."

Liz smiled to herself, thinking of the tough woman her little sister had become, so different from their mother – and from her, or at least from the woman she originally thought she was. "I know," she said with a laugh. "I was stuck in a fifties mentality."

"More like nineteenth century. Women got the vote, remember? And I just got a credit card, without a man's signature. Get with the times."

"Right, and I got a loan. Mr. Hancock at the bank told me he remembered Rick and wondered why he never came back. Then he shook my hand and said I was the first woman to ever get a farm loan and he was happy to sign it. He laughed when he told me his wife would be proud of him."

Liz hugged her knees. A smile spread across her cheeks as her eyes took in the half empty closet across the room. Rather than the big empty void it felt like when Rick left, it was now a wide-open space waiting for something more. "Krissy, he made me feel proud. Now I realize I was so caught up with how I was going to get the grapes harvested, I couldn't think of anything else. I had to get money, but I was frozen. I couldn't hear what you were telling me. I needed money and not only to finance my business . . . Hey! Listen to that. My business!" Liz let out a booming laugh.

"I'm thrilled for you, Liz, though I can't help it. I'm still so aggravated. Outraged, really, why that son of a bitch isn't obligated to pay anything."

"I'm just relieved he came back and signed the papers. Plus, I get the better deal," she said, her hand firm on the receiver. "I get to live off the land, to use his words." Yet Liz could not stop her stomach from churning. As proud as she felt about owning a business, so much depended on that rich earth she would live on and what it would bring. "You know, Kris, he's banking on me to fail."

"Prove him wrong. You can do it."

"I can. I will. It's just going to take a long time. And paying him every damn week – it's ridiculous."

"Think of it this way," Kristin said. "Rick won on that count, but that's all he won. I just feel sorry for the kids if he really goes to California. They'll never see him."

"They haven't seen him yet," Liz said, feeling the same crushing ache in her heart that she felt every time Noah ran to answer the phone. "I thought he was better than that."

"Farewell to illusions," Kristin said. "He's like his mother."

"Yeah, I'm afraid you're right."

Kristin's positive tone danced through the phone wires. "You're going to have a very successful winery," she said. "And Rick will have nothing – exactly what he deserves. I highly doubt he'll go to California. He can barely find his way around here with all the grass and booze in him. Let him grow his tomatoes and sell 'em roadside."

"Oh, don't be so cruel, Krissy. Remember you once loved him."

"That was a different Rick – and don't you ever forget it."

My wise little sister. Liz smiled to herself, imagining Kristin's finger pointing at her, emphasizing each word. She needed to engrave them in her mind.

CHAPTER 50

Liz and her team, each with a crystal wine glass in front of them, stood around their polished tasting table. The old pine slab was dressed with freshly cut spring flowers, ready for the debut. Liz, the first to taste, lifted the delicate glass. The petite crystal, from her mother's treasured stemware, held one ounce of their very first endeavor into winemaking. Their premier vintage. Its luminescent pale yellow lit up the fragile glass. Pregnant with anticipation, the women didn't utter a word. Even the air was silent.

Liz brought the crystal to her nose, closed her eyes, and sniffed. A slight, slow smile spread across her cheeks as she inhaled notes of grapefruit and green apples. Then, with her lips on the edge of the glass, she tilted the stem and sipped. "Smooth. Crisp," she whispered, for fear of celebrating prematurely. "Exactly what I wanted." A sigh escaped her mouth and the slight smile turned to a wide grin filling her face.

Bobbi fanned hers. "Whew!" she said. "But can you taste the citrus?"

Liz took another sip, a tiny one, afraid to waste a single drop. She swished, letting it coat her mouth, then swallowed. Its crisp taste lingered. Her eyes sparkled. "There's just a hint. Perfect." Then, as gently as a mother kisses her newborn, Liz kissed the thin edge of the crystal and nodded to Bobbi who was practically dancing on her toes. "We did it," she said as happy tears welled behind her eyelids. "Your turn."

Bobbi lifted her glass, inspecting the color and viscosity, then sipped and licked her lips. "Yes, we did," she said, and the two women, winemakers and friends, turned to each other and hugged.

"My turn," Sandra said, and lifted her glass off the table.

"Me next," Nancy, with her new short haircut, called out, shaking her head up and down like a little girl impatient for her turn on the carousel. She stood next to Sandra observing every tiny movement of her mouth and throat as she savored the flavors. Sandra ran her tongue across her lips, then pressed one hand to her heart as she nodded to Nancy whose glass was already at her lips.

The room throbbed with excitement. Relief mixed with pride consumed Liz. She wanted to be still, to absorb the moment, yet at the same time she wanted to dance and sing and hug everyone in the universe. Silently, she told herself not to get too excited, that this was only the first varietal. There were more waiting.

With the edge of the glass against her lips, Nancy's smiling eyes twinkled above the rim. She tipped it back and the crisp, golden wine filled her mouth and slid down her throat. She raised the crystal high in triumph. "To Liz," she said. "And Bobbi."

Liz opened her arms wide. "To all of us," she corrected. "I couldn't have done any of this without you."

A cacophony of voices filled the room, Bobbi thanking Liz for the opportunity, for giving her a new identity. "I never dreamt I'd be a winemaker," she said, and Sandra and Nancy reminisced about their first day in the vineyard. "I was so petrified I'd kill a plant," Sandra said. Nancy added, "Who knew grapes could grab your heart?" Liz grabbed them all into a group hug and they swayed together, their arms draped over one another like vines extended over their supports stirred by the wind, each with their own thoughts.

"Okay, ladies," Sandra said, extracting herself from the group hug. She stood erect, commanding attention, holding the wine bottle high in the air. "Now we bring this original vintage to the world!"

Liz laughed. "Or maybe just the Valley?" she said. "I would like to open a little tasting room – once everything's bottled."

Bobbi scanned the rustic room. Oak barrels lined the shelves, refrigerated tanks claimed their space on the gray cement floor. "Where would we put it?" she asked.

"Right here," Sandra said. "Or over in that corner." She pointed across the room to the only spot free from winemaking paraphernalia. "There's enough room for a small counter. All we need are some plastic cups and a pitcher of water."

"And customers," Liz added. "Plus, we've only got three varietals. That's not enough to open a tasting room." Through all her excitement, she couldn't help her stomach clenching as she looked up at the barrels filled with reds fermenting.

What if all I get are these three whites? Unconsciously, her finger scraped the skin around her thumbnail. What do I do then?

"Girls," Nancy said. "This is all a great idea, but these wines need names."

They all nodded. Liz and Bobbi looked at one another, shoulders lifted, palms flipped up.

"I've been so consumed with other worries," Liz said, "I couldn't think of any. But now, that they're actually here, I guess they need a birth certificate."

The women threw out ideas: Bountiful, Bethany's Wood, Noah's Hillside. None felt right.

"I want something, at least for this very first vintage that . . . I don't know . . . something that brings all of us into the name." Liz said. "Let's sleep on it. Come up with something unique, like us."

Bobbi nodded. "Good idea, but let's not wait for the reds. It's spring. A perfect time for white wine and this one, especially, is ready to meet its audience."

CHAPTER 51

Several weeks later, when daffodils bloomed through the countryside, Sandra walked up and down Hill Valley Road nailing freshly painted signs to telephone poles. "Winery – Open for Tastings – Saturdays and Sundays 1-4 p.m." Word spread throughout the valley about the new winery owned and operated by women. To their delight, on opening day, cars crunching gravel under their tires pulled up the road. Women, men, young, and old leaned against the makeshift bar made from a long piece of avocado-colored Formica left over from Lou's kitchen remodeling. They set it on four oak barrels and began pouring.

"Sisters of the Vine," said the tall, stately woman with long brown tresses pointing to the label on the bottle of wine in front of her, its black letters simply scripted across a plain white background. She brushed some feathered wisps of hair from her face. "Good name, but it needs a jazzier label."

Nancy glanced at the unadorned paper she and the women had painstakingly glued on each and every bottle. "It is kind of vanilla," she agreed, "but the name tells our story."

"That's why I'm here," the woman answered. She extended her hand, nails freshly manicured. "I'm Marcia McLeod. My husband and I own a liquor store in Poughkeepsie and when I heard about your winery, I told him we should come over and try some –maybe we'd want to sell them."

Nancy's face lit up. Liz, who was at the other end of the counter chatting with a young couple, felt her heart leap. No, not leap – jump and twirl. Somehow, she managed to continue talking to her customers while her mind raced, imagining her wines on store shelves. She looked at the young man and woman across from her and remembered when Rick took her to her first winery and, being underage, she was afraid to taste anything – and how he had connived her into doing it. But he didn't have to use any tricks to get her to grow grapes. That was her idea. And, she mused, picturing bottles of Riverview Vineyard wines lining store shelves – maybe even restaurant menus if she was lucky – now it's all mine. She smiled at the couple when they asked to taste another and even managed to say "Sure," as she picked up the bottle of Vidal Blanc. "This one is more robust, perfect with chicken or pork." She felt so accomplished, so professional that, for a second, she wondered if she was the same woman who'd dropped out of college after only one year to get married and have her husband take care of her. Though my skin's the same, she reminded herself, I am not that woman. I'm a winemaker! Then she watched Nancy remove a little plastic tasting cup from the top of the pile and pour an inch of the chilled wine for the McLeod woman. Liz's heart palpitated.

The woman laid her shoulder bag on the counter, took the cup from Sandra, and buried her nose in it. "Mmm, nice bouquet," she said, then added, as if questioning her immediate response, "well, maybe a bit too citrusy." Liz's chest tightened; her breath hitched. "Not overpowering though," Marcia McLeod added, and Liz was able to breathe. From her end of the counter, Liz eyed Mrs. McLeod as she lifted the glass to the light. "The color is good," she said, then took a sip and Liz, again, barely breathed, barely even noticed the wine she was pouring for her full-figured customer fill the glass. "Smooth, well balanced," Marcia said. "It reminds me of my grandmother's house in California with her lemon and orange trees." A sudden giddiness came over Liz, and she danced over to where more bottles stood on the floor behind the counter. She sang out to her young couple that this other bottle was perfect for Easter dinner. And then she heard Marcia McLeod's next words. Her disgusted tone shook Liz to the core. "Now I have to convince my husband."

"Is he here?" Nancy asked looking around. She noticed a tall man in a red flannel shirt in Bobbi's little tour group. He seemed to be hanging back, not even listening to Bobbi's explanation of how they made the wine.

"No," Marcia said. "I couldn't get him to come with me. You see, he doesn't think women can make wine – that it's a man's domain." She shrugged. "What can I say? He's never heard of a woman winemaker. He doesn't believe it."

Those four words hung in the air. Liz bristled. They stung like a Band-Aid being ripped off skin. She threw Nancy a look, her brows upturned. Nancy knew what she meant and forced herself to remain perky, the consummate sales person.

"I get it," she said. "Liz is the first woman winemaker in the Hudson River Valley, maybe the country. I'm not really sure about that, but she is a pioneer and, honestly, there is no man behind the scene." Nancy turned to where a case of Sisters of the Vine sat on the floor. She caught Liz's eye and her questioning expression met with a thumbs-up from Liz. "Here," she said handing Marcia a bottle. "Take this home, make a nice dinner for your husband, and serve it. Then, if he likes it, tell him our story." Marcia reached for her wallet. "No, it's on us," Nancy said, waving away the attempt. "Somehow I think, pretty soon, you'll be buying more than one bottle from us."

"My husband's tough," Marcia said. "I'm not sure I can get through his prejudice, but I'll try. Anyway, I know *I'll* enjoy the bottle. Thank you." She then asked to taste the other varietal and Nancy, using her experience from the florist shop she used to manage, continued pouring and chatting with her about how Liz, a single mom, found her grape pickers and assistants – all women. "She stepped off her porch, walked down her mile-long road and recruited stay-at-home moms who had absolutely no knowledge of winemaking, or even picking grapes, to come and help her." Nancy flipped her hand. "And here we are," she said, then tapped the cork on the bottle named Aura.

The man from Bobbi's tour, who hadn't bothered to taste a single drop, was walking with his palm on a young woman's back pushing her toward the exit. "It's a great story," he said, throwing his words over his shoulder as he stepped out. "But people have to buy it – and that's not only the wine."

CHAPTER 52

The steel refrigerator tank that Liz had bought used from a nearby winery stood ready and waiting on the cement floor. Dwarfed by its size, Liz stood next to it and looked up at Bobbi on the top rung of the ladder. "Are you ready?" she shouted.

"In a sec." Bobbi lifted the rubber pump-hose from where it rested on the oak barrel and moved it over to the left a bit. "Okay," she shouted down to Liz. "No more crimps. Here it comes."

The wine sloshed through the hose and filled the dull, dented stainless steel tank. Soon it would be ready for the final tasting.

"Crap!" Liz shouted looking at the wine pouring into the tank. "It's still not right. Not exactly red milk, but definitely not the deep color we want."

"No worries," Bobbi said, her fingers on the rubber tube, feeling the fluid streaming down. "We'll blend it with another varietal – the Chambourcin's ready. It'll be perfect."

Liz wasn't sure it would be, though she wouldn't admit that out loud. She had to stay upbeat, send positive vibes out to the universe. No matter how anxious she was each time they had tasted one of their finished products, she tried to embrace the idea that if she sent out positive thoughts, she'd be rewarded with positive outcomes. She'd read that in a magazine article and, thankfully, their white wines had proved her correct. Now it was the reds' turn. So far, the Chambourcin seemed fine. They'd added sugar and adjusted the pH level, but this one . . . the Cab Franc . . . well, she hoped Bobbi was right. And she prayed the other two still in their oak barrels, not quite ready for their birth, would be okay.

When the hose was totally empty, Bobbi shut the pump and unhooked it from the barrel. She lifted it onto her shoulder and made her descent slowly, rung by rung. Liz pulled her end from the tank and, with Bobbi's help, washed it out, rolled it up and stashed it in the big storage closet her dad had built.

Liz peered into the refrigerator tank at the oddly colored juice that should have been wine by now. A heavy sigh escaped her throat. "I won't call this by its grape name," she said, "cause it doesn't look like it."

"And you don't want to hurt its feelings?"

"Right." Liz laughed. "When it's all done" – if it's ever done, she thought, then quickly kicked out that negativity – "I'll name it. I waited nine months to name my kids, so why is this any different? My children came out okay. This wine? It needs an incubation period, like in a neonatal ward."

Bobbi took an empty gallon jug from the closet, climbed a little step ladder, opened the top of the second refrigerator tank, the one that held the already perfect red wine waiting to be bottled, and scooped some Chambourcin. She leaned over and handed it to Liz, then climbed down and slid the ladder over to the tank holding the poor-colored varietal that Liz refused to call by its name. Up and down she went, over the next ten minutes, scooping gallons of the perfect wine and pouring them into the problem. The color refused to change.

"I'll do some," Liz said, then climbed the ladder.

"What if we add some more yeast?" Bobbi asked.

"No. I don't want to do that. Let's give it another gallon or two and see what happens. I hate to have to dump this whole batch."

Liz made several trips up and down the ladder, mixing Chambourcin with Cab Franc – all disappointing. "This is the last time," she told Bobbi, then swallowed hard thinking about how much would be wasted.

"Okay, close the lid and we'll let it sit for a day or two. The color has to change eventually. It'll be a unique blend, like us."

Liz tilted her head. "Well, that's one way to look at it."

"Come on. Nothing more we can do today," Bobbi said, shrugging out of her zippered sweatshirt. "I need to feel the sun. It's so cold in here, you'd never know it's July."

Two Adirondack chairs sat on Liz's patio in the back of her house, inviting the women to sit and let the sun seep into their overworked shoulders. She and Bobbi headed over. Whatever thoughts were running through their heads stayed there. Work-weary, neither could utter a sound. Halfway there, Liz stopped and raised her face to the brilliant blue sky. Silently, she gave her usual prayer. "God, Goddess, Mommy, all the powers that be – make this batch a good one. Please."

Liz sat on the red-painted chair and laid her head against its wooden slats. She put her feet on the white plastic table she used as an ottoman and sighed. "I can't believe it's almost harvest time again. Two more months and we start all over."

"We did it," Bobbi said, her face tilted upward, catching rays. "And they're selling. And more orders are coming in for Sisters and Aura, thanks to Sandra. She's going to more restaurants today introducing our wines, getting them to put them on their menus. She's quite the marketer."

"Yeah. I'm so glad she came to pick that day. I never imagined all this when she asked if I needed more help."

Bobbi agreed, letting out a little laugh.

"And we can't forget Marcia McLeod," Liz said. "Her husband was a pain in the ass at first, but he just ordered another case. Guess he believes in us now."

"Speaking of doing it without a man, have you heard from Rick? Did Noah ever get a birthday card?"

"Nope. And he's crushed. It's really been hard on him. His father's a prick."

"You didn't say that to him, did you?"

Liz shook her head. "No, I swore to myself I wouldn't bad-mouth Rick – he *is* their father, even if he forgot. Bethany called him all kinds of names when he missed her birthday, but no matter what she said, how angry she was, she cried for days. There was no way I could console her. Now I think she's hardened to it. She won't even mention his name and, sadly, Noah follows her."

Bobbi merely shook her head, her eyes downcast. Liz figured she was thinking of her own kids and how their father wasn't even able to send them a birthday card or watch them blow out the candles on their cake – and that Rick could. What a shit he was. Would he ever see his kids again?

CHAPTER 53

"He's good-looking," Sandra said, with a quick glance at Liz who was standing next to her at their makeshift bottling line. It was a late July afternoon and the women were bottling their new unique, aromatic blend that still didn't have a name. Hints of berries and chocolate emanated from the wine. Eyes back on the bottle and pressing the ends of soft hot wax around the rim, she added, "And he's got the cutest dimple in his chin, like Kirk Douglas."

Liz wrapped her piece of red wax around the cork, adhering it to the bottle she was working on. "I don't care what he looks like," she said, "as long as he can design a label."

"He's got a great reputation. Everyone says he's an artist. And to top it off, he does his own printing. He's got a shop in town."

"Where'd you meet him?" Bobbi asked. She stood opposite, pressing corks into wine bottles then handing them across the table to Liz or Sandra to complete the bottling.

"At tennis." Sandra put the finished bottle in the case on the floor, then righted herself. "And he suggested the name Harmony when I explained how we mixed Chambourcin with Cab Franc. Actually, he thought what you did was quite clever, when I told him about how we almost had milkshakes instead of wine."

"Harmony," Liz said quietly to herself tasting the word in her mouth. She said it again, then looked at the women around the table. "I like it, and not only because the wine's blended. No," she shook her head, "it's that we're in harmony."

Positive murmurs filled the air around the bottling line, "Mm, hmms" and "Yeahs." It was all coming together like a beautiful symphony. Liz felt her cheeks spread into a warm smile. Harmony. She played with the word in her mouth. Yes, a good name.

Bobbi glanced up from her corking. "When do you guys talk?" she asked Sandra. "Not during your game?"

"Of course not. I don't even play on the same court as him. We all have coffee afterward in the lounge, and everybody knows about the vineyard, so when I mentioned we needed someone to design labels, Jim said he could do it. He even made a sketch – two grapevines wrapped around each other. Wait, I'll get it." Sandra walked over to the tasting table where she'd dropped her pocketbook, carefully stepping around the twenty cases they'd already bottled. She dug inside her bag and pulled out a scrap of white paper. "Here," she said, coming back and handing it to Liz. "What do you think?"

Liz looked at the penciled drawing. "He's good. He even got the hillside and the trees way in back." She gave it to Bobbi. "But I'd like it in color – deep purple grapes, green leaves on the trees. What do you think?"

"I think I'd like to meet this guy," Bobbi said, her chin dipping down. She handed the sketch to Nancy and added quietly, as if talking to herself. "And not just 'cause he can design labels."

Six pairs of eyes shot right at her. Bobbi lifted a shoulder and gave the women a coquettish smile.

"You're serious?" Nancy said. "You want to meet a guy?"

Bobbi looked at her friends, all with their eyebrows raised. "Is that terrible of me? It's been five long years since Glen's been missing and . . . I know he's not coming back."

A hush filled the room. The wood-paneled walls, the cement floor, the cases of bottled wine and shelves of empty oak tanks seemed to hold the four women in a warm hug. Liz looked across at Bobbi and blinked the mist from her eyes. "Wow," she said with an imperceptible shake of her head. "You never even hinted. I had no idea you wanted to meet someone."

"Neither did I, 'til recently. I don't need a man to take care of me. I've been doing that for a long time – with my mother's help of course. It's not that. No, not at all. It's just, I had a beautiful love and I miss that."

Liz, again, blinked the moisture from her eyes. A beautiful love. How lucky. How fortunate. I had Rick for much longer, and I can't say those words.

"Okay, ladies, come on, back to work," Bobbi's in-charge tone cut through the heavy air. She grabbed another open bottle of what would now be called Harmony and with her other hand picked up a cork and pressed it into the top. "I say we talk to this label artist and see what he can do for us."

"Us? Or you?" Nancy asked.

"Come on. You know what I mean." Bobbi ran her thumb over her wedding band then, with the heel of her hand, pressed the cork down farther.

CHAPTER 54

Bobbi kicked off her boots and stepped into Liz's kitchen looking like the abominable snowman in her baby-blue snowsuit. Sandra was at the counter scooping coffee into the pot. "Hey," Bobbi said, "wasn't I supposed to meet you in the vineyard? Where's Liz?"

"Still in the shower. I've got Ella with me. She has a bad cold and when I told Liz I couldn't come today, she suggested I do her office work and she'd prune instead."

"So, you're going to pay the bills?"

Sandra shrugged. "Why not? She trusts me." With her index finger, she lifted her glasses.

"Of course. That's not what I meant. What about *the* check. The one for Rick?"

Sandra chuckled. "Oh, no. That's hers. She has her own special way of writing that one. You know, when she goes to that bench behind the vineyard."

Bobbi nodded. "I hope that serenity helps her get past her anger."

"Me too. I know money is tight, though I do think she's a bit more at ease now, since we're selling. We're in four restaurants — that new one is fancy with tablecloths and cloth napkins," she said, doing a shimmy, "and two stores. Today I'm going to call some more liquor stores farther out in the Valley about carrying our wines."

"Good luck. Because I've got to tell you, I don't want to work anywhere else. We may not get paid much . . . Liz does what she can and . . . well, I love being a winemaker." Bobbi smiled at Sandra and sipped her coffee. "Yum. You added hazelnut. That's what smells so good." She looked around the kitchen and peeked into the living room. "So, where's Ella now?"

"In Liz's bed."

Imitating Liz's voice, Bobbi quipped, "I've got juice and crackers. Ella can stay in my bed and watch TV." Bobbi laughed, remembering the few times she'd brought her own kids to work when her mother couldn't watch them. Once, when she and Liz inspected the new label designs from Jim, who she wasn't interested in after all. The man was married! And the other time, when they ordered the stainless steel tanks they now used instead of oak barrels.

Sandra chuckled. "Yup, that's exactly what she said. Where else can you find a job that lets you bring your sick kid to work?" With a damp paper towel, she wiped stray coffee grounds off the counter, dropped it in the garbage, keeping everything neat and clean, then poured herself a cup. She turned to Bobbi. "You know, when I came to pick grapes that first time, I never expected to be working at a winery. I figured it'd be fun – a day in a vineyard – somewhere I'd never been. And now, after two harvests together," she raised the cup overhead, "you can call me a lifer. I'm not going anywhere."

Just then, Liz walked out of the bathroom, wrapped in a towel, brushing her teeth. "Hey, you girls talking about me?" she asked, her mouth full of foamy Crest, the toothpaste bubbling from her lips.

"Oh, gross, Liz," Sandra squealed. "Get back in there."

"Yeah, hurry up," Bobbi added. "We've got a vineyard waiting."

Liz stood among the icy vines and looked out over her snow-covered farmland. The roots were nurturing their plants like pregnant mothers to their unborn children, waiting for spring. The winery, with its old barn roof covered in an alabaster hat, stood across the gravel driveway. Sweeping white snow drifts carpeted the ground, and, set against the silvery scrim of the valley, icicles hung like dangling earrings from the roof of her farmhouse. "My cottage," Liz said. The scene reminded her of an antique picture postcard one might come across rummaging through an old trunk. Overcome with a deep melancholy, Liz stepped backward and let the pruning shear dangle at her side. She let out a heavy-hearted sigh. A distant memory crept into her mind – she and Rick standing in this same vineyard sweating, digging their very first post into the soil while Noah and Bethany sat on a blanket munching graham crackers. She looked up and saw that very same post, and its brothers and sisters, standing straight and tall like sentries supporting the original vines, the same ones she was pruning today, almost eight years later. Eight years, she thought. And I'm a winemaker, a vineyard owner – a girl who hated raking leaves on that little lawn in New Jersey where I grew up, who couldn't imagine myself with dirt in my fingernails, who planned to teach a few years and then have babies and my husband would take care of me. Isn't that what my mother had said – the way it was supposed to be? Where was that girl from the nineteen-fifties?

Bobbi, busy snipping in the next row, looked up. "What's the matter?" she asked catching Liz staring out into space.

"You know, Bobbi, I love what we've made here, this life, making wine, all of us women together. And I adore my vineyard." She threw her arms out as if she could hug all the land like she did her children. "But I don't know how much longer I can keep doing this. Every month I pray I can tear off that coupon and send it to the bank."

"What coupon?" Bobbi asked.

"The one for my mortgage payment." She snipped off a thin tendril. "I'm scared," she admitted, and peered through the mass of leafless vines to look at Bobbi. "I don't know how I can keep doing this." With the shears lifted high over her head, she cut off another thin shoot. "Everything costs so much. Sure, we got a good price for the oak barrels we sold and that paid for the new steel ones." Lowering her head, she silently investigated the vines, choosing which to prune next. The words spilled out. "It's not only the mortgage. I know we're selling, but the bills don't stop coming. There are bottles, labels, corks, advertising . . . and then the tractor breaks down! Not to mention taxes which, by the way, have gone up." She snipped a few more unwanted skinny shoots. Her head shot up and she spit out, "And then there's that goddamn check I have to send Rick every week!"

"At least he's not having a say in the business," Bobbi reminded her. "You've gone through two harvests without him – without a problem." She spoke in her lay-it-out-on-the-line way and threw a hand upward, leaving the question hanging in the air.

"I know, I know, that's what I wanted." Liz threw the clippings on the snow. "It just seems like he's always there. Every damn week I have to think about him. Just what *he* wanted." She scowled. "And it makes me sick. It's like a tumor too difficult to remove." Liz lopped off another long, lanky vine hating how she felt yet having no idea how to get past it. "The last few years with him were hell. It felt like I was going through a war." She brushed off some stray twigs from the faux fur trim on her jacket and dumped them on the ground. "Yeah, I know I agreed to pay him his share, but hell, it's choking me. And I've got eighteen more years of it. Sometimes, when I think I'm going to have to sell the land, that there's no way I can keep up all these payments, I yell at myself. *No!* It's like I want to stick it to him. Show him I can do it. That I'm not running back to my father like he said I would. Then I realize that's not it. It's *me* I want to prove it to – that I *can* do it!"

Liz continued cutting off unwanted shoots as words spewed from her mouth. "So what if there aren't any women winemakers – does that mean I can't be one?" She threw down some more limp tendrils and kicked the snow. "The hell with that!"

"Amen!" said Bobbi.

Words kept coming, erupting like steaming, boiling water bubbling out of the pot. "If I didn't have to pay Rick, I could use that money. Buy shiny new equipment, not old and used, get a machine to do the bottling, pay off my mortgage . . ." Suddenly, as if someone turned the knob and shut the heat, Liz stopped talking. She stared into space. The clipper hung loose in her fingers. "Or . . ." she said more quietly to herself, "maybe open my own store." Her voice trailed off thinking of all she could do with the extra funds, if only she didn't have to pay Rick.

CHAPTER 55

Snowsuits and boots were traded for shorts and sneakers. Bright green leaves covered the vines. With the warm summer sun beating on her shoulders and a sweaty red bandana wrapped around her forehead, Liz yanked out dead plants from Rick's long-ignored, weed-infested vegetable garden.

"I was wondering when you were going to clean that out," Bethany said, coming up behind her mother. The thirteen-year-old's midriff top showed off her golden tan.

"Like I've had any time," Liz grumbled, pulling a tall, tough weed out of the dirt. "If it bothered you so much, you could have done it."

"Sorry. I didn't mean it that way. It's. . . well. . . it's a mess and . . ." Beth pulled on the fraying fringe of her cutoff jeans.

Liz looked over her shoulder at her daughter and wondered where all those curves came from. She certainly didn't look like that when she was Beth's age. Her face heated simply remembering her utter embarrassment undressing in gym class, still in a training bra when some of her friends were already wearing a 34B. Bethany was growing up so fast and now with a steady boyfriend . . . Liz had qualms about it that kept her awake at night. She remembered make-out parties in friends' paneled basements when she was sixteen, not thirteen. And the guys were the same age. With everyone else around, petting – if it was even attempted – remained above the blouse. Morés were a lot stricter back in the fifties. At least, they were for her. But Bethany's boyfriend was older – and he had a car!

"Sweetheart," she said, checking her tone. Liz glanced at the dead vegetable garden and then at her daughter. "I understand." She knew Bethany couldn't stomach looking at anything that reminded her of her estranged father. The hurt was too deep. "But really, I could use your help sometimes." Liz never had to ask Noah for a hand. The land bore itself deep into his soul just as it had for Liz. And Bethany, well she barely put her fingers on a rake or clipper unless Liz demanded. Liz knew her daughter would rather be out with Drew than in the vineyard or winery, but a little help would be nice sometimes.

"Yeah, well, Drew's picking me up. We're going to the lake." She cleared her throat and picked at the threadbare fringe again. "Maybe when I get back. What are you going to do with this spot when it's all cleaned out?"

Liz smiled, imagining the wine and cheese party she was planning for her pickers. "Grandpa and Uncle Ken are going to make a patio here." Liz pointed to the large forgotten area now full of weeds and dirt. "We'll get a picnic table and chairs and I'll plant some pots of flowers. I love those purple ones that smell like vanilla. Heliotrope, I think."

"Sounds nice." Beth adjusted the straps on her skimpy top, pushing them off her shoulders. The blouse barely covered her perky breasts.

Liz wondered how she didn't have a hole through her tongue with all the times she bit back words. Instead, she said, "And you can have friends over, have a barbecue. We'll get one of those new gas grills."

Bethany nodded. "Okay, Mom, gotta go. I'll help when I get back."

Sure, Liz thought. She watched her daughter run off to the driveway as Drew's car pulled in. He stepped out and waved to Liz. "Hi, Mrs. Bergen. My dad said to tell you he'll have the new design ready by the end of the week."

Liz waved. Sighing, she turned back to work, to the blight on her beautiful land. Bethany and Drew's relationship worried her and not only the age difference and a teenage boy's raging hormones. If he broke up with her daughter, who would be devastated as any young girl would be, losing her first love, would Liz be able to keep the business relationship she had with his father? Jim's label designs were beautiful, especially the one for Harmony, the first he did for her. It was ironic that, before they knew he was married, Bobbi had wanted to meet Jim and instead Bethany got a steady boyfriend from the deal. Liz hummed "Young Love," a song from her teen years by that heartthrob Tab Hunter. She bent over and grabbed a long, lean, dead stalk. "As if humming or singing could ever wipe out worries," she mumbled and yanked the dried-up stem. It slipped from the dirt dragging a straggly vine with it, one where fresh green beans had once dangled. Liz threw it in the pile on top of the other weeds and laughed, thinking about how she now cooked vegetables from frozen packages. Thank you, Mr. Birdseye. Maybe they weren't as tasty, but oh-so-much easier. And that wasn't only about preparing vegetables.

CHAPTER 56

Two months later, on the new cement patio lined with pots of fragrant flowers bursting in purple, yellow, and orange, Liz's grape pickers gathered for a Labor Day party. The redwood wine cart, a gift from Bobbi, Sandra, and Nancy, was filled with bottles of Riverview wines. A block of strong New York cheddar sat on a teak cheeseboard, purchased especially for this occasion, along with a soft French Brie and a mild Holland Gouda. Next to it was a wicker basket, also brand new, filled with crisp crackers. Everything about the day said "new," and Liz embraced the word like a mother would a child she hadn't seen in years. She hugged it tight to her chest, breathed it in, and swore she'd never let it go again.

"Hey," Sandra said, holding up a wine glass half-filled with Harmony, the rich red color glistening in the sun. "Everybody's buying this. Marcia ordered another case. So why don't we enter it in a contest?"

Liz laughed. "It's an interesting idea, but we'd never win. The men probably wouldn't even taste it when they saw our name."

"Maybe it's judged blind," Rose said. "You know, no names on the bottles." Rose, as all the other grape pickers, had been with Liz from day one when she'd handed clippers to women who had no idea of winemaking.

"They have to know which vineyard it comes from," Liz said. "Although . . ." She poured a little of Aura in her glass and swirled the liquid, staring at the luminescent buttery-yellow hue. "They might not know *my* name. So what if I get a period? I am a vintner." She laughed and lifted her glass in triumph. "If we do it . . . and that's if . . . it'll only be New York competitions, like the Farm Show."

"I didn't mean international," Sandra said, giving a two-fingered nudge to her glasses. "I'm not suggesting we compete against French wines."

French. They all cracked up.

"Why not?" Nancy asked. "Our grapes are French hybrids."

"No, ladies," Liz said. "We'll stay local." They all agreed and she sat back listening to the hum of their voices as they chatted about entering competitions, picking grapes, and so much more. A smile filled her face, imagining her own mother, when Rose, who would be her mom's age, made her announcement. "My husband can't believe I'm doing this – and that I'm loving it. It's the first job I've ever had, even if it's only for a few weeks a year." Liz wondered if her mother would have had the same reaction. She probably would have been stunned that her daughter even had a vineyard. It certainly wasn't the life she had envisioned for Liz, or the one Liz had pictured for herself growing up. Reminiscing about that girl, her breath slowed. She stared off into the ether, the women's voices lovely background music. A grin slowly filled her face as she realized she liked the woman she was becoming. Dotty, who would also be the same age as her mom, broke through her musings.

"I'm proud of my little paycheck," Dotty said, sitting tall, doing a little shimmy. "I went to Lord and Taylor, not the drug store, and bought a Revlon lipstick. And I didn't have to ask my husband for a cent."

"Oh, the days I didn't have to ask for spending money," Nancy sighed, "when I was working full-time."

"What made you stop?" one of the other women asked.

"My husband. It was fine before we had kids," Nancy said with a shoulder lift, as if it was obvious, at least to him. Why would she work full-time when there were little ones at home? "So now, this is perfect. Part-time work, my own cash. It's great."

Warmth tingled through Liz. She wanted to drink in the moment, to forever remember the joy of this day. Two years ago she never could have imagined this – to be surrounded by so many friends happy to be helping her, wanting her to succeed. She hoped she would. *No. I will.*

"All right, ladies," she said, cutting through the happy chatter. "Let's do it. And let's enter Aura and Sisters of the Vine too. Let these guys know we're alive!"

CHAPTER 57

The early morning sun, sliding through the trees, cast ribbons of light on the stone bench where Liz sat in her hooded sweatshirt, checkbook and pen in hand. "Six bottles of wine," she said as if the orange and gold leaves could hear her. "Maybe it's not much to some vintners, but to me . . ." After learning she'd have to send two bottles for each wine she was submitting to the contest, Liz had calculated what the cost would be. Actually, what the loss would be. "That's six bottles I won't be selling," she had told her dad the night she'd made that crazy decision to enter the New York Farm Competition. "And don't forget the cost of shipping, which isn't cheap either."

Liz twirled the pen in her hand remembering her father's response and the gleam in his eye when he'd said, "It's worth the gamble, Lizzy. Your wines are selling well." She'd felt as light as a leaf blowing in the wind.

And now, with this weekly task at hand, that happy feeling turned dark, as black as ink. She looked across from the wooded hillside where she sat to the vast open space filled with acres of grapevines bathed in the dewy morn. A few more days and the 1974 harvest season would be over. The last of the fruit would be picked and join its sisters already turning into wine. Bobbi was in the winery building making her magic, giving Liz the time she needed. Every Wednesday it was the same. After a cup of coffee, Liz walked up the hill, sat on the cold stone bench and wrote the one check that made her stomach roil.

"Damn!" She slapped the checkbook against her thigh. "Rick's out of my life. I wish I could erase him from my bank account. Get rid of this one stinkin' line item. Our budget would look so much better if it didn't have this cancer on it."

Liz picked up the ballpoint pen and filled in the space labeled "To the order of." Richard Bergen, she wrote and lifted her head. Okay, Richard, she thought, here we go again. You get your money, but look what I get. Two wonderful kids, beautiful land, sumptuous grapes, and exquisite wine. She bent her head, filled in the amount, signed the check, and let out a laugh. "Yup, and bills up the ying-yang," she said aloud. "But they're *my* bills. For *my* business. And you don't get an ounce of that!" Liz clicked the pen closed and slipped the check in the envelope. She pulled the eight-cent stamp from her pocket, licked the back, and stuck it in its corner. The payment was ready to be mailed to Rick's lawyer, the same place she sent it every week since Rick's address was unknown – at least to her. With the envelope sealed, she stood, shoved the checkbook in her jeans back pocket, then clasped her fingers together, flipped her palms up, and stretched to the sky, releasing the repugnant taste that filled her mouth.

"Back to winemaking," she announced to the trees then made her way down the hill to the winery building. At the bottom, she stopped, as she often did, turned, and lifted her eyes to the majestic vineyard. She patted the checkbook lying against her bum. Yup, if it wasn't for Rick, I'd probably be teaching school in some suburban town, maybe living in a split-level on a quarter acre with a little flower garden out back. Maybe even have a husband who loved me. She shook her head. But I wouldn't have this. This place, this grass, this dirt . . . these grapes. They were all my idea. Not his. So, Richard, take your check and shove it. Even if this contest is a stretch, I'm sending in that wine. It *is* worth it.

CHAPTER 58

Seated at her kitchen table, Liz was filling the ledger with numbers. She stopped, pen in hand, and stared at the ceiling. She saw nothing but the black bicycle with the red stripe on its front fender. How would she break it to Noah that she couldn't afford it? His blue bike they'd bought at a yard sale a few years ago was getting too small for his eleven-year-old body, and he'd bemoaned that lots of his friends had already graduated to a ten speed like the one he craved at Sears. She so wanted to surprise him with it. Noah never asked for much, and it broke her heart that she wasn't able to. The numbers simply did not add up.

The jangle from the telephone pierced through the quiet air, shaking Liz from her thoughts. It was barely 9 a.m. on a gray, cold Saturday. The kids were still asleep. She walked over to where the phone hung on the kitchen wall and lifted the white receiver.

"Hi, Riverview Vineyard, this is Liz." Ever since opening the winery, Liz used the same greeting every time she answered the phone. One line for both home and business was less expensive than having two phone numbers.

"Hello. This is Richard Bogart from the New York Wine Association. I'd like to speak to the owner of Riverview Vineyard."

"I am the owner."

"Oh. I believe you said your name is Liz?"

"Yes."

"Well then, Liz, I'm calling concerning the wine competition you entered." Her breath hitched. "We'd like you to send us a crate of your Harmony."

"My Harmony?" She felt like a puppy cocking his head at what his master was saying. "Why?"

"Because . . ." She could almost hear the smile in his voice. "We're asking all the winners to send us their wine."

With her belly fluttering, she digested his words. "Okay," she said. "So . . . why *my* wine?"

"Because Riverview Vineyard won the gold medal."

Her chest pounded like a drummer in the Rose Bowl parade. A squeal escaped her lips, then a quiet "Oh my God." Flabbergasted, her mouth hung open, but words wouldn't come.

"And, Liz," Mr. Bogart said, interrupting the brief silence. "Your winery also won silver medals for the other two wines you entered."

"Oh my God! I did? Really?"

Mr. Bogart laughed. "Yes. You really did. One gold and two silvers."

"Holy sh . . . Wow! Incredible! Thank you." Then, as his request set its feet, a thunder cloud crept up her spine. Without a trace of shame or embarrassment, she simply asked, "Are you going to pay me for the case?"

Mr. Bogart chuckled. "No, we don't pay for the wine. We're going to serve it at the awards dinner. We hope you will attend, as well as your winemaker."

Liz felt her chest expand. "Actually," she said. "I am the winemaker. Though I will be happy to bring my assistant along."

Liz heard the surprise in his voice when he said, "That's wonderful. We will be showcasing the gold medal winner and would be honored if he would pour the first glass."

Liz couldn't stop herself from smiling. *Won't they all be surprised?* Adrenaline rushed through her veins. Mr. Bogart gave her the particulars, and she kept crossing and uncrossing her legs forcing herself not to jump and squeal. Then, after saying good-bye, faster than a finger snap she hung up the phone, grabbed her slicker, ran across the linoleum, and flew out the side door screeching "We won! Oh my God, we won!" loud enough for the vines on the hillside to hear.

As she was halfway down the front walk, the storm door slammed. "Mom," Noah yelled hiking up his pajama bottoms, running down the path strewn with wet leaves. "What are you screaming about? What happened?" Bethany, in her flannel nightgown, zoomed past her brother. "What's going on? What'd you win?"

Liz stopped and, hopping from one foot to the other, threw her arms in the air. "The gold! Harmony won the gold."

Both kids halted in their tracks. "The gold?" they screamed with wide open eyes. "In that state competition?" Noah said. "That's ace! I knew you could do it."

Bethany grabbed her mother and together, rocking side to side like happy little kids, they sang "the gold, the gold" over and over again. Noah joined in. Even the trees seemed to be dancing, their damp branches swaying in the breeze.

Breathless, Liz pulled back. Still dancing, the words tumbled over her tongue. "I've got to tell Bobbi."

"Right. Go!" Noah said and Bethany gave her a little push. "Yeah, go! Far out! This is awesome!"

Liz ran the rest of the way, stones kicking up as her slippers slapped the gravel. She pushed open the big old wooden door yelling, "Bobbi! We did it! We won!" She pulled her from the tank where she'd been racking wine, siphoning off the unwanted sediment, and danced a polka around the tanks.

"Wait, wait," Bobbi said laughing, forcing Liz to stop. "We won?"

"Yup!" Liz flopped into a chair against the side wall. Exhilarated, tingling all over, she repeated the telephone conversation she'd just had – word for word. "He's going to be so shocked when two women show up." Then she covered her face, giggled, and shook her head. "I can't believe I actually asked him if he was going to pay for the wine." She looked at Bobbi whose eyes sparkled like brilliant diamonds. "But, hey, it's a whole case."

"You're unreal," Bobbi said. "Of course you're sending it. It's the best marketing we can do. And we're going to that ceremony. Wearing dresses."

"Yup. Syracuse, here we come!" Liz said. "Even if it means staying in a shack."

"Liz, we can afford Motel Six. And my mom will stay with my kids. I'm sure your dad will stay with yours." Bobbi bounced up and down. "This is so cool!" she sang. "First prize! And you thought we were nuts to enter."

Jubilation practically shook the walls. Despite the misty rain outside quickly turning to snow flurries, everything in the winery was as bright as a summer day and smelled as wonderful with the heady scent of fermenting grapes infusing the air.

Later that night, Liz was back in the winery to finish racking and clean the hoses. She felt her heart fill with love and appreciation thinking about Bobbi. They were a good team, and with Sandra and Nancy filling out the roster, well, it seemed they couldn't be beat! Yet as happy as she was, she couldn't get over feeling guilty about her kids. She knew they could fend for themselves while she was in the winery working. They'd done it so many times over the three years since she'd thrown Rick out with Bethany making dinner, even if it was just a can of tomato soup and grilled cheese. She wasn't much of a cook either. TV dinners and frozen pot pies were staples in her kitchen. Liz smiled to herself. The kids were great, despite everything. Beth had run out secretly that afternoon and bought a cake – and had a wine bottle drawn on it with red icing. Even so, Liz couldn't stop beating herself up. It seemed her days were never over; there was always something that needed her attention and kept her working late into the night. Sometimes it was at the kitchen table, which served as an office desk. That made her feel better. At least, then, she was in the house. But there were the nights spent in the winery after everyone else went home to their families, nights like this one, performing a labor-intensive job. Still, it was all worth it. Visions of that red and black bicycle zoomed back. Liz felt her lungs expand. She took a deep, satisfied breath, smiled, and got back to work.

Two more hours slipped by unnoticed and then exhaustion took over. Liz could hardly see straight. Before leaving, she walked along the aisles flanked by the gleaming steel cylinders silently working their magic fermenting her grapes. Her hand gently brushed from one to another. Though she was completely depleted from the long day, the sight of them filled her with pride. With a tired, satisfied smile she made her way around the room, then lifted her ski jacket off the hook by the door, shrugged it on, turned out the lights, and headed back to the house.

A full moon illuminated the dark night sky. Liz made her way up the path. Her feet knew every stone and pebble. Through the silence, she could almost hear the sound of snow as it coated the branches of the old Sycamore with soft white fluffs of cotton. Pausing for a moment, she drank in the cold, crisp air to clear her head, then tightened the blue wool scarf around her neck and face to keep her damp nose from freezing, and picked up her pace. She could hardly wait to get home and sink into bed, hoping that tonight, after a long and physically exhausting day – and the good news – she'd be able to sleep.

Ahead, the soft glow from the front porch light created shadows on the snow and stopped her in her tracks. Her two-hundred-year-old clapboard farmhouse was painted in silhouette. It was bewitching. "How lucky I am to live here," she exclaimed. Her purpose, her reasons for never giving up when faced with so many obstacles became clear in that moment. "This is why we bought the land," she said. "It is simply beautiful." With snow falling on her shoulders, coating her lashes and brow, Liz made a proclamation. "This land doesn't truly belong to me. I'm its caretaker, like all the others who came before me." With her arms wrapped around her body in a tight hug, absorbed in the beauty, she continued thinking, nodding. *I get to care for it . . . for Bethany and Noah, and one day . . . their kids.*

CHAPTER 59

Liz turned left onto Interstate 81 and checked her rearview mirror to see if her father's car was behind them. "We're coming with you," Lou had said when Liz asked him to stay with the kids so she could go to the award ceremony. "There's no way I'm going to miss seeing my daughter get her medals." Just as her eyes had welled up then, they teared again now, remembering the feel of his loving arms around her, the pride in his voice. With a smile spread across her cheeks, she turned up the radio and hummed along while Linda Ronstadt belted out "You're No Good." Listening to the lyrics, Liz felt at one with the air and sky, the birds and trees. *Yes, I am over you. I am feeling better.* She continued humming and smiling through the chorus.

"I wonder if he'll be there," Bobbi said.

"Who?"

"Rick." Bobbi motioned to the radio.

"Why would he be at the award ceremony?"

"Because," Bobbi answered slowly, "he's been working at a winery. At least that's what I heard."

"So what." Liz punched the air above her. "I won, not him. And I'm flyin' high!" She kicked up the volume and joined Linda Ronstadt, then laughed. "That song was made for me!" She drove on for another minute, Ronstadt's voice fading as her thoughts jumbled. She glanced at Bobbi. "Is Rick in the Valley?"

"No. Somewhere in the Finger Lakes."

"Is he the winemaker?"

"I don't think so. I heard he's working the tasting room. I'm sorry, Liz, Matt Woods told me. He wasn't sure I should tell you. He didn't want you to worry for no reason."

"I'm not. He's not going to be there."

Bobbi kept quiet and Liz drove on, her mind on overtime, her stomach twisting. The song ended. A mile or two later, she glanced at Bobbi. "Okay, I've got to admit it. I'm scared. And mixed up. Do I want Rick to be at the award ceremony or don't I? Of course, I'd love him to know we won. *And* that I did it without him. But I'm not sure I could be nice about it. Part of me wants to shove the medal in his face and the other, well, I feel sorry for him."

"Really?"

"Yeah, I do. Honestly, I've been thinking about it. Rick always said he didn't want to be like his mother." She sighed. "I don't know what changed. Was it me? Was I really emasculating?"

"Stop! Don't do that to yourself again. You didn't force him to drink or take drugs."

"But to go to other women — or *woman?*"

"Come on, Liz. He was a shit and still is."

Liz agreed, but then shrugged as if saying yeah, but still . . . She drove on in silence. Ugly memories ran through her head. Her stomach cringed as it did every time these past three years when Christmas and her kids' birthdays came and went with nothing from Rick. Not even a card. It broke her heart watching them go through all the cards that came in the mail. They never said a word, but she knew they were searching for something from their father. Her teeth clamped together so tight her jaw hurt. Her chest heaved heavy breaths until she finally blew out a thin, slow steady stream, exhaling tension, anger, anxiety. "You know, Bobbi," she said, still looking straight out the windshield. "I tried hard to put my anger, all my bitterness, in an imaginary box tucked away inside me." Her head turned to her friend for a moment. "Never to be forgotten, though."

"Yeah, but . . ."

"I know. It was eating me up. I was devouring chips, cookies, everything in sight. It was poison and not doing me any good. I had to stop. And I thought I was succeeding. With the vineyard producing and the winery doing so well — and now these awards . . . I've been feeling good, on top of the world. And, I've got dreams."

Bobbi smiled at her. "I could tell. You look happier. Your eyes are brighter."

"Thanks. But now I hear I might see Rick again and it all changes."

"I doubt he'll be there, Liz. And even if he is, you're walking away with three medals!"

"No. I'm not. *We* are." A huge grin spread across Liz's cheeks and she sat taller thinking of those medals hanging on her winery's walls. She drove on trying hard to kick negativity out the window, forcing it into the ether.

CHAPTER 60

Later that evening, seated with Bobbi and all the contest officials at a large round table covered in gold and white linens, sparkling wine goblets in every size, and shiny silver cutlery, Liz surveyed the crowd. Her dad and kids were at a table to the left. The Master of Ceremonies gave his opening remarks and she listened with half an ear, more interested in who was in attendance and what they were wearing. She was glad her sister insisted she buy the black silk spaghetti strap sheath with crystal beads glistening on the low-cut bodice. She fit in well, and it was fun to get dressed up again. It had been years since she'd worn makeup. She pressed her lips together, feeling the creamy, new pink frosted shade, and heard a familiar laugh. Her shoulders tightened. She scanned the room once more, but didn't see him. And then, the emcee announced her name.

"Come on, Bobbi," she said, extending her bare arm while telling herself to stop freaking out. "This is your award as much as mine. Let's go get it." That sparkly feeling, as glittery as her couture, took over.

As they pushed back their chairs and stood, Liz felt someone's eyes boring a hole into her skin. It's only my imagination, she told herself again, then turned to inspect the crowd anyway. And there he was. At a table just to the side of the stage. Hidden from her seated view. Holding the hand of a younger woman with a chest the size of the Appalachians. He met her eye with an icy glare that could have turned wine into vinegar.

Liz glanced at her own nonexistent cleavage. No, she told herself, he can't intimidate me any longer. She pulled her shoulders back, grabbed Bobbi's hand, and marched to the podium.

The emcee looked from Bobbi to Liz. His lifted brow said he was surprised, and the tilt of his head and emphatic nod said impressed. He proffered his hand to each of them in turn then addressed the crowd. "Riverview Vineyard is unique. The first winery in the state of New York with a woman as sole proprietor *and* winemaker." The emcee continued describing Harmony – "a robust bouquet and smooth mouth feel" – as he held the bottle for all to see. "As soon as these two talented women return to their seats, we'll be pouring samples for everyone. So raise your glasses with me to congratulate these ladies then get ready for a magnificent treat." He handed Liz the gold medal and Bobbi the silver plaques. The applause was deafening. Shutters clicked. Flash bulbs flared.

Liz tingled all over at the sight of Lou, Bethany, and Noah standing, cheering, and hugging, a grin the size of Texas on her father's face. She never felt so proud, so strong, so happy with who she was and what she'd accomplished. Unable – or was it unwilling – to stop herself, she glanced toward Rick's table, grateful that there was no line of sight between him and her family. He downed what was in his glass in a single gulp then gave her a sinister look, his hand in the air rubbing his thumb and fingers together. She shivered then shook it off. This was *her* night!

Bobbi seemed not to notice – or if she did, she didn't let on. They reached for each other's hands and made their way back to their table feeling like they were floating on air, their feet barely touching the ground, accepting congratulations from everyone.

On their way, a strong, hard-worked hand reached out to stop them. Hank Scanlon, that misogynist she used to sell her grapes to, pulled her over. Liz cringed. In a stage whisper he said, "I guess you didn't need him anyway. Good for you. Congratulations."

CHAPTER 61

Standing on the top rung of a step-stool in front of the tasting table, Liz reached up and penciled a black dot on the wall. "Think it'll be high enough?"

Bobbi handed her a gold medal on a black velvet ribbon – the first they'd won back in 1975. For three years in a row Harmony had taken first place at the New York Farm Show, and this year, Sisters of the Vine won first in the Hudson Valley Wine Competition, adding a gold to the silvers it had previously won. "Hold it there and let's see," Bobbi said as she stood back to check if the medallion hung too low. They didn't want it to bump into the wine bottles standing proud on the wood shelves just a few inches below. The sun, streaming from the open, wood-planked door, made the wines glisten like diamonds and rubies. Over the moon with all this unexpected glory, they wanted to give each medal its own place of honor in the former barn that now had the clout to call itself an award-winning winery. Liz got goose bumps whenever she thought about their stunning success.

"It'll be fine," Bobbi said, "but what if, instead, we draped the medals on the bottles, like necklaces?"

"Ooh. I like that idea," Liz said, stepping down from the step-stool. "Then we can hang a banner on the wall – one with our logo on it and maybe some images of grapes or wine bottles to fill it out. I'll get Jim to work something up."

When they'd won gold and silvers in their first competition, Sandra had pressed for a proper logo. "Something we can use to advertise the winery itself – not just the individual wines."

Reluctant to spend the money, Liz hesitated, but Bobbi chimed in. "She's right, you know. If we're going to promote the tasting room, we need something, some kind of image, to identify us."

The result was to everyone's liking. A grassy hillside with a bright sun shining on perfectly aligned rows of green vines. Riverview Vineyard, in a sweeping feminine script, stretched across the landscape. And, tucked into the bottom right-hand corner, a small Venus symbol.

Liz walked over to the table where the medals waited to be displayed. She handed Bobbi one gold and one silver and took the same for herself. They draped them over the necks of the winners and then, together, dressed the bottle of Harmony on center stage.

"Why don't you come with me tonight?" Bobbi said, stepping back to inspect their work, like a mother would to a child whose hair she'd tied in a bow.

"No. Thanks though. I hate that bar scene. It's like we're on display."

"Like these bottles?" Bobbi pointed at the winners.

"Yeah, but I don't want anyone to buy me."

"Oh, Liz. Scotty's isn't a meat market. It's fun. Come on, you need to get out, get away from work. No one says you have to jump in bed with a guy. Just dance. Talk. You might enjoy yourself."

Liz tilted her head from side to side, weighing the idea. "I don't know. I'll think about it. First, I've got to see what the kids are doing."

"Don't give me that. Bethany will be with Drew, and Noah will be with his friends. You're free to go out on a Friday night."

Liz shrugged. Sure, she could use some fun, but a bar? She'd never gone that route; she hadn't had to with getting married so young. Is this now how she'd have to meet a guy? And did she even want to? No, not yet. But dancing . . . jeez, if Bobbi can do it . . . "Oh, hell," she said. "Sure. I'll go. I haven't danced in forever."

Later that evening, Bobbi stopped her car in front of Liz's house and honked. Liz ran out and climbed into the back seat.

"I feel like I'm back in high school" she said, then looked at the red-headed woman seated next to her. "We met one time, didn't we? You came for a tasting."

"That's right," she said and pointed to the brunette with the Farah Fawcett feathered look riding shotgun. "That's the other part of our threesome. And now, we're a foursome." She gave Liz a warm welcoming smile. "It's about time we all got together. We've heard so much about you."

"All good, I hope." Liz joked, feeling the invisible hug. "It *is* about time." And she meant it – not only about going out with Bobbi and her friends and maybe making some new single girlfriends, but going out in general. After Bobbi had left that afternoon and Liz told her kids she'd be going out at eight, they were so happy it made her realize she'd been living like a monk, tending her vineyard and making wine as if she too lived in a monastery. No more, she told herself. I deserve to have fun.

Bobbi pulled into a parking spot in front of the club, its name lit in blue neon, and shut the engine.

"Wow! Look at you," Liz said as Bobbi exited the Chevy. "Where'd you get those shoes?"

Bobbi looked at her red high-heeled mules. "Like 'em?" she asked, as she sashayed across the parking lot. "Like Sandy in *Grease*."

"And do you plan on meeting your own Danny Zuko? It won't be hard in those jeans." Bobbi's new dark-denim Sassoon's along with her red crop-top showed off her svelte figure. "You look incredible," Liz said. "Not at all like a winemaker."

"Though I am proud to be one," Bobbi said. "I just needed a change from tees and flannel shirts and worn out Levis. And you look pretty good yourself, you know. We needed this night. Let's go have some fun."

Inside was a circular bar one step down from a large dance floor. A five-piece band was playing a medley of Elvis songs. In her scooped-neck white peasant blouse, borrowed from Bethany, and hip-hugger bell-bottoms, Liz felt like a teenager, not a thirty-eight-year-old divorced mother of two. Guys and girls, crowded on the floor, shook their hips to the beat. Bobbi grabbed Liz by the arm. "Come on, dance." All four girls joined the fray, shimmying and shaking, their faces lit with delight. The band segued into an Isley Brothers hit from Liz's senior year in high school. Everyone gathered into a circle singing along. Arms flew in the air as everyone yelled "Shout" on the chorus. Breathless, Liz clapped and swayed.

She felt someone's eyes on her back, checked over her shoulder, and spotted a guy in a chambray shirt tucked into the narrow waist of his Levis, his sleeves rolled halfway up exposing tanned forearms. He winked and smiled. She liked the way his eyes looked behind gold-toned wire-rimmed aviators. Although a little uncomfortable, it was also titillating having a man's eyes on her.

As the boisterous song ended and the band rolled into a dreamy tune, Mr. Chambray Shirt shouldered his way through the crowded floor. "Would you like to dance?" he asked, extending his arm to Liz. She felt herself blush and hoped the dim light in the room hid her reddened cheeks.

"Sure," she said. Her friends evaporated as he led her into a slow dance with a firm hand on her waist drawing her in close. Liz held back a sigh that so wanted to escape. It was so delicious having a guy hold her again, and a handsome one at that. He smelled of soap and spice and she forgot her earlier worries. Bars weren't so bad after all.

Like honey bees to summer flowers, she was drawn in to his embrace. He was a smooth dancer, a strong leader, and she wished the dreamy songs would go on. After three slow dances though, the beat kicked up and the crowd flooded the floor.

"Can I buy you a drink?" he said, as Olivia Newton-John's voice blasted the air. Bopping to the beat, belting out the words, everyone sang along to "You're The One That I Want," and Liz wondered if Mr. Chambray might be. Then she silently scolded herself. What are you thinking? You don't even know this guy. She simply nodded to him and turned, making her way across the dance floor. Feeling his eyes on her the entire time, she strode to the bar and took a seat.

CHAPTER 62

"A winemaker," Eddie said, standing angled toward Liz, who perched on a high bar stool. His tanned arm rested on the shiny, wood-grained bar-top, his blue-gray eyes on hers. "That's impressive. Where?"

Liz appreciated the awe in his voice, quite different from the condescension she'd expected when she answered his question. The way he'd phrased it was so simple. "So, what do you do to keep yourself busy?" She did not like the way that sounded. Just because she's a woman, did he assume she didn't work? That she spent her day shopping and lunching with friends? He'd certainly never ask a man that same question. Though, in his favor, he did sound impressed – rather than laughing it off as if she'd made a joke – that women could be winemakers.

"At Riverview Vineyard," she said.

"I don't know that one. Where is it?"

"About a half hour from here. Why don't you come for a tasting one day? I'll show you around."

"Sounds good," he said. "Are you open tomorrow?"

"Yes. We're open every day, from eleven to five." Since the awards, business was booming, and she'd put Nancy in charge of the tasting room. Work in the vineyard was all-encompassing. It never stopped, and an exhausted Liz had finally realized she could not be everywhere. "When you come, ask Nancy to get me. I might be in the vineyard, or the office. Or you can ask my dad, Lou. He'll be the one pouring tastes with an unlit pipe between his teeth."

"Oh – is this a family business?"

"In a sense." Liz tilted her head and smiled. "All the women that work there, we feel like a family, though really it's mine. My winery and . . ." she hesitated for a second, then added, "and my vineyard."

"Wow! Did you grow up there?"

"Not at all." She told him she was from suburban New Jersey. "I never even mowed a lawn and hated raking leaves. But this farm? I fell in love with the land as soon as I saw it with its hills and valleys and the mountains and river that surround it. And somehow, I became a grape grower." She shrugged, feeling her chest expand but trying hard not to boast. "Though eventually, growing them wasn't enough. I had to see the grapes flourish from tiny vines into bottles of wine."

Eddie's smiling eyes told Liz her success did not affect his manhood. He seemed genuinely impressed. Then those lovely eyes hooded. "Wait," he said, obviously trying not to sound put off, but curious. "Is there a man involved in all this, besides your father? Like a husband?"

"No. Not anymore." She shook her head and gave him a coquettish smile. She couldn't help herself. And with that information out of the way, she felt comfortable flirting and assumed he did too – except for the sign in the hall leading to the restrooms that announced: "Next time bring your wife." It was printed in bright red letters for all men to see. Even though Liz had laughed when she first saw it, it did give her pause. "And what about you?" she asked pointing to his bare fingers. "Did you leave your ring home or don't you have one?"

Eddie waved his hands in the air. "Single man here. Never been married."

Liz reached into her purse and pulled out a pen. "Okay, then, I'll write the directions." She reached for a paper napkin.

"Write your phone number too," Eddie said looking over her shoulder as she scribbled on the napkin. The words tickled Liz. It had been years since she'd heard that request, and they sounded as good now as they had then. Back then, though, she had no idea how much hurt could come from handing over seven digits.

Liz clicked the pen shut, slid off the bar stool, and handed Eddie the paper, leaving her glass of rosé on the counter. "Well, I'd love to dance with this single man again," she said, and he took her hand and led her onto the floor.

CHAPTER 63

"It's beautiful," Eddie said standing in the midst of grape vines spread out over the hillside. "Who picks these?" He looked around at the abundant clumps of berries. "And how long does it take for these to become real grapes?"

"Oh, about another six weeks," Liz smiled to herself at his confusion over real grapes and the berries now on the vines. Once, she had no idea of the difference either, and now she knew more than she'd ever imagined about the fruit. "I've got a whole team of pickers," she said. "You could join in, if you want. It's fun, and the more hands harvesting the better."

Eddie didn't look like he thought it would be fun. "I'm not much of the farmer type," he said.

Strike one, Liz told herself. "So what type are you? You know what I do, but I never asked what kind of work you do."

"I'm an attorney, in a practice with three others in Poughkeepsie."

"Perry Mason?"

Eddie laughed. "No, Wills and Estates, some tax stuff, real estate. Boring, I suppose, if you compare me to the TV attorney. I'm hardly ever in court."

"So if I commit murder, you won't be able to represent me?"

"Don't worry," he laughed. "I'll find you somebody. Now show me your winery and let me taste those medal winners." Liz liked the way he joked with her. He seemed like an easy-going guy, and, as they walked down the hill to the winery, she hoped maybe he would help out one day. After all, harvest wasn't only on weekdays, and she wouldn't mind spending a Saturday or Sunday with him – if she ever found the time.

Liz took Eddie to the back of the winery, behind the tasting tables that were buzzing with customers, to where the tanks, clean and shiny, were waiting for this year's juice. "Right now, nothing is going on here," she explained. "Soon though. Our grapes are all French-hybrids, not Cabernet Sauvignon or Chardonnay. You're probably more familiar with those."

"Not really. I'm more a scotch drinker."

Strike two. "Well, anyway, that's why nothing is humming right now. Soon, though, Bobbi and I will be back here crushing while my team is out there picking. That's when all the fun begins. Not that summer isn't fun too. We joined a few festivals this year and had a great time introducing our wines and concocting all kinds of recipes with them. Bobbi's great at that. Come on, even if you're not a wine drinker, you'll like her blueberry slush made with our Vidal Blanc. She crushes fresh blueberries, adds a splash of seltzer, and voilà! It's great over ice cream too."

With her proprietor's genuine smile spread across her cheeks, Liz stepped behind the rectangular tasting table and greeted her customers as if she'd known them for years. "If anybody wants, I'll be happy to take you to the vineyard and show you where these wines came from. You can meet their parents, in a sense." Nodding to a chorus of yes and sure, Liz told them to "finish up, buy whatever you want, and Nancy will hold it here for you. Let's say we meet out front in fifteen minutes." Then she turned to her father. "Dad, please pour my friend here, Eddie, a taste of Blueberry Slush."

Lou removed the meerschaum from his mouth and said, "Sure." He nodded his hello to Eddie, yet when he walked back to the shelves where the bottles were kept, he glanced at Liz with an upturned brow as if asking, "Friend? Since when?" Liz waved off his question with a giggle and a shake of her head, then went on to chat with a new face down at the other end. Fifteen minutes later she announced, "Okay, everyone. The vineyard tour starts right outside this door. Hope you've got your walking shoes on."

The tour, the day, Eddie's visit, all made Liz feel taller than her five-foot-four stature, and she jabbered all afternoon with everyone about grape growing and winemaking, their kids and hers, the valley and its beauty and the Hudson River running through, and anything else that came up. All of this was a bonus, an aspect of grape growing she'd never imagined, and she wanted to hold tight to it forever.

Another month went by with Nancy running the tasting room while Sandra dealt with advertising and marketing and Bobbi sprayed garlic juice around the vines to protect them from deer. Liz joined her in laying netting over the ripening berries to keep the birds at bay and she constantly checked the colors, the deep red/black that would make their Cab Franc and other red wines and the yellow/green for the whites. Daily, Liz went to the vineyard and gently pressed the ripening fruit, testing it for softness. She watched their growth to estimate harvest time, which looked like it would be in mid-September, maybe two weeks more. This period of veraison, when the vines are transporting their stores of energy from the roots into the grapes, gave Liz's muscles a slight rest. It wasn't as labor intensive as when she pruned or harvested, or crushed and pressed, or raked, which she still did not like, but as in every season there was no real rest and often she'd spend some time on the couch at the end of the day with an ice pack on her shoulders or lower back and her phone pressed to her ear chatting with Eddie. With him living a good three quarters of an hour from Liz, they only saw each other on Saturday nights and often they met halfway at a club or restaurant. No matter how often he said he preferred the concrete world of cities, Liz didn't understand why he was so opposed to coming out to the farm.

"Why don't you come out here this Saturday?" she asked one night, the telephone stuck to her ear after thirty minutes of talking about their week and baseball, with Pete Rose ending his streak. Liz didn't care that he'd hit in forty-four consecutive games and tied the National League record, though she pretended she did.

"Actually, I was hoping you'd go to the Yankees game with me. It's a doubleheader and I've got two tickets."

"Oh, I'd love to, but you know I can't be away from the winery for all those hours." *Seriously, a doubleheader?* Though it would be wonderful being with him, sitting in the sun eating hot dogs, drinking beer.

"Come on, Liz. Take a day off."

She pictured how it would work out. She'd have to drive to Eddie since he lived closer to the Bronx, though that was still another hour away, and with traffic and an entire nine innings – no, she corrected herself, eighteen. Could she do it? They weren't picking on Saturday. The next round needed another week, and Bobbi could handle everything else. It was only one day. She juggled her thoughts, weighed them all.

"I'm sorry," she said, seriously meaning it. "I can't. I can't be away from here for that long. There's too much to do and customers and . . ." She shook her head even though he couldn't see it. Was this strike three? She hoped not.

CHAPTER 64

Liz luxuriated in the odd silence of the house. Bethany was spending a few days at Drew's, anxious to be in town for New Year's Eve, and Noah, on his winter break from school, was with Grandpa Lou at Rutgers, his alma mater. The Scarlett Nights were playing a contentious game against UCLA, and Noah, with his dribbling prowess, dreamt of playing for Rutgers one day.

Liz slid down the brown and rust tweed sofa, tucked the afghan around her bare feet, and replayed the conversation she'd just had with Eddie. Since her kids wouldn't be around, he wanted her to come to him for New Year's Eve. "There's a great place not far from here," he'd said. "They're having a band and buffet dinner – even a breakfast is included if we want to go back in the morning." Liz smiled and felt herself blush again, recalling his voice when he said "though I'd rather have it in bed." It was deep and sensuous. She pictured crumpled sheets tossed around their naked bodies, her bare leg draped over his muscular thigh, his arm around her, his thumb stroking her pink nipple. She hugged the afghan close and dozed off imagining the bedroom's musky scent. Half awake, thoughts of basketballs and college tuitions crept back in. Next year she'd have to deal with college costs for Bethany, even if she did go to a state school. She hoped her daughter would finish four years before marrying Drew. With a start, she was fully awake. It seemed as if she never had a moment's rest from bills and all her responsibilities. Despite increased sales and medal winners, her profit and loss columns were as shaky as a toddler's first steps.

Liz didn't want to worry her father or ask him for money, and she certainly wasn't about to discuss her finances with her kids. With the repairs on the tractor and all the advertising for the holidays, she felt stretched. It scared her, kept her up nights. She absolutely would not, could not, miss a payment to Rick. He'd take her to court and then what? Yet she was afraid she wouldn't have enough to make her mortgage payment this month. Ads eventually paid off, but banks did not like "eventually." As much as she would have liked to be able to discuss her problems with Eddie, she had a feeling she knew what he'd say. "Sell the farm." Eddie was not able to grasp why she worked so hard. Perhaps it's because she never told him everything that happened with Rick and how she swore she'd make this work. He understood she enjoyed her work, but not that this farm with its vineyard and grapes were as much a part of her as her fingers and toes.

Whenever she fancied a future with Eddie, not that they'd ever spoken about it, Liz knew it wouldn't work. So why did she keep going out with him? It was definitely wonderful having his arms around her. The sex was good and he was fun, a great dancer, a good sense of humor and a Democrat, thank God. Plus, she felt fabulous hearing his compliments. "You're beautiful," he'd say, even when she wasn't wearing makeup and was sure her hips were too big and her tummy too soft, or "She's incredible" when he introduced her to one of his friends. Eddie seemed proud of Liz even if he didn't comprehend life on the farm. He might wear jeans on the weekends, but Eddie was a jacket and tie kind of guy. He liked living in the suburbs with sidewalks and stores and restaurants a minute away.

"Enough," Liz said and threw the afghan over the back of the couch. "Eddie's arms can't help me. I've got to figure something out." She had to come up with a solution to pay her bills and keep her business going.

Liz hurried to her file cabinet in the kitchen, took out her financial statements and spread them across the table. She sat examining numbers, income, and expenses. A tight ache started at her jaw and climbed up her head, pounding her temples. After a few more minutes going over the balance sheet, worrying her cuticles the whole time, she grabbed the papers, shoved them back in their manila folder, stuffed them in the cabinet, and slammed it shut. Grabbing a piece of cheese from the refrigerator, she gobbled it up and climbed in bed.

"Okay, Liz," she said out loud, "you need a plan and you need it now!" She lay in bed staring at the bare white ceiling. Her mind explored every possibility, every way she could get the money to pay her mortgage. Even though she was hanging on by a slender thread and knew she could lose everything, Liz refused to depend on Lou and prove Rick right. I'll do this myself, she vowed. I will not fail now. Unable to drown her anxieties in sleep, she watched the inky sky turn gray, then amber, as a plan hatched.

The following morning, after a quick breakfast of coffee and toast smothered in sweet butter, Liz rummaged through the file cabinet again. This time she pulled out additional papers, compiled a stack, and tucked them, along with her financial statements, safely in her new leather envelope. Then she showered and got ready.

Liz took her time getting dressed, making sure her skirt, sweater, and boots matched. Today was especially important. Her decision was made. She applied some blush and mascara, then stepped back from the mirror and took a critical look. She turned sideways, looked over her shoulder, then front again. A slight smile played on her lips. *I look good – smart and professional, though I could stand to lose some weight.* The smile morphed to a familiar frown. *So, what else is new?* She grabbed her coat from the hook, slipped it on, and buttoned up against the frigid December air. With her pocketbook slung over her shoulder and her hands in warm gloves, she tucked the envelope in the crook of her arm. It held all the important papers.

Driving down the country road into town, Liz kept repeating her mantra. "I can do this. Think positive and things will work out." Six years ago, that attitude helped when she'd knocked on neighbors' doors. She hoped that same energy was still in the air because she had no idea what else to do.

CHAPTER 65

Liz pulled her car in front of First Valley Bank, shut the engine, and swung her legs out the door. The icy chill stung her exposed knees just as it stung her thoughts. *Will he remember me?* She smoothed out her coat, stood straight and, with a determined stride, crossed the sidewalk and pulled the door open. A warm blast of air welcomed her. Liz strode to the first teller's window.

"Hi, good morning," she said in a neighborly way. The teller placed a stack of bills in a drawer and looked up. "Is Joe Hancock here?"

"Sure, honey. I'll check if he's free. Have a seat. It'll be right back."

In a few moments, Liz was led into the loan manager's corner office. The room was quite plain, the same as it was when she first came in for her farm loan, and the framed picture of his family still sat on his tidy desk. Her neck and shoulders, too, felt as tight as they had back then.

"Hi, my name's Elizabeth Bergen," she stated with cheery confidence using her full, formal name. This was important business. "We met several years ago," she said, extending her hand across the desk. He stood and shook it.

"Yes. How could I forget? You have a vineyard, and you needed a loan to buy supplies to make your own wine." He motioned for her to sit. "How's it going?"

Liz told him about the winery and the stores and restaurants that sold her wines, as her shoulders loosened. And she proudly mentioned the medals they'd won and the women who worked with her.

"So this is an all-woman winery?" he said.

She felt her scalp prickle, then drew herself even straighter and said, "Yes."

"Impressive. So what brings you in today? What can I do for you?"

Liz slid the newspaper articles from her leather bag. She placed them on his desk, hoping they would be enough ammunition to get what she wanted. "In addition to the loan, which I have been paying back regularly, I have a mortgage with you. I have a check to give you for this month, but as you'll see I'm short a few hundred dollars." Barely taking a breath, she added confidently, "I'm having a special event next weekend for the holidays featuring our rosé. I'm sure it's going to sell really well." She leaned in closer. "I'm very excited about it. It's fresh and crisp and has a wonderful bouquet. And it's only eight dollars a bottle. People are going to love it." She sat back, erect. It was crunch time; everything depended on this. "Mr. Hancock, I would like to personally ask you if I can have an extension of four weeks on this mortgage payment. I know I can make it. This wine is going to be a big seller."

She spread out the articles from the *Newburgh Express* and *Morning Call* on his desk. "If you'll take a look at these, you'll have a better understanding of what Riverview Vineyard is all about." Her voice was full of pride and passion. She spoke the language of an experienced vintner that loved every aspect of wine making.

Mr. Hancock rose from his chair, came around to the front of the desk, and leaned over to have a better look.

"That's you, pressing grapes," he said, pointing to one picture. "And look at all those tanks," he said of another photo. "All these vines grow right here in Vogel?"

He stared at the newspaper article and repeated quietly, "Impressive." Then he looked at Liz. "I understand you've got a lot of expenses; it costs a lot of money to run a business. So what makes you so sure you'll have the rest of the payment in four weeks?"

She began with the self-assurance of a successful businesswoman. She didn't want to sound desperate. "My wines are selling really well. People are pouring in from all over on weekends, tasting and buying, plus we're in several stores, as I said, and four restaurants. Later today, we're meeting with another interested restaurant in New Paltz. I honestly believe this young rosé is going to put me over the top."

"That's all well and good," Mr. Hancock said. "But it is not enough. I will have to see your financials."

Liz felt her throat constrict. She hadn't wowed him, as she had hoped. Once he sees these numbers, he'll never give me that extension, she thought as her fingers reached into the leather envelope. Slowly, she extracted the folder that held the papers she was certain would be her downfall. There was no way to turn this around.

With her stomach churning, Liz followed the loan officer's eyes as they perused the expense sheet. He stopped at one line, then picked up another of the papers she had given him. He stared at it. Liz wondered which number had caught his interest. Each one could be explained. Each was necessary. And they all added up to a negative balance sheet. She knew that did not portend well.

"You have a very large repair cost listed here," Mr. Hancock said, tapping his finger to the legal size paper. "What's it for?"

"My tractor. I had a huge repair on the engine."

"Yes, they can cost a great deal," he said. "Yet they are a necessary expense. I suppose you need a tractor for your work."

"Absolutely."

Mr. Hancock nodded and carried on looking at the columns of numbers. All was quiet, except Liz was afraid he could hear her heart pounding against her chest. He then pulled the papers together, stacked them and slid them across to her.

"Mrs. Bergen, I can tell you believe in your winery, and it's obvious you love what you do." He hesitated a moment. Liz prepared herself. Okay, as much as she hated to, this one time she would ask her father for a loan. But if these negative numbers continued, well, she'd just have to accept the fates. Sell the farm. Tears crept into her throat. She blinked so they wouldn't pool in her eyes. "Elizabeth," Mr. Hancock continued. "Is it all right if I call you that?" Liz nodded, afraid to utter a word. "I've been in this business a long time, and I know a good risk when I see one. From all I see on your financials, this was a one-time outlay of money. A large one, yes, but I understand it. Therefore, I am going to grant you that extension."

Liz bowed her head in relief then stood, feeling light and giddy, though allowing only a sweet smile to appear. She reached across the desk and shook his hand. "Thank you so much for having faith in me and my vineyard, Mr. Hancock. I'm grateful for the chance you've given me, and I won't disappoint you." Releasing his hand, she reached over to pick up the papers and stopped midstream, turned toward him, and let a bit of her perkiness sneak in. "Why don't you come out to the winery next weekend? We do tastings all day and I'll give you a tour. Bring your family."

"We might just do that." He hesitated a moment, then tilted his head in contemplation. Wondering what he was thinking about, Liz's skin prickled until a smile spread across his face. "My wife and daughter have been trying to come up with something unique for wedding favors. Maybe, if my daughter likes your wine, we could make some type of arrangement."

"Absolutely!" After thanking him again, Liz danced out of the bank picturing splits of her wine at each guest's seat. Mini bottles with a picture of the bride and groom on the label. Oh, how she hoped his daughter would love her vino.

CHAPTER 66

Sandra hung her parka on the hook by the side door and stepped into Liz's kitchen. "I'm here," she said, expecting to see Liz sitting with a cup of coffee, as planned. Bobbi would be in the winery all morning, and she and Liz were supposed to go over orders from the new restaurant in town. "Where are you? I've got some news." Sandra walked into the living room to check. Liz wasn't there.

"In my office," Liz called out. "Turn around."

"Office? I was just there." The kitchen had always doubled as Liz's office, the Formica table her desk, with a file cabinet and shelving shoved in a corner. Sandra turned. She spotted Liz through the archway that led to the dining room, or dinette as Liz called it. It was the word her mother had used for their small dining room in New Jersey. Sandra stepped in. Spotting two oak desks set on opposite walls, she pointed and asked, "Where'd you get them? And what did you do with the pine table?"

"It's in the attic. I've got some ideas for it. Not now though." Liz stood and pushed the swivel chair aside. "You like this?" she asked, all perky and cheery. "I wanted to surprise you. We have a real office now." She pointed to the wooden shelves on the walls over each desk and the bookcase in the corner filled with books and magazines on winemaking. "This one's yours." Liz tapped the top of one desk then pulled open the drawer on the right side. "It's a file cabinet. Now we have two."

"This is fabulous," Sandra said.

"I knew you'd love it. We need a real office with the business growing. So while you were out of town visiting your parents, I went to an auction at an old hotel in New Paltz. It was closing and auctioning off practically everything. I even bought these." Liz pointed to the Art Deco desk lamps with green glass shades. "All we need are some pictures on the walls and we're all set."

"And a telephone," Sandra added, nudging the wire-rimmed frame of her new glasses.

"Yeah, they're coming to install the jacks tomorrow, though still only one number."

Sandra smiled at her frugal friend. Liz might be the owner yet she never let the women refer to her as their boss. They were a team. Friends. "Sisters," like the name of their wine.

"So how did it go?" Liz asked. "Are your parents moving here?"

Sandra shook her head. "No, they gave up that idea. They're not ready to leave Brooklyn. Even though I could use their help now that I'm working full time." She adjusted the aviator frames again. "It's okay. As long as I can keep leaving by three to be home for the kids."

"No problem. I always say, family first. So what is it?"

Sandra stood and threw out her chest. "Riverview Vineyard now has a new venture. Personalized bottles." She raised her arms as if she'd won a race. "Mr. Hancock gave me the idea. When he came with his daughter and she said she'd love us to make favors for her wedding, well, I figured, why not capitalize on that idea. Her wedding isn't until June. We could get started now. So I called caterers in the valley and made a deal."

"You did?" With a wrinkled forehead, Liz voiced her unease. "You never said anything."

Sandra sat and swiveled toward Liz. "I wanted to surprise you with something too. I thought it'd be okay. You said I should use my ingenuity, to be creative in marketing. So . . ." She shrugged.

"You're right. I did. Please, go on." *Was it all right, though? Do I really want Sandra making decisions without consulting me first?*

"You sure? I . . . I'm sorry if I overstepped." She played with her glasses and hair again.

Liz knew Sandra was correct. And that she was uncomfortable, which made her feel awful. She was well aware she couldn't do everything herself. That's exactly why she had suggested Sandra should create marketing ideas. She trusted her. So why were the hairs on the back of her neck standing up? She shook it off, realizing this was *her* problem, and smiled "No, you didn't," she said. "It's fine."

Sandra's eyes lit as bright as the light from the new lamp. "Okay, then. So now, in addition to the Hancock wedding, we have three more and one corporate party in April."

Liz's brows raised.

"I know, it's next month, but we can do it. We'll be ready." With a tilt of her head, she asked Liz if she was on board. Liz scooped her hand, motioning her to continue. "I thought that we would work all this through the caterers. You'll set the price, and we'll up it of course. They'll charge the customers directly and pay us sixty percent. How does that sound?"

"Interesting. Go on."

"I made sure we can keep the names of the wine, just make new labels adding the couple's names or, like you had suggested to the Hancocks, put their picture on it. And for businesses, we'll add their name or logo. Jim will figure it out."

Liz steepled her fingers and laid her chin on them in contemplation. *This is creative, but am I glad she did it?* She pursed her lips in thought. Her head started spinning with ideas. A moment later, she looked up and gave Sandra a crisp nod. "Brilliant. You are phenomenal."

CHAPTER 67

"I don't see why you can't take a week off," Eddie said, his forearms planted on the speckled Formica table rimmed in chrome. He was seated across from Liz in a corner booth in the diner just down the road from her bank. After two weeks of constant snowfall keeping people inside, this sunny Saturday with the temperatures rising into the high forties had Eddie and many others escaping their homes. The parking lot was full and patrons crowded together, waiting at the door for the next free seat. "The women can handle all the work," Eddie said. "You say you've got a great team."

"I do, but there's so much more. And we'll be bottling in a few weeks. I have to be here."

"We can go before bottling starts. Come on, Liz. Come to Florida with me."

Liz's hackles raised hearing the name of that state. Images of a girl in a flowered dress standing under a Royal Palm made the blood pound in her head. She didn't want to admit that it still affected her. She was over Rick but would she ever get past the fact that he wanted someone else? "I'll think about it," she said with a tight nod. Silverware tinkled and dirty plates rattled on trays carried by busboys. "This is for a vacation, right?" Liz held her empty fork in midair. "Not work?" Eddie nodded and continued talking. Liz played with the salad on her plate, moving tomatoes, olives, and onions round and round, half listening to his plans on teaching her to play golf – just what she wanted – and how they'd take walks on the beach, sit with their toes in the sand watching seagulls dive bomb for scraps of food dropped by other sunbathers, and sip fruity drinks with little paper umbrellas while watching the sunset. Oh, why was it that Eddie refused to understand she could not leave? She was Riverview Vineyard. She had to be on site. Sure, the women could handle a week without her, but could she handle a week away? It was like leaving her babies with a favorite aunt, and she never did that when Bethany and Noah were little. Was it because she and Rick didn't have the money to go on vacation? That was part of it, though honestly the idea never occurred to her. Maybe it would have been good for their marriage? Too late now. What does it matter anyway? Liz would never have left her kids for a week, even with a favorite aunt, so why would she leave the business? Like any other seven-year-old, it needed its mama.

"So, how about it?" Eddie said leaning forward, his voice all bubbly and loud. "I can book the flights tonight when I get home."

Liz kept her eyes on the salad. "Aren't you staying the weekend?" She watched the blue cheese dressing coat the lettuce leaves, her lips pressed tight together.

"You know I don't enjoy this rural world. There's nothing to do here." Eddie lifted a shoulder. "I was amazed you even agreed to have lunch with me, considering it's a weekend and you say that's your busiest time."

"It is. Though not only weekends. I really am busy. I . . . I can't take a week off."

"Can't? Or won't?"

Liz met his piercing eyes. There was a little ache in her chest.

"Eddie," she said softly, shaking her head a bit, sorry she had to admit what had been on her mind. "This isn't working. I'm not the woman you want."

Eddie sat back against the red vinyl booth. His shoulders slumped. "I knew you wouldn't go away with me. I figured I'd try, that maybe you'd see my point. I like you, Liz. I really do and we could spend a lot more time together if you weren't so incredibly consumed with work. I feel like I'm always in competition with it. If only you could trust Bobbi and Sandra and Nancy."

Liz held her chin high. "I do trust them." She unlocked her jaw and forced a soft tone to keep the irritation from her voice. "Eddie, Riverview Vineyard is not some part-time job, something fun to keep me busy. It's my life. It is up to me to make this business a success." As hard as she tried, frustration took a seat and refused to leave. "Yes, I have a phenomenal team and I do depend on them, more than you can imagine. But the business lives and dies with me." The waitress came by with a full coffee pot. Liz put her hand over her cup and Eddie waved her away. With less power in her voice, and a little more regret, she continued where she'd left off. "Eddie, I realize it's hard for some men to see a woman in charge. You're not used to that. You have secretaries and gal Fridays. None of them are in control. But I am. I'm in a powerful position."

Eddie wrinkled his nose, like there was a bad smell.

"Yes. Powerful. My winery may not be as large as Gallo or as successful as Mondavi. But it's mine and I am going to do everything in my power to make it a huge success. Even if that means not going to Florida, or anywhere. For now, this is where I have to be."

Shortly after, pulling out of her parking spot, Liz told herself she had done the right thing. As much as she would miss the fun they had, and the sex, Eddie would never understand her. If I'm going to be with a guy, she thought as she drove down the street, he needs to know he's never going to take first place. That spot is reserved for my children, the ones who grew inside my body and the ones that grow on my land. Will I ever meet a man who can deal with an independent woman? And does it really matter if I do?

CHAPTER 68

A terracotta pot filled with bright red geraniums sat in a corner of the front porch, as joyous and bright as Liz. Seated at the edge of her wicker chair, words tumbled from her mouth as birds chirped from the trees.

"Slow down," her father said. Lou, smoking his favorite pipe, relaxed on the wood rocker opposite his daughter. The scent of jasmine mixed with spicy cloves filled the air. "You want to build a banquet hall? Here, on the farm?"

"Yes, imagine it. We could have weddings right here. Instead of us supplying the caterers, they could supply us, in a sense. People always need venues and what better place than a vineyard? They could have the cocktail hour among the vines and then come to the hall for the reception. Maybe even have the ceremony here. Can't you just picture it? A bride in her white dress, a groom in his tux, standing among grape vines holding hands. The photos would be stunning."

Lou looked out toward the gravel road that led from Hill Valley Road all the way to the house and the winery. Acres of empty green land surrounded both. "Your land is beautiful," he said, turning to his daughter. "When you and Rick first bought it, I was worried. I couldn't imagine what you would do with thirty-five acres."

"Me too," Liz said with a little laugh. She remembered her father's skepticism at the time, his distress that she had failed to get her BA.

"And then you planted the vineyard. A brilliant idea and you've done marvels with it."

Wrapped in a blanket of her father's love, Liz tingled all over.

"So, forgetting the trees, your own small forest actually, how much usable land do you have? Eliminate where the house and winery sit, and obviously the vineyard."

"I don't know. Another twelve, fifteen acres maybe, forgetting the road. I can't build on that. Enough room, though, for a banquet hall."

Lou stood. Chewing on the end of his meerschaum, he walked over to the end of the porch and looked out on the open land. "I've got another idea," he said. "Follow me."

"What?"

"Just come." Lou stepped off the porch. "It's something I've been thinking about."

Liz followed, her dad already several steps ahead. She knew that walk. It was the same stride he had when she was a teen living in New Jersey and drove the family car to pick him up from work. He always came down the street, to where she was parked, with a determined stride, his carriage straight and tall, a fedora propped on his head. It was as if he couldn't wait to slide into the driver's seat and head home. Liz hurried to catch up, wondering what he was so intent on now.

Lou stopped at an open space, far enough from the barn to leave the winery on its own plot of land. Emerald green grass spread out all around. He turned to his daughter. "Rather than building a banquet hall, how about we construct a subterranean winery?"

"Underground?"

"Absolutely. Think of it as nature's refrigerator. You wouldn't need the climate control system you have now, and it's the perfect environment for wine to age. No temperature swings, no issue with sun coming in."

She was stunned by his words. Over the past several years, seeing the pride in her father's face, hearing his applause every time she took home a medal, Liz was finally getting past the guilt she carried, the guilt that had set its feet deep inside, rooted to her core. And now, this? "Sounds like you've done some research, Daddy."

Lou's bright eyes told Liz all she needed to know. "When you brought up the idea of a banquet hall, I thought now's the time to suggest this. Honey, why not make the barn into a venue for weddings and other events and build a winery below ground?"

Her eyes opened wide. She tilted her head; images played like a movie in her mind; her mouth slowly turned upward. She looked at her father and gave him a little nod. "Great idea," she said and suddenly her face pinched. "I can't. It'll cost a fortune."

"Yes, it will be expensive," Lou said. "I want to help."

"Oh no. I will *not* take your money. If I do this — and that's if — I will get a loan."

"Elizabeth, honey, let me invest in you. I invested in your sister and brother, in their futures…"

"How?"

Lou answered in a serious voice, almost a whisper. "Paying for their college educations." Liz winced. "I know, I wasn't able to do that for you, though Lizzy you have proved you didn't need it. I am so proud of you, of all you've accomplished. And it's only the beginning. I am sure of that."

Liz reached for her father and, with their arms wrapped around each other, tears filled her eyes. He held her, rubbing her back as she pictured rows of steel tanks humming underground, turning her grapes into grown-up wine. And with a beautiful tasting room upstairs complete with a shiny oak counter, U-shaped, filled with customers.

She unclasped her arms and stepped back. "Daddy, I do want to do this. My way. My loan is almost paid off and I'm sure I can get another. First though, I have one more expense to take care of."

CHAPTER 69

Liz pressed the glued label onto the bottle. "Harmony," she said, lifting the wine bottle for all to see. "Remember when we named this?" The women were seated on folding chairs around the counter they had perched on tall sawhorses. An old piece of Formica Liz found at a garage sale doubled as a labeling table now, at other times their bottling line. It was a well-used, five-foot-long piece of speckled laminate saved from the garbage heap.

Bobbi, focused on filling the labeling machine's tube with more thick industrial glue, simply murmured "mmm hmm." Sandra and Nancy mumbled the same, their noses wrinkled, trying to avoid the stench, their eyes focused on the labels they were adhering. This labor-intensive job took eagle eyes to make sure the labels, showing deep-purple grapes entwined with chartreuse clusters, were applied perfectly, no crimps in the paper, no weird angles on the finished product.

"Well, girls, we're harmonizing again," Liz said. "With a whole new endeavor."

The women looked up, bottles in one hand, gluey labels in the other.

"I spoke to my lawyer yesterday," Liz continued seeing the wonder on their faces. "I'm going to pay off Rick and, once I do that, we're building a new winery."

"Wait. Hold on," Bobbi said, placing the tube in its slot in the manual labeler. The others put down the papers they were holding, sticky side up, giving Liz their full attention.

"What do you mean you're paying off Rick?" Bobbi asked. "All at once?"

"Yes, I am getting that line-item off my books."

Sandra laughed. "That's a good way to refer to him."

"That's all he is," Liz said. "Rick never thought I'd make it, and now I don't have to wait years to give him his share writing weekly checks. One more and I'm done."

"That's great," Bobbi said. "So what's this about a new winery?"

Liz stood and threw out her chest. "We're going subterranean, ladies, like wineries in France. And on the main floor, a real tasting room – not like this." She waved her hand around the barn. "It'll be complete with a beautiful, shiny, large oak counter and gorgeous antique tables filled with gift items, maybe some bakers racks too. I like the wrought-iron ones." Liz told them about her conversation with her father and how the existing winery would turn into a banquet hall.

"I love it," Sandra said. "All those people that hire caterers and have their events in VFWs and Elks Clubs, firehalls, all sorts of ugly places, they'll come here." The women buzzed talking about the chairs and tables they'd need to purchase, the colored cloths and silverware. "We can go that route," Sandra said. "Or have them rent everything from the caterers. Less upfront expense for us, and less inventory."

"That's all to be decided," Liz said. "We've got big things coming. You already have specific roles. Now it's time to give each of you an official title."

With forearms on the counter, eyes and ears open, they listened as Liz went on. "You know the vineyard is my happy place, that I'd rather be working there than anywhere else. Although when I'm not, I want to be out talking with vendors, making more connections, selling more wine." She faced Sandra. "You've been phenomenal at that and you'll still be my marketing guru, but now you are officially Riverview Vineyard's Office Manager. You do know how much I depend on you."

"Yes. And thank you, but I've never needed a title to do my work. I love being part of Riverview."

"I know. But I'll feel better. Don't get me wrong," Liz said, pointing her finger toward the women, her eyes wide open, like a mother reminding her children of something very important. "I'll still have my hand in every part of this business." She lowered her finger and smiled, then sat and put her arms comfortably on the Formica. "Now you'll each wear a manager's hat. Be in charge of your own part." Liz focused directly on Bobbi. "You, my right-hand gal, are now Riverview Vineyard's winemaker."

Bobbi recoiled. "No. You are."

"I'll still make wine. We'll do it together, like always," Liz said. "Though once this new winery is built and we convert the barn to a banquet hall, I'll have even more to do than I have now. So you will take the reins on winemaking. I need to know someone will be here doing every bit that needs to be done. That way I have the freedom to put my energies in other places, other aspects of the business, some I might not even be realizing now."

With her hand on her chest, Bobbi looked at Liz. Genuine delight shone from her green eyes. Bobbi was as happy as a little girl skipping through a meadow.

Liz turned to Nancy. "And you, my consummate salesperson, will be in charge of the new tasting room, ordering the items we'll sell. I'd like to offer items from local potters, maybe ceramic wine glasses and coasters, stuff like that, and other things from women artisans in the Valley. I'll leave that research to you, our Tasting Room Manager. So you see," she said smiling at her team, "we're harmonizing, like a symphony. Bobbi's the brass, Sandra the strings and Nancy . . . She looked up quizzically.

"The percussion," Sandra said. Liz laughed at her own forgetfulness.

"And you are the conductor," Nancy added.

"You can be my Leonard Bernstein any day," said Bobbi. "I'm happy to follow your lead. I only hope you're not saddling yourself with another loan."

"I am applying for one," Liz said, "though it's not saddling me. I can afford it. And, I'm going to sell the diamond."

Bobbi's head drew back. "I thought that was for Bethany."

"Beth doesn't want it. Her exact words to me, when I said she could have the ring when she and Drew got engaged, were, 'No way am I ever going to wear a rock that huge.'"

"Engaged?" The women sang out, sounding like a chorus.

"No, not yet." Liz waved her hand. "It was only a mother-daughter conversation one day. Bethany says that the diamond means nothing to her. It shouldn't even be called an heirloom, that an heirloom is something handed down from generation to generation from a beloved grandmother or great-grandmother or some well-loved relative. And we all know that was certainly not Rick's mother."

"Well then," Bobbi said, "do something really special with it."

Pleased with herself, Liz gave a sharp nod. "I plan to."

CHAPTER 70

With one hand on the open refrigerator door and a bowl of blueberries in her other, Kristin turned and stared as Liz walked into the kitchen, her face pinched.

"Who was that?" Kristin said, referring to the phone call Liz had taken in her office. "You look awful."

"My lawyer. Seems Rick wants more money."

Kristin recoiled. "You agreed on a figure and he signed off on it." She put the berries on the counter. The pie could wait. "Jeez, it's been seven years," she said. "What the hell?"

"He wants a new survey done. He swears the land is worth more now. That's not the issue, though. Adele and his lawyer spoke, and they agreed he isn't entitled to any more even if the land is worth more." She threw up a palm. "As you said, we settled on a figure and that was final, although Rick was not happy about it. Adele said he pitched a fit."

"Not surprising." Kristin pulled out a kitchen chair and sat. "So what now?"

Liz laughed, although there wasn't an ounce of joy in the sound. Plans for their July Fourth party the next day seemed insignificant now. Still, she was glad her sister was with her. Liz stood with her back to the sink, arms folded across her chest. "Now he wants the diamond."

"Really? Are you going to give it to him?"

Liz took a deep breath, shaking her head, thinking about the consequences. Her stomach quivered. "If I give him the ring, he'll sign the papers. I'll be done with him. Forever."

"And if you don't?"

"Then I've got eighteen more years of writing his damn name every week, having to think about him. I want it over."

"What did your lawyer say about it?"

"She said the ring was a gift. Legally mine. I am not compelled to give it back. It's my choice."

Liz walked over to the table, grabbed a chair, and yanked it back, as if it was Rick's neck. "Get a hold of yourself," she mumbled, realizing anger wouldn't get her anywhere. Wishing she hadn't quit smoking – she sure could use a cigarette now – Liz plopped on the chair. As the anger dissipated, doubt and confusion crept in. Would he sign off on the lien and take the money? Or would he insist she keep paying him weekly if she didn't give him the ring? *That bastard! I wouldn't put it past him. On the other hand, would it be so terrible if I kept paying him?* Liz took a deep breath. *Yes, it would. I want him out of my life.*

She placed her elbows on the table, clasped her hands, and laid her chin down. "I had plans for that ring," she said, staring off into space, then looked at her sister who had a pained expression on hers. "I'm all right, Kris. Really, don't worry." Liz sat back. "You know, I haven't had the ring appraised since I got it. I don't even know what it's worth now but I'm sure it would get me what I want – or at least a part of it." Her eyes glassed over, picturing the new tasting room, as her fingers slowly swept along the kitchen table as if it were the highly polished, genuine oak counter she envisioned. There would be customers, or guests as she preferred to call them, crowded around the large semi-circular bar top, facing shelves of glass that showcased their medal winners sparkling in the spotlight. Adorning the walls, she saw framed professional photographs of her vineyard in each season, and, outside, a deck where guests would sit munching on platters of fruit and cheese, sharing a glass of wine. And music on the weekends. Yes, we need music – maybe a guitar player or a trio.

Liz looked at her sister. "I have so many ideas. Why does he have to be a problem?"

"He doesn't. The ring is yours. Believe me, he'll take the money – without it."

Liz shrugged. "Maybe."

CHAPTER 71

Liz slipped the bank check into a business envelope and laid it on her desk, opened the top drawer, dug deep into the back, and extracted the tiny orange one that held the key to her safe deposit box. Holding both in her hand, she pressed them to her chest. Finally, she whispered and looked out the picture window. Her vineyard, budding with flowers, greeted her anxious eyes. Just as America, the previous week, celebrated the Fourth of July, Liz was about to celebrate her own independence from a tyrannical king.

With the two precious objects tucked safely in her Etienne Aigner bag, bought specifically for this auspicious day, Liz slung it over her arm and walked out to her car. She turned the ignition on and hoped the ominous July sky wouldn't open. She had to get to the bank and then her lawyer's office looking sharp, hair perfectly coiffed, makeup fresh.

Ten minutes later, she angled her car into the empty space in front of the bank and stepped out into sunshine peeking through the clouds. She hoped that boded well for the rest of her day.

Joe Hancock stepped out of his office. "Good morning," he said to Liz, who was standing next to the table with the coffee urn, shifting her weight from one foot to the other, waiting for the next available bank officer. "What brings you here today? Don't you have an important meeting?"

Liz warmed realizing he remembered their conversation when she'd come in last week asking for an additional loan. She had paid off the first, in record time, and Joe had been wonderful when she said she wasn't sure how much she could afford – how much of a loan they would allow her. "Liz, what you can afford is not the concern," he'd said. "The question is, how much do you need? Whatever it is, we know you're good for it."

"Yes," Liz said. "The meeting's at noon. First, I need to get into my safe deposit box."

Joe cocked his head. Whatever question he had in his mind, Liz knew that, as a banker, he'd never ask. She respected his professionalism. She had learned a great deal from him about how to relate to customers, and to vendors when she was negotiating costs. Joe Hancock was more than her banker. He was a trusted friend, yet she kept quiet. This decision was hers to make. She did not want any more advice.

Liz signed her name in the notebook on the wooden stand outside the gated room where patrons' precious papers and jewels were locked up tight. Joe entered, leaving the door open and climbed the step ladder, opened the oblong metal box with his key, then Liz's. The only other key to Box 672. A slight smile spread across her face as she pictured Rick trying to get into the safe deposit box where the ring originally sat. By now it was in someone else's name.

Joe walked out, handed Liz the narrow box, and led her to a small private room.

Alone in the cubby, Liz sat on the straight-backed chair, lifted the metal lid, and took out the ring box. Gently, she removed the gem from its slot on the black velvet cushion. Holding it between her thumb and forefinger, she twisted the marquise right and left, up and down. It sparkled. Liz wondered what it was worth. And was it worth giving it to Rick? She would be free of him. The day would go smoothly. But was that all she really wanted? Was that enough? Liz had never taken the easy way out of anything, except for quitting college, and look how that turned out. She was a different woman now. But did she still have enough fight left in her? She knew there would be a big one if she didn't give Rick the diamond.

Liz opened her leather bag and gently tucked the ring box into a side pocket. She closed the clasp and let her hand lie on the soft leather for a moment, as if caressing a baby's head, then walked out and waved good-bye to Joe, sitting in his office. As she drove to her lawyer's, Liz pictured the white, delicately scented flowers growing on her vines. Soon they would set fruit and mature into plump grapes. Would this gem, wrapped in velvet, set its own fruit? Or would it die on the vine? She had an hour to decide.

CHAPTER 72

After stopping at a coffee shop where she mulled over the pros and cons of giving Rick the diamond, Liz arrived at Ms. Samuels's office with fifteen minutes to spare. She sat in her car with the windows open, a summer breeze blowing, shifting her thoughts one way, then another. A pickup truck, filthy and full of dents, drove into the parking lot and pulled next to Liz's silver Camaro. She felt sorry for the owner. Either he can't afford a new truck or he has no pride in himself, she thought. Even when she was barely able to afford a used car, Liz had kept it clean. Despite her insecurities, she'd masked herself in confidence. And the more she did that, the surer of herself she became. Outward appearances mattered, and not only for how others viewed her.

The driver, a Charles Manson look-alike with hair down to his shoulders and a straggly beard and mustache, stepped out of his truck. He turned and waved to Liz, then came around to her driver's side window, arms swinging, jaw set. She gasped. Rick didn't look like this at the awards ceremony. What happened to him these past five years? In an instant, no matter what she thought before, her decision solidified. It was as strong as the diamond itself.

"You got the ring?" Rick barked.

Liz wished her window wasn't wide open. She turned in her seat to face him and leaned back a bit. "No, Rick. I don't."

"I told your lawyer, no ring, no deal."

"I understand." Liz kept her voice calm. "If you insist, I'll simply keep paying you every week, as I have been doing for the past seven years. You will eventually get the money."

"Nope. Not good enough. I want that money now."

From the look of him, Liz figured he needed the money for drugs. The diamond too. She hoped he wasn't in any serious trouble, other than being hooked on drugs and alcohol, which was bad enough. There was no way in hell she would enable him. He was due the money, whether in one lump sum or over the years. That had been their separation agreement, incorporated in their divorce decree. The ring, on the other hand . . . maybe that's why his mother gave it to me? Liz wondered about that. Maybe she knew her son better than I thought – better than I did. Liz chuckled to herself. If it wasn't so sad, it would be funny.

"Rick, I have the bank check in my pocketbook. All we have to do is go inside and sign some papers. If you insist on getting the diamond, well, that's extortion. I will go inside and let everyone know why the deal is off. We'll have to go to court and who knows how long that will take, or what the outcome will be. So, Richard, if you want the money, I suggest you walk through those doors with me. Satisfy the lien."

One half hour later, after thanking her own lawyer, Liz extended her hand to Rick's. With her freshly manicured nails polished Peaceful Pink, she shook his, a strong, firm handshake. "Thank you," she said. He nodded.

"Wait," Adele Samuels said as Liz turned to leave. "How about joining me for lunch?"

"Oh, I'd love to, if you don't mind waiting a little. I have a date with a jeweler."

THE END

ACKNOWLEDGMENTS

Becoming a published author later in life has been an incredibly thrilling adventure. Having one book in the hands of readers was a dream come true. Now, with two, I'm overwhelmed, jubilant, elated! I am grateful to so many people who have been part of this wonderful journey.

First, I send an enormous thank you to the team at Black Rose Writing for their faith in this story and for wrapping my "second baby" so beautifully and bringing it into readers' hands.

To Pamela Taylor, my fabulous editor. Once again you've done your magic. Thank you for your talent and your friendship. I'm so fortunate to have you by my side.

I send a huge thank you to my writing buddies, Pat Williams, Bunny Shulman, Bea Lewis, Carren Strock, Judi Askinazi, Lucette Bloomgarden, Joe Berardino, Lea Becker and Jacquie Herz. Your sage advice and gentle, generous critiques have made me a better writer. I look forward to many more Tuesday afternoons together.

To my beta readers at Spun Yarn, a huge thanks for spotting the anachronisms that I missed when changing my story's time-line – and for all your other suggestions, even those I didn't use. I truly appreciate all the time you took with my book.

The 2020 Debuts and The Rogue TGIF writers have wrapped me in a community I never imagined being part of when I started this journey. Thank you for your friendship, your encouragement, your energy and sharing. I look forward to many more years traveling this road with you.

Elaine Pivinski, my high school friend, deserves a special thanks. I'm so glad we reconnected. Thank you for sharing your story and gorgeous vineyard with me and for answering all my questions about winemaking and grape growing.